dark future

ROUTE 666

AMERICA, TOMORROW. A world laced with paranoia, dominated by the entertainment industry and ruled by the corporations. A future where the ordinary man is an enslaved underclass and politics is just a branch of show-biz. This is the Dark Future.

The followers of Joseph are on a pilgrimage to the Holy Land. Led by the charismatic Elder Nguyen Seth, the faithful have just been presented the state of Utah by the President. However, with the wastelands of America populated by bloodthirsty gangs and worse, someone has to guide these "lost lambs" through the valley of the shadow of death to get there, and that someone is US Cavalry Trooper Leona Tyree. However, as the journey nears its goal, Leona begins to have her doubts about Seth: is he really the benevolent humanitarian he seems to be, or is his agenda something far darker? Savage satire and outrageous action combine, with mind-blowing results.

dark future

ROUTE 666

Jack Yeovil

BLACK FLAME

For Karen

A Black Flame Publication
www.blackflame.com

First published in Great Britain in 1993. Revised edition published
in 2006 by BL Publishing, Games Workshop Ltd., Willow Road,
Nottingham NG7 2WS, UK.

Distributed in the US by Simon & Schuster, 1230 Avenue of the
Americas, New York, NY 10020, USA.

10 9 8 7 6 5 4 3 2 1

Cover illustration by Jaime Jones.

ISBN 13: 978 1 84416 327 4
ISBN 10: 1 84416 327 X

A CIP record for this book is available from the British Library.

Printed in the UK by Bookmarque, Surrey, UK.

Publisher's note: This is a work of fiction, detailing an alternative and
decidedly imaginary future. All the characters, actions and events
portrayed in this book are not real, and are not based on real events
or actions.

When it was first published, parts of *Route 666* were set slightly
earlier than now. For this new edition, Black Flame has gently
revised certain dates to bring this title into line with the other
extraordinary tales from the Dark Future.

AMERICA, TOMORROW

My fellow Americans —

I am speaking to you today from the Oval Office, to bring you hope and cheer in these troubling times. The succession of catastrophes that have assailed our once-great nation continue to threaten us, but we are resolute.

The negative fertility zone that is the desolation of the mid-west divides east from west, but life is returning. The plucky pioneers of the new Church of Joseph are reclaiming Salt Lake City from the poisonous deserts just as their forefathers once did, and our prayers are with them. And New Orleans may be under eight feet of water, but they don't call it New Venice for nothing.

Here at the heart of government, we continue to work closely with the MegaCorps who made this country the economic miracle it is today, to bring prosperity and opportunity to all who will join us. All those unfortunate or unwilling citizens who exercise their democratic right to live how they will, no matter how far away from the comfort and security of the corporate cities, may once more rest easy in their shacks knowing that the new swathes of Sanctioned Operatives work tirelessly to protect them from the biker gangs and NoGo hoodlums.

The succession of apparently inexplicable or occult manifestations and events we have recently witnessed have unnerved many of us, it is true. Even our own Government scientists are unable to account for much of what is happening. Our church leaders tell us they have the unknown entities which have infested the datanets in the guise of viruses at bay.

A concerned citizen asked me the other day whether I thought we were entering the Last Times, when Our Lord God will return to us and visit His Rapture upon us, or whether we were just being tested as He once tested his own son. My friends, I cannot answer that. But I am resolute that with God's help, we shall work, as ever, to create a glorious future in this most beautiful land.

Thank you, and God Bless America.

President Estevez

Brought to you in conjunction with the GenTech Corporation.

Serving America right.

[Script for proposed Presidential address, July 3rd 2021. Never transmitted.]

proLogue
the book of Joseph

I
Utah Territory, 1854

"Elder Shatner, look," said Brother Carey, pointing to the high country. "Thou canst see a horseman, alone."

Hendrik Shatner turned casually in the saddle. In the light of the coming dawn, the lines of the ancient and rugged table rocks were becoming visible. Young Carey saw true. A rider was picking a careful way, silhouetted against red-threaded sky.

Hendrik shivered with sudden insight. If he stopped and dismounted, he could draw a clear rifle bead before the horseman was out of sight. It would not be a certain kill at this range, but he had made more difficult shots.

His rifle hung from his saddle horn in its soft leather sheath. Store-bought in the East, it had been his companion for a good few years.

In the desert stillness, the report of the shot would carry for miles, probably as far as New Canaan. He could not risk alerting the Gentiles. Still, his gut-twinge told him this bloody business would go better without the unknown stranger drifting through. He wished he had availed himself of the skills of the Brethren's Paiute allies and learned how to bring down a hawk with a silent arrow.

"Is't one of the Indians?" Brother Carey asked.

Hendrik shook his head. The horseman sat on a saddle and wore a hat. His gaze was fixed on his rocky path. To him, the deep crack of the canyon would be a river of dark. The raiding party were bottom-crawling creatures of the shadow. Hendrik tried to believe the stranger was unaware of them.

"A *Gentile*," Carey spat.

"Most like, brother."

Carey had been raised in the Brethren of Joseph. His parents, early converts, had died on the Path, run out of one town after another, pestered Westward. The young man had gathered up an unhealthy store of vengeance. He was not alone among the Brethren. Each man of this party had made his blood sacrifices.

"We'll see them Gentiles off, elder," Carey said.

"That's the general idea."

The rider up in the high country would be some ragged mountain man, drifting west, never settling. Hendrik might have gone that route himself at one time or another, before his brother put on the mirrored spectacles and saw the future laid out like a map. The horseman would not be one of the Gentiles who had fixed on the played-out mining town of Spanish Fork. The pioneers had planted their grain and renamed the place New Canaan.

The grain shouldn't have taken, but neither should the crops planted at the Josephite settlement. The Lord made the desert flower for the Brethren of Joseph; now Gentiles picked around the edges of the territory, crowding the outcasts. Of course, it seemed strange that the Lord should have placed that deep-water well for Gentiles to find rather than the elect. Hendrik recalled that a similar situation had obtained in Old Canaan before Joshua rode up with his trumpets.

In the dawn quiet, Hendrik heard tiny sounds: hooves on sand and the occasional rock outcrop, the muted rattle of harnesses, the squeak of saddles, the breath of horses.

This was a necessary action. The Brethren had left too many settlements behind, been driven off good land by soldiers and bandits. Here, in deserts no one but an Indian could want, the Path of Joseph petered out. This was where the Shining City must rise to the glory of the Lord. It was either that or a communal grave.

"We'll send 'em runnin' back for the States," Carey vowed, vehemently trying to convince himself. "This be the Land of Joseph. *Our* land."

"And theirs," Hendrik indicated.

The Paiute rode silently. Hendrik had expected the party to separate into its constituent elements but everyone was mixed in. The Indians were blanketed huddles on scrawny mounts, interspersed with Josephites in broad-brimmed black hats and long, peg-fastened black coats. A sprinkling of Chiricahua were present alongside the Paiute, wanderers well off their usual trails.

The Brethren of Joseph were at peace with the Indian, if not with the United States. Among the elect was the Ute, who had been at the side of Brother Joseph from the first. He was taken, even by Indians, as one of their number, if rarely welcomed as a red brother.

The Ute had scouted this path and now rode near the head of the party. Even in the twilight, he wore his peculiar mirrored spectacles. It was hard for most to imagine his eyes, though suggestive glimpses troubled Hendrik's nights. The Ute had the coat and hat of a Josephite but his face was burned the colour of blood. Josephites abjured adornment, but the Ute wore a necklace of knuckle-bones.

"Gentiles whipped my pa, back in Kentucky," Carey said, steeling himself. "Tied him to a wagon wheel, opened his back to the bone, left him to die. And Gentiles hanged Elder Joseph. Thou knowest that better'n anyone."

Joseph Shatner, founder of the Brethren of Joseph, had indeed been hanged. Hendrik had heard the verdict handed down against his brother, had tried to raise his voice amid the hurrahs of the crowd. The charge was sorcery, a capital crime in certain backward counties of the State of Massachusetts. The law had lain unused among the statutes since the Salem Witch Trials.

"It has to stop somewhere," Carey continued. "The whippings, the hangings, the bullets in the back. We've found the place where we ought to be, and we must take our stand."

Hendrik had heard this speech before, in the war with Mexico and in the campaign against the Seminoles. Before fighting, each man convinced himself the cause was just, that he was doing the right thing. Trouble was, the Mexicans and the Seminoles must feel the same way, or else why would *they* bear arms?

A shaft of early light angled down into the canyon. The horseman was gone. Hendrik saw round black hats ahead, bobbing like mushrooms in a pot of water. There were about twenty Josephites, with maybe ten Indians mixed in. It was a fair-sized war party.

"Any rate," Carey said, "we're going to see them Gentiles off."

"Like I said, that's the general idea."

II
Boston, 1843

HENDRIK SHATNER COUNTED himself unfortunate to be in the company of not one but two madmen.

"The *only* irrefutable argument in support of the soul's immortality," the poet announced, "or, rather, the only conclusive proof of man's alternate dissolution and rejuvenescence *ad infinitum* is to be found in analogies deduced from the modern established theory of nebular cosmogony."

The air of Samuel's tavern was thick with bad whiskey and worse talk. If one took into consideration the storm-clouds of tobacco smoke gathering under the low ceiling, the aromatic powders upon the faces of every woman present, and the natural odour of the male clientèle, the atmosphere was hardly calculated to soothe the nostrils.

Hendrik was at least accustomed to the eccentricities of his brother, Joseph. This Eddy, Richmond-bred, but currently out of Philadelphia, was some new species of lunatic. Hendrik was afraid Joseph and the poet would lock horns in a contest of drink-sotted feeble-wits, which would outlast the night and conclude only with the both of them in their graves.

As debate thundered, Molly O'Doul, whom Hendrik knew to be a not infrequent paramour of Joseph's, pouted and wriggled by his side, failing to distract him. If matters continued, Hendrik would feel obliged to relieve his brother of this particular burden of the flesh.

Hendrik abused his throat with another swallow. It raised stinging tears in his eyes. He had spent too much time in the crowded East; he should head for the open West again, soon. He had not been to California since the territory was ceded by Mexico. There were stories of cities of gold.

He shook whiskey fire from his brain and returned his attentions to the vagaries of the conversation.

Eddy declaimed against the current state of American letters, not a topic of any particular interest to Hendrik, with occasional footnotes as to the essential nature of the universe. The poet and essayist had come to Boston, which he insisted upon calling "Frogpondium", to attend the deathbed of the *Pioneer*, a monthly magazine that had published his scribblings and then had the indecency to expire before paying him for his efforts. Eddy was aghast to discover that the periodical, published in this very town, had lived its brief life without extending its fame, and thereby his own, to Samuel's Tavern.

"Have you not read my tale, 'The Tell-Tale Heart'? My poem, 'Lenore'? My celebrated essay 'Notes Upon English Verse'? The *Pioneer* took them at ten dollars apiece, but monies have not, I regret to say, been forthcoming. The demise of the periodical is a most severe blow to the good cause, the cause of Pure Taste."

Hendrik was given to understand that Eddy, a self-declared genius, had not much prospered from his literary efforts. Like Joseph, he could talk up a blue streak but was only minimally able to transform his energies into remuneration.

"I have expectation of securing, through my contacts with the family of President Tyler, a government post, a sinecure in the United States' Customs House. This position will finance my literary endeavours, freeing me from the pestilential need of providing for myself and my dependants. Until that welcome time, so close as to be within a breath's grasp, I'm afraid I shall have to trouble you to settle a greater portion of the worthy Samuel's bill."

Despite Eddy's penury, the goodfellows drank steadily for two hours. Hendrik could almost no longer feel the lump of Mexican shot that had lodged in his leg as he galloped away from San Antone. Usually, he took that as a sign that his evening's liquoring was over and that he should transfer his affections to beer. In the current circumstances, he called for another shot. Ernie, the pot-man, was ready with an unstoppered bottle and exchanged a sympathetic look with Hendrik. Evidently, he was more than familiar with the windy likes of Joseph and Eddy.

At Molly's summoning, a cluster of drab girls gathered around, loitering like coyotes just beyond the firelight. Hendrik was not yet far enough along the whiskey turnpike to discern the attractions of these painted specimens, but he knew well enough that before the bottle was emptied he would make out some startling and hitherto unperceived beauty among the unpromising herd.

Joseph, eyes bright, had taken a shine to Eddy, whom the brothers had come upon when the tavern was a deal less populated than now. Alone and muttering, he had been scattering spittle over the pages of the book he was reading. He was going through a poem by Longfellow, underscoring phrases stolen from other sources, and his first outburst had been a bilious attack on monied plagiarists. Now the conversational topic had shifted, Eddy was arguing mysterious matters with Joseph.

"Our perceptions must perforce be inexact," Eddy said, taking some new tack. "A veil hangs before all things and we cannot push it aside. My belief is that devices can be constructed, poetical devices or physical, which would enable us to see clear through this fog as a telescope penetrates the night skies."

"Aye, there's truth to be seen," Joseph said, taking another gulp of liquid fire. "The Lord's Truth."

Hendrik knew the preaching fever was almost on his brother. It was Joseph's habit to pursue the pleasures of the bottle, generously sharing them with fellows like this poet, until entirely in his cups. Then Joseph would be possessed of a deep revulsion for his sinful ways and would feel compelled to get up on a table and rail against the generality of mankind. His usual topics were those faults that ran strongest in his own character – drink and dissipation.

"If we could but shake the casts from our eyes," Eddy continued, "what wonders would not be disclosed to our revivified sight? We could remake the world on ideal lines."

"Changes are coming, Eddy. The Lord's changes."

While Hendrik had knocked around the territories for most of his adult life, Joseph had stayed in the States. His travels had all been interior, and wayward.

If he had been more given to speechifying, Hendrik would have silenced Joseph and Eddy, criticising them for drawing conclusions about the nature of the universe from observations made exclusively in taverns, chapels and the gaudy houses of Massachusetts. A man had no right to an opinion of the world until he had seen the unpeopled desert stretching to the Western horizon, waded through Florida swamps forever expecting a Seminole blade in his throat, outraced the soldiers of Mexico while comrades fell at the Alamo, passed a year in the wilderness without seeing another human soul, held in his hands a treasure in dust that would shame the courts of Europe, losing said fortune along a punishing trail, yet counting himself wealthy indeed to come down from the mountains still breathing.

"This world does not please its maker, Eddy," Joseph said. "It is populated by foul harlots and men of low character."

Molly's comrades were not offended. Joseph always knew girls in Boston taverns. Originally, he had set out to preach to fallen women but at some point, early in his career as a reformer, he had undertaken to fall along with them. He had passed more than a few nights in jail cells on account of his association with soiled doves.

Eddy ignored the painted child who was cosying up to him, though when the polite coughs with which she endeavoured to secure his attention turned into racking spasms that spotted her kerchief with blood, he began to show singular excitement.

Joseph was able to keep up a flow of chatter, though he had a constantly replenished glass in one hand and the substantial bosom of Molly O'Doul in the other. For some reason which Hendrik thought best to leave behind Eddy's universal veil, Molly was providing coin enough to settle the party's bill.

Suddenly, Joseph slammed down his glass, sloshing liquor on the scarred bar, and cast Molly roughly aside. He leaped up from the stool upon which his backside had been perched, tearing his hat from his head and hammering his breast with both fists. His remaining fringe of hair, wet with whiskey-sweat, stood out in tufts from his scalp.

"The Lord is upon me," Joseph shouted, "and I must speak His Truth!"

The hat skimmed, forgotten, through the air and crumpled against the wall. With an agility that always surprised Hendrik, Joseph leaped upon the bar and strutted like a performer upon a stage. Eddy's large, watery eyes goggled and his tiny mouth fell open. At this, even the poet's prodigious flow of talk ran dry. The coughing child – Kitty or Katie or somesuch – looked down as if expecting a thorough chastising.

The regulars at Samuel's had seen this before. Ernie was ready with his cloth to wipe any drink that was spilled by Joseph's boots, and with his leaded shillelagh to silence any unwise customer who might complain at such wastage. A few of the girls clapped; nothing so endeared Joseph to women as his ability to convince them the fires of hell were nipping at their petticoats.

Joseph sucked in a lungful of smoky air and Hendrik assumed the draught would be good for a full hour of sermon. Afterwards, Eddy might feel obliged to counter with a recital of one of his poems. As free shows went, it was one of the more expensive. Listening to rot gave a man considerable thirst.

"Sisters, brothers…" Joseph began.

His flow died and his mouth stilled. His eyes fixed upon a face in the crowd and words became ashes on his tongue. His cheeks and forehead flushed an angry crimson.

Hendrik turned to discern the object of his brother's gaze. The lump in his leg shifted sharply and he gritted his teeth at the pain.

He could still hear the crack of that rifle shot. Then, he had thanked the Lord, for if the ball had missed his leg and penetrated his horse's ribs, Santa Anna's men would have brought him down and his pains would have been at an end. Now, he cursed the tiny scrap of dull, unreachable metal.

Standing alone, near the back of the room, was a man in nondescript clothes. His face might be carved of wood: cheekbones knife-edged, mouth a thin line. His eyes were concealed behind extraordinary spectacles, black wooden frames with silvered mirrors for lenses. Whatever Joseph saw in those mirrors, smote him to unique silence.

III
Utah Territory, 1854

THE SKY WAS the colour of flame, scattering bloody light on wind-carved mountains and deep-etched rifts. When the canyon widened briefly to admit the light, their shadows lay before them, spindle-legged and scrawny, dark against reddish dust and rocks.

The party made its way through a narrow fissure which cut deep into the rock. A primordial blow, struck by the hand of God, had cracked the land in two. Another shift might restore the unity, and crush them all like paste between hard faces.

Hendrik had learned that everything was alive.

Brother Carey's horse paced evenly. The young Josephite's long rifle jogged against his back as he bent his body either way to avoid overhangs. Hendrik carefully kept to the centre of the path. The walls of the passage were rough. A scrape against an outcrop could take off clothes and skin.

At the head of the column, the Ute whistled like a night bird. The sound cut the quiet like a dagger's edge. Beside the Ute, Brother Clegg, who had once been a soldier, held up his hand and whirled it in a signal.

Step by step, the party emerged from the passage and fanned out as if drilled. Their horses stood in the shadow of the mountain, at the top of a gentle slope. Below was New Canaan.

The community was a collection of rough dwellings and fragile, irrigated squares of wheat. There was little timber around; most homes were assembled from old stones, roughly fitted together like cairns.

Still-smouldering hearths allowed smoke to trickle from chimneys into the sky. The party had little time. These sodbusters would rise with the sun.

Hendrik dismounted. His leg thrilled with pain as he came down on the hard ground, but he did not cry out.

IV
Boston, 1843

THE MAN IN the mirrored glasses claimed to be of the Ute, but Hendrik knew he was no Plains Indian. He might be a native of Arabia or a Chinaman or an inhabitant of the moon, but he was not from the West. He could just about pass, with his thin face and leather skin, but he had about him a quality not of the Americas.

The back room at Samuel's Tavern was usually reserved for dice or cards. If extra payment was made, one could conduct business with Molly or her sisters in the relative warmth and comfort of this place rather than in the foul-smelling alley outside. The confined space was infernally hot. The only light came from the stove, which cast glow-ing bars of red on faces and walls.

Fires burned in the Ute's spectacles.

The company was much reduced. Hendrik, Joseph, Eddy. And the Ute. Hendrik was in a fog as to how this party had assembled, and what bargain had been struck between them.

Now, Eddy and Joseph leaned forwards, hellfire striping their attentive faces, each fixed upon the bogus Indian as if held rapt by a speech. In fact, the Ute was silent.

The drink had burned out of Hendrik's brain, leaving behind a ruin of aches. Midnight was long past but dawn was a way off.

From inside his jacket, the Ute produced a book. He laid it, open, on a table. The pages were covered in neat sym-bols, cipher or foreign script. The ink must be silvered, for the writing caught firelight and seemed to waver on the page.

"Words of fire," Joseph breathed. "The Truth is written in flame."

Eddy shook his head, denying something.

"Do not reject this revelation, brothers," Joseph said.

The Ute took off his fabulous spectacles and laid them on the book. His eyes were deeply shadowed, lending his upper face the empty-socketed look of a skull.

Joseph reached out for the spectacles and picked them up. Hendrik wanted to tell his brother to throw the damned things on the floor and stamp them into fragments.

The Ute turned to look directly at Hendrik. Minute sparks shone in his eyes.

Hendrik was pinned to his chair. The heat hung heavy on him.

Joseph set the spectacles on his face and adjusted them. He gasped in amazement. Tears emerged from behind the reflecting circles and trickled down his cheeks.

"I see," he breathed. "I see… Truth."

He snatched up the book and turned pages, as if absorbing paragraphs of sense in a second. He hurried on, nodding and laughing and sighing. Lenses flashed as his head bobbed.

"Lord," Joseph said, not profaning the name, but invoking, praying.

Hendrik did not know what was happening. The room was stifling, heat squeezing the head and pinioning the limbs. Eddy was intent on Joseph, impatient for his turn.

The Ute sat as still as a stone.

Joseph had been well up on his scriptures as a child, but possessed of a wild streak. He had run with the barefoot and savage Irish. Their parents, respectably Dutch-speaking after generations in the New World, had expected to be shamed by him. But it was their first-born, abandoning law books for the West, who had proved the greater disappointment. They were both dead now, buried in a cold and crowded churchyard.

After minutes that stretched like hours, Joseph took the spectacles from his face and, hands not shaking, laid them down. He was transformed. Hendrik saw a new calmness. His brother had won battles with himself. He beamed like a happy baby, but his smile was frightening.

The Ute's gaze swivelled, neck moving like a snake, and he looked to Eddy.

The poet swallowed and took the glasses. He put them on, looking not at the book but at its owner. For a moment, he stared the Ute full in the face.

A scream began deep in Eddy's chest and exploded from his mouth with the force of a cannon-blast. In the tiny room, it was as loud as thunder, as high as the wind.

Eddy stood, stool falling away, and staggered as if smitten. Hendrik was on his feet, arms out to catch the poet. He met surprising resistance. The little man fought like a bobcat, screeching as if dying.

"What is it?" Hendrik asked, seeing his own face in the mirrors over Eddy's eyes. "What do you see?"

They fell against the stove and Hendrik felt searing pain in his hip. The poet broke loose and twisted around, the skirts of his coat flying, upsetting the table. Hendrik smelled his own scorched clothes. The Ute seemed mildly interested in the commotion. Joseph was still transported to the heavens. Words scattered among Eddy's screams.

"The maelstrom at the heart of all," he babbled. "The colossal maelstrom, always sucking, devouring, destroying! The void inside the night's maw, where darkness and decay and death hold illimitable dominion over all…"

The poet threw himself against a door, his whole body shaking, and battered it with his fists. He was snivelling and sobbing, liquid tracks pouring down his face. The latch was displaced and the door swung outwards into the alley.

"*Tekeli-li*," Eddy screamed, a birdlike jabber, "*tekeli-li, tekeli-li, tekeli-li…*"

The poet turned and ran, caroming off the wall opposite and tearing away into the night. The Ute bent down and picked up the spectacles. Eddy had dropped them. Hendrik heard him in flight, a clattering of boots on cobbles and an extended garble of terror.

Hendrik stood in the alley with the Ute, struggling with his own panic. The poet's nonsense had in it something of the screeches of the Seminoles, the howling of wolves, the drone of the Mexican *degüello*. They were all the sounds of death. Moonlight fell all around. Hendrik looked to the stranger, who held out his spectacles, offering them with a sly curve of a smile.

Eddy had fallen silent or was beyond earshot. Joseph was alone inside. Hendrik looked at the glasses, so odd and innocent in the Ute's weathered hand.

The offer was still there.

V
Utah Territory, 1854

BROTHER CAREY STRIPPED to the waist, arranging his neatly unpegged clothes in a parcel which he fastened to his saddle. His skin was pink in the early light, unmarked. Hendrik's own chest and limbs were a map of his campaigns, each engagement marked with a scar.

The Paiute waited patiently, holding aloft torches whose growing flames were barely visible in the early morning light. The Ute laid out the pots of paint on an unrolled skin.

Carey finger-streaked his face blue and red, and drew designs on his chest, circling his nipples with angry eyes, drawing a toothy mouth on his belly. He looked like no sort of Indian Hendrik had ever faced.

Pretending to be savages was an American tradition, dating at least to the Boston Tea Party. The pretence masked a deeper truth. Europe was used up; now, America was the battleground of Darkness and Light. His brother had wrapped the whole thing around the Cross of Jesus, but Hendrik knew this was an older conflict and that, in ways he would never understand, it was nearing its end.

Armageddon would be a city in America. The foundations were already marked out with lines of blood.

The Ute squatted by the paints. Hendrik could see his own savage face reflected in twin miniature. He was painted like death, face blackened, black outlined with red.

Today, the Brethren of Joseph and their allies, the people of the Paiute, would ride against the invader. This was the Brethren's territory, no matter how the claim might be disputed. If the action meant war with the United States of America, then the Josephites were prepared to take arms and protect themselves.

The Brethren had been provoked sorely. And the Gentiles had fired warning shots at the Indians.

Satisfied with his war paint, Hendrik returned to his horse. He fastened his belt around his waist. His Bowie knife hung heavy on one hip, his .36 Colt was holstered on the other. In a pouch that hung from the back of his belt, his razor nestled.

In all the meetings, the elders had agreed that the Gentiles were to be run off the land. A good fright should accomplish that. There was no reason to harm them.

No reason.

Clegg inspected the new-painted Brethren, commending them as complete heathens.

Hendrik took his hat from the horn of his saddle and set it on his head, then mounted his horse. The Indians called the Josephites Black Bonnets. A torch was given to him; he held it aloft, a signal for all. He looked up at the sky and saw no birds. He scanned the horizon and saw no strangers.

"Them Gentiles won't know what's hit," Brother Carey said, laughing with no humour. "They'll keep running till they've sea around their boots."

Hendrik let his torch fall, flame slicing through the air...

VI
1843–1848

AFTER THAT NIGHT in Samuel's Tavern, Joseph Shatner was a reformed man. He permanently and publicly abjured drink and dissipation. He persuaded Molly O'Doul to join him in abstinence. Saintliness spread to Molly's sisterhood.

Hendrik took the pledge for his own reasons but found little comfort in purity.

Joseph still preached; now his sermons were conducted in chapels and meeting halls, not in ale-houses and on street-corners. He spoke, eyes burning with the fire of the Lord, of the revelation that had come unto him. The Book was opened. Shining cities would rise in the West, dedicated to the glory of God. Sin was to be obliterated utterly.

The Ute was perpetually in attendance, hanging back, never speaking. Most took him for Joseph's manservant. He seemed to smile now, though it was impossible to gauge whether his stone features actually changed their habitual configuration. He still wore the spectacles.

Always, the offer was there for Hendrik. He could look through the spectacles, like Joseph, like Eddy.

How bad could it be? Joseph had found purpose in his vision, had seen the path to a shining city. He had followers. His congregation donated money. Joseph was better clothed now, always in black. His followers copied his style, his distinctive hat. Even more women clustered around him. Many of the better sort. Sister Molly was among the most respectable of the Brethren of Joseph. Joseph had renounced carnality, but Molly had something of the position of a consort. In order to get to Joseph Shatner, many of the men and women who would most have scorned Molly O'Doul had now to deal with the former drab.

Hendrik made inquiries about Eddy. The fellow had, as he had insisted, some small measure of fame in the world of letters. Having returned to Philadelphia posthaste, his pen was more active than ever. His genius flowed unabated, though it was reckoned morbid and unhealthy. He could not have been seriously harmed by what he had seen, what he *imagined* he saw, through the marvellous mirror-glasses.

So why was Hendrik afraid?

THE CHURCH GREW. Brothers wore black frock coats and circular hats, sisters looked like widows in black bonnets and smock-dresses. There were many such sects in New England, all apparently thriving, talking of Utopian communities to be built in the unpeopled West, or giving dates in the imminent future which would mark the Day of Judgement. Creeds flourished: Mormons, Mennonites, Danites, Millerites, Hittites, Shakers, Esoterics, Hutteriah Brethren, Quakers, Agapemonists, Seventh Day Adventists. But, Hendrik knew, the Josephites were different. Even the Mormons, who had their own spectacles, were less plagued by miracles than the faith founded by his brother.

When Hendrik and Joseph reoccupied their father's town house, it became the headquarters of the Brethren. Between sermons and gatherings, Joseph Shatner shut himself away with the Ute. Hendrik tried not to know what passed between them but Joseph could not resist sharing the wonders that were disclosed. He was setting everything down in his own testament, *The Path of Joseph*.

Joseph tried to share his revelation. His Brethren were receptive to the message, so why not his brother? If only Hendrik would look through the marvellous glasses, then he would truly understand.

Hendrik remembered Eddy's cries. If Joseph had seen a shining city, what had assaulted the eyes of the poet?

"*Tekeli-li, tekeli-li, tekeli-li…*"

The echo of Eddy's babble resounded in Hendrik's skull.

He considered setting out for California, but something kept him in Boston. Perhaps he knew that no matter how far he went, the Church of Joseph would spread to encompass him. His responsibilities, however they had been neglected in the past, were with his brother. He was the head of the family, even if Joseph was head of the Brethren.

The Word of Joseph spread. *The Path of Joseph* was published, despite vandalism at the contracted printers, and disseminated among believers. Converts flocked to Massachusetts and many found temporary accommodation in the Shatner household. Sister Molly presided over chaste dormitories. Rules were handed down: buttons were forbidden as fripperies, coffee was condemned as an impure stimulant, "thee" and "thou" were required forms of address.

Rumours spread. Irresponsible gossips alleged Josephites practised animal sacrifice, that the Sisters were held as communal property by the Brethren, that Gentile children were kidnapped into the Church. These absurdities reached the less scrupulous periodicals, that hastened them into print. Wild stories gained great currency and idlers competed to embroider the legends with grotesque frills. It was said the Christ that Joseph Shatner worshipped had goat's horns.

Gradually, public meeting places ceased to be available for Josephite gatherings. Brethren were abused in the streets, sometimes severely, and the Shatner household was daubed with paint and filth by unknown vandals. Local ordinances were passed limiting the rights of Josephites to worship, to own property, to hold public office. With each slight, Joseph became more sure of himself.

HENDRIK REMAINED ON the Council of the Brethren but the true inner circle was restricted. It consisted of Joseph Shatner and the Ute. Hendrik tried to learn more of the Ute. Little that was concrete emerged, though Hendrik consulted frontiersmen who concurred with him that the man in the mirrored glasses was unlike any Indian who ever walked.

In the basement of the Shatner mansion, Joseph built a private chapel. He passed many nights there, secluded with the Ute. Peculiar smells seeped upwards and filled the house. When Hendrik asked his brother what went on in his night rituals, Joseph told him he was seeing further, piercing more mysteries, rending aside the veil…

"You wear the spectacles?"

Joseph nodded and held his brother by the shoulders. "Thou too must look through the lenses, Hendrik. The Revelation was for us three. Poor mad Poe could not understand what he saw. Only I have accepted the gift of sight. It is not too late to see the city, my brother."

Hendrik shook Joseph off.

In September 1846, Hendrik returned late one night to find the house afire, an angry mob gathered around. As he made his way through the crowd, Hendrik heard stories from all sides. He could not believe a fourth of them.

Recently there had been a rash of disappearances among children of good families. Investigating the crimes, the authorities, acting upon anonymously provided information, had breached Joseph Shatner's cellars and surprised him in his chapel in the midst of some rite. Hendrik heard a dozen obscene accounts of the scene that had been disclosed. Two children, allegedly, had been recovered.

At the edge of the crowd, watching the house burn, he found the Ute. Hendrik started forwards, but the Ute gripped him by the arm and held him back. The upper windows blew out with the heat, showering glass onto the cobbles. As they fell, the shards sparkled with fire. Hendrik heard his brother calling for him. Joseph, hatless and bloody, was in the grip of stern officers.

He cried out as he was dragged away. The arrest was not easy. Among the mob, many of Joseph's followers impeded the officers. Shouts were raised. Some sang "The Path of Joseph", the Brethren's anthem. Gentiles tore up cobblestones and used them as missiles, putting officers in the uncomfortable position of shielding the man they had arrested. A sheriff discharged a pistol into the air but was not rewarded with silence.

Two empty-faced children, swaddled in blankets, stood with one of the officers, regarding the fire with no especial interest. They were Joseph's accusers.

Finally, Joseph was wrestled into a closed cart. As it trundled off, mobs pounded on the cart and Josephites pounded on the mobs. Running fist-fights spread through the streets. Hendrik heard more shots. A fire engine arrived, amid a tintinnabulation of bells, too late to save the Shatner house but in time to prevent the spread of the conflagration to the neighbouring residences. Water gushed and steam rose.

The Ute released Hendrik and gave him something. The mirror glasses. Fierce indignation burned in Hendrik's breast. The timbers of his father's house cracked and fell in upon themselves. From the heart of the dying fire came a roar as of a stricken lion.

"Yes," he said.

He put on the spectacles.

FOR AN INSTANT, the night sky was a blaze of white and the flames were black. The Shatner house stood not in the city of Boston but on an infinite plain of white sand, of salt baked under a pale sun. Joseph was alone.

No, *not* alone.

The distant echo of Eddy's "*Tekeli-li, tekeli-li, tekeli-li*" sounded from the throats of horrid, birdlike things.

★ ★ ★

Hendrik tore the glasses from his face and gave them back to the Ute. He had almost, but not quite, accepted the gift. In that moment, he truly became a follower of Joseph.

Within days, he was calling upon his long-forgotten legal education and fighting in court. No respectable lawyer would undertake to appear in defence of Joseph Shatner, who was accused of disgusting offences. A few wretched apostates drifted away from the Church, but an overwhelming number stuck by their new faith as its founder was pilloried. Hendrik was not surprised when Sister Molly told him the flow of new converts was unabated. Martyrs attract followers.

During the nights before the trial, five Josephites were killed in the city. Only one of their murderers was apprehended; he was later acquitted, indeed commended, by a Gentile jury. Brethren were refused service in stores. Josephite homes and meeting houses were razed.

When sentence of death was passed, half the courtroom erupted in cheering. Josephites sat stunned. Hendrik had expected no less and burned with a cold fury. When the judge's hammer silenced the dancing merriment, Joseph bowed and thanked the court, claiming "I go without regret to Golgotha."

Joseph Shatner was hanged in public on 5th October, 1846. The judge ordered that no member of the Brethren of Joseph should be permitted to attend and officers rigorously enforced the ruling. Hendrik, believing he had a special dispensation, put on Gentile clothing – the buttons, so recently abjured, were already awkward to deal with – and took his place in the crowd.

Joseph died with the catcalls of a Gentile mob in his ears. And a smile on his face.

Driven out of New England, the Josephites followed the path west. The Ute was their scout and Hendrik their wagon master. From all over, converts came. The Word of Joseph spread. There were miracles a-borning in the western wilderness.

Across desert, mountain, river, rock and plain, Josephites made their way. They faced hostile Gentiles and savage Indians. They were robbed and killed, abused and burned, whipped and battered. Treasured possessions turned to millstones and were abandoned along the trail. Still, the pilgrims endured. With each blow, the faith became stronger. Many died singing "The Path of Joseph".

As he travelled, Hendrik often dreamed of the plain he had glimpsed. It was featureless and white, extended to an unimaginable horizon in every direction. There was no cover, nothing to interrupt the monotony of the landscape. He saw no other moving, living thing; and yet he knew, with the echo of Eddy Poe's screams and of the bird-things, that he was not alone.

Westward rolled the wagons, ever westward…

VII
Utah Territory, 1854

HENDRIK SPURRED HIS horse as the party charged, whooping like wild things. Reins held fast in his left hand, he leaned over to one side, trailing his torch through the wheat, leaving a wake of fire. Crackling flames spread and thick smoke drifted from crops that had been painfully wrung from unpromising soil.

He let the torch drop and straightened, urging the horse to plough through an irrigation flue. His steed reared up, hooves kicking, and the water-bearing structure – adapted from abandoned mining apparatus – collapsed all around them.

The human din was incredible. The party screeched like creatures of Hell and rode at the houses of New Canaan like a stampeding herd.

A blinking Gentile emerged from the nearest building, slipping suspenders up over his shoulders, hair awry from recent sleep. Brother Carey side-swiped the man as he rode past, pitching him back at his doorway. As the Gentile's head cracked against his lintel, Carey yelled triumph and wheeled around, coming back for another pass.

Hendrik saw the pistol in Carey's hand kicking before he heard the shots. Bloody wounds burst out of the Gentile's chest.

VIII
1849

THE UNITED STATES provisionally ceded tracts of stony land to the Brethren of Joseph, but the persecutions did not cease. In the east and south-east, Josephites were branded as sacrificers of small children and hounded out of towns. In the south, Josephites were barred from owning slaves. Congressmen railed against the Brethren as Devil-spawn. Gentile parsons preached abomination from pulpits.

Hendrik, seeing the bloody footprints the elect left in their wake, came to understand sacrifice. The Ute led them on and remained at the settlements while Hendrik returned to shepherd the next pilgrims. In the west, the Brethren discovered the savage force of their new faith.

The blood sacrifices began. Hendrik, trying to rid himself of his dreams, offered up his own blood many times. When he had to fight for the Brethren, he did so without compunction.

He fought with a greater conviction than ever before. Indians lay in the wake of the wagon trains, mutilated so their ghosts could never enter the spirit lands. Outlaws were hanged from trees or left where they fell, rotting warnings for their kind.

Don't tangle with the Josephites, people said, whispering. Many of the malicious stories Hendrik had heard, he made true. If a Gentile stood in the path of Joseph, it was no sin to shift him with a bullet or a stone or the razor.

In his own sermons, begun hesitantly but with growing fervour, Hendrik preached that Gentiles were no better than beasts. He spoke of the fire and the rope, and the debt that could only be paid in blood. For every drop of Josephite purple, a quart of Gentile blood must be spilled.

As he preached, Hendrik would open his palms with a razor. Many of his congregation followed his example. Among the Josephites, an elite arose who carried razors about their persons, always ready for a blood sacrifice.

Few turned aside from the path. Most of them returned eventually. Apostates were scourged righteously.

The blood rose around Hendrik.

Finally, he fell away from the path. The dreams were not blotted out by blood. The Ute's smile seemed to have become a deathly grin. Hendrik was weighted down by the sacrifices.

He fled east and ran into an old friend.

IX
Baltimore, 1849

HENDRIK WAS AFRAID the Brethren had despatched their agents, human and otherwise, for him. He could not see a black hat on the street without running for cover. He kept his razor open in his pocket.

The Ute must have decreed that he be returned to the fold. To the elect, the Word of the Ute was as the Word of Joseph himself. The brother of the founder could not be allowed to turn apostate. Hendrik was determined to be killed rather than be taken back to the settlement. One last blood sacrifice.

He considered his options. If he made his way to New York, he could find passage on a ship for Europe. The Ute's influence did not yet extend to the Old World. He would make a life for himself in England or Holland. He would die before the Word of Joseph reached Europe.

But he was being followed.

The streets were full. Elections were a few days away and corner-speakers campaigned furiously despite the strong winds and soaking rain. Hendrik sensed rather than saw the black hats.

He ducked into Gunner's Hall, a thronged tavern, and there, at the bar, haunted and alone, was Eddy Poe, coughing over drink. The poet saw Hendrik coming and flinched, but was too drained to run. Hendrik understood how he must feel.

It was strange; here was the only other man living, so far as he knew, who might understand his plight.

Eddy, hollow-cheeked and poorly dressed, seemed twenty years older. He wore a moustache now. Hendrik thought his pale face might be powdered. He was living in Richmond, travelling north to deliver lectures on "The Poetic Principle", reciting his own modestly famous verses.

Over the years, Hendrik had sought out Eddy's work, imagining in the fever dreams and horrors paraded across the page what the poet must have seen through the spectacles. His tales were crammed with the unquiet and unforgiving dead, with vast and malignant cosmic entities, with plague and premature burial. He had to admit Eddy hardly seemed the cheeriest of souls in the pieces published *before* that encounter in Samuel's Tavern.

Eddy, for his part, had followed the careers of the Brothers Shatner. Several times, he admitted, he had felt the impulse to light out for the Josephite Settlement.

Again, Hendrik asked Eddy what it was he saw.

The poet shrugged.

"I believed I beheld the face of the worm. Or the mechanicals of the cosmos. I cannot be sure. The lasting impression is philosophical, not visual. I have come to think we were subject to some trickery of the light, some distortion of the glass, but that a deeper truth was poured into our souls. Not one day has passed but that I have not shuddered at the memory of that accursed night."

Hendrik confessed to a similar affliction.

Eddy was struck with a fit of coughing. Hendrik realised the poet was sorely ill.

"It tore the heart out of me," Eddy managed to say. "Since then I have walked with the dead. I cannot look upon the face of a loved one without seeing the worms burrowing beneath the skin."

Hendrik surveyed the well-lit room. There were several black hats, bobbing behind the sea of faces. The noise of people was oppressive, and the heat, contrasting with the chill of outdoors, hard to stand. The revellers' coats steamed.

"They are here," Eddy said, blankly. "The conquerors."

Faces flowed into one another. The crowd grew thicker. Steam spotted the ceiling. The noise increased. Hendrik tried to stand away from the bar but the press was impossible. More and more people, many in black, poured into Gunner's Hall like sand. He was wedged tight. Smoky yellow light flooded the room. Hendrik blinked, water in his eyes.

He still struggled and listened. The noise was a babble; no matter how he tried, he could not focus on any one voice, or discern any actual words. The sound was human and yet not language, an alien hubbub akin to the rhubarbing of minor stage players called upon to simulate background noise. But this was not background, this was deafening.

Eddy tried to speak, but his words were lost, drowned. Hendrik's ears hurt and his body was pressed against the rail of the bar. Looking into the mirror behind the bar, he saw the crowd had coalesced into one mass, clothed in a vast patchwork of materials. The morass was dotted with distorted heads topped by familiar hats. The crowd, one creature, flowed all around, washing against the corners of the room like water, climbing the walls. Bodies stretched like rubber and merged like melting wax. The level was above the waist already.

Blood trickled from one of Hendrik's ears. Eddy was being sucked under, a chequered tide slipping around him. The noise, a painful yammering, smote Hendrik like a cudgel. He could not fill his lungs. His mouth was full of the taste of sickness. His ribs strained and threatened to stave in.

The mirror bulged outwards, unable to contain such a living mass, and exploded into a million fragments.

The noise shut off and Hendrik was released, falling to the floor. A spittoon overturned, spilling tobacco slime under his palm.

Wiping his hand on his trousers, he stood.

Eddy, coughing still, clung to the bar as if it were the wheel of a ship in a storm.

They were alone with a roomful of statues, looking out through the smashed mirror onto a familiar plain. A thin horizon separated white land from white sky. The remaining spears of mirror fell out of the frame and scattered across the plain, sucked by an unfelt wind.

The tavern doors pushed inward and the company was joined. A man, his head hooded, staggered in, arms stretched out, and wound a way between the statues. The dummies represented the drinkers who had been in Gunner's Hall when Hendrik had first entered, posed in attitudes of revelry, grins painted on their faces, prop tankards lifted.

The newcomer's head lolled unnaturally and Hendrik recognised his brother. Joseph reached up and snatched off the hood. His face was discoloured and the top of his spine poked out of the skin under one ear. A waxy mould spread under his face and a red rope-weal ringed the stretched neck like a cravat. The apparition, its voice-box crushed, could not speak. It staggered towards the bar and came to a halt, eyes swivelling between Hendrik and Eddy.

Another had slipped into the room. It was the Ute, dressed as a Josephite elder, eyes reflecting in the shadow of his hat-brim.

"Not enough blood," the Ute said to Hendrik. "Not nearly enough…"

Hendrik knew he was entrapped again, that he must return to the Path of Joseph. He stood away from the bar and Joseph clapped a cold hand on his shoulder.

He surrendered his purpose.

Eddy stayed by the bar, turning to look at the Ute. The mock Indian took off his mirror glasses and held them out again. Eddy was trembling throughout his body. A tiny dribble of blood emerged from between his lips.

Hendrik saw the Ute's broad, black-covered back as he faced down Eddy Poe. The poet looked at the offered spectacles, then up at the Ute's face. His trembling froze.

"Friend," Eddy said, "what can be discerned with these adornments is as nothing set beside what I see in your eyes."

Eddy turned away and the Ute put his glasses back on. The dummies moved again, voices buzzed all around.

Joseph and the Ute were gone. Hendrik was jostled.

"Eddy…?"

The poet shook his head but would not turn. In the intact mirror, Hendrik saw Eddy's stricken face. He looked worse than the apparition of the hanged Joseph. Hendrik backed away, with increasing haste. People got in the way and he could no longer see Eddy. He turned and ran from the tavern. The icy rain outside washed away his fear.

A Josephite party would be gathering soon to leave for the Settlement. He would return to the Path. Only blood could free him.

X
Utah Territory, 1854

HE PULLED HIS Bowie out of the Gentile's neck-vein and was blinded by the burst of blood. Hendrik shook his eyes clear and looked into the dying face. He saw nothing he had not seen before. He scored a deep line across the settler's forehead with his knife-point, then lifted the hair. It came away in a ragged cap. The light went from the Gentile's eyes.

Hendrik gave voice to a shout of savage victory.

Eddy Poe had been discovered in Gunner's Hall, having been missing for some days, by an acquaintance who surmised he was deathly sick. He wore ill-fitting clothes believed not to be his own and was in a semi-conscious state taken for severe intoxication. Conveyed to the hospital of Washington Medical College, he babbled constant delirium, addressing spectral and imaginary objects on the walls.

"*Tekeli-li, tekeli-li, tekeli-li…*"

All around, New Canaan burned. Hendrik had lost count of those he had sacrificed this morning. His painted skin was crusted with drying blood. Scalps lay strewn in his wake. He did not keep trophies.

When a doctor told Eddy he would soon be enjoying the company of his friends, he broke out with much energy and said the best thing a friend could do would be to blow out his brains with a pistol. Raving for a full day or more, he exhausted himself and, quietly moving his head as he said "Lord help my poor soul", expired.

Baltimore newspapers reported that the poet's death was caused by "congestion of the brain" or "cerebral inflammation".

With Brother Carey, Hendrik hunted down Gentile families. He razored off a mother's eyelids and forced her to watch as Carey eased his jackknife into her sons' throats. Her anguish was an offering. Gathering the woman's hair in his fist, he slid his blade around her skull, feeling the razor-edge scrape bone. He scalped her alive then stove in her brains with his boot-heel.

He yelled to the skies, to his dead brother, to goat-horned Jesus. Blood flowed into the American earth around his boots. He waded through the rivers of his sacrifices. Fresh water from the prized well of New Canaan would run pink for years.

His war cry choked and he had to catch his breath. Three Paiute braves stood a little way off, watching the Josephites make sacrifice of the Gentiles. The Indians seemed appalled. The practice of scalping had been introduced to the Americas by the French, Hendrik knew. Savagery came from men's hearts, not their skins.

"From this day," said Crow Who Mourns, the Paiute chief, indicating Hendrik, "you are Bonnet of Death, killer of women and children!" There was no condemnation, exactly, in the Paiute's naming. But there was a recognition that Hendrik Shatner was not of the red man.

"This is a new land," he shouted, a hank of long, bloody hair in his fist, "and we are the new people!"

The Gentiles had been taken by surprise. The men, having invested so many hours of agony in their crops, tried first to save the fields, leaving their families for the knives and guns of the Josephites. They had quickly seen their mistake. There were bloody black hats in the dust and Indians had fallen too.

But Hendrik was invincible. He might have taken another ball in his leg, but he could feel nothing.

Bonnet of Death, killer of women and children, abandoned his Bowie in the chest of an old man and continued to make sacrifice with his razor. The blade was thick and slippery with blood but its edge was not dulled.

Animals, freed from pens, ran loose. Josephites put bullets into goats and horses, though the Paiute let the animals pass. Crow Who Mourns had made treaty with the Josephites because a hard winter had carried off too many of the animals of the tribe, and he needed to replenish livestock through raiding. Unheeding pain, Brother Clegg charged at houses, tearing with his hands, scattering stone, uprooting timbers, felling roofs.

In flashes, Hendrik saw the white plain extending around the burning blotch of New Canaan. The plain could absorb any amount of blood and flame.

The Ute strode through it all, approving the sacrifices, silently killing where he could. Eddy Poe had been one more sacrifice, important enough for the Ute to take a personal interest. Hendrik understood that the poet had been some crazed kind of three-fifths genius. The greater the potential that was lost, the greater the offering. He wondered if men or women of genius had died this morning in New Canaan. Was there a child among the dead who would have been a painter, a discoverer, a singer?

In the centre of the nascent town was a half-built church, a raised wooden floor and the skeleton of a tower. A bell, laboriously conveyed through the desert, stood ready to be hauled up. At intervals, Josephites would fire shots at the bell, producing an unresonant dinging.

Brother Carey found a preacher, stripped of his collar but still wearing his black shirt, and pinned him down on the churchless floor, piercing his hands and feet with knife-thrusts. The Josephite had emptied his gun minutes ago. The preacher opened his mouth – to pray? to curse? – and Carey jammed a stone into it. Brother Carey fell upon the Gentile and stabbed him again and again in the belly, ripping free the ropes of his innards, strewing them across the boards.

Hendrik walked towards Brother Carey and the preacher. As he stepped, he froze. Carey was distracted by some sound and looked away. Hendrik saw the perfect circle of his black hat for an instant before its centre became a red splash. Carey fell dead on his still-living sacrifice, his face shot away. At that moment, timbers burned through and the church tower collapsed like a straw house.

Hendrik went to a crouch, alert, taking cover behind the bell. Someone with a rifle had intervened. He remembered the horseman of the dawn and, with a dizzying certainty, knew the stranger was Brother Carey's murderer.

He looked to the fields. They had burned down to stubble. Thinning smoke poured into the air, a veil over the landscape. Through the gauzy wisps, Hendrik saw the horse and the rider. They advanced deliberately through the burned fields. Hendrik lost himself in the shimmer, a great tiredness falling upon him.

The horseman could not possibly reload his rifle in the saddle. Hendrik stood up, ready to chance a bullet, and stepped away from the bell. The boards under his boots were slippery. He was shivering again, shocked awake. The cries of the dead pressed in on him. Again, he had made sacrifice and not been freed. The white pain still waited. He cast his razor away.

No Gentile stood. Josephites had fallen too, and Indians. Animals and men kicked their last, leaking life into the soil, seeding the dirt. Maybe these sacrifices would be the foundation of Joseph's shining city.

The horseman advanced, empty rifle held easily. Hendrik saw a battered face under a battered hat. A long duster lifted in the breeze around his flanks.

To Hendrik, the saddle tramp looked like an executioner from God. He strode past Carey and his kill, stepping off the floor that would never be covered by a church. After a dozen strides, he was walking on the crunchy black stubble of the field. His bootsoles warmed in the thick ash. A ripe, cooked-corn smell hung in the air.

Hendrik thought he must have sacrificed ten or twenty Gentiles. He was Bonnet of Death. He stopped shaking. The stench of blood was as strong as the smell of the corn. His offerings had been rejected. Despite it all, he was not free.

Somewhere, a goat-horned Jesus was laughing, and in his laughter was Eddy's "*Tekeli-li, tekeli-li, tekeli-li…*"

The horseman dismounted and slipped his rifle into a long holster by his saddle. A pistol hung on his hip.

Hendrik unholstered his Colt. It had been forgotten until now; neglected in favour of more personal killing irons. The gun was heavy in his hand. With his thumb, he eased back the firing hammer.

The horseman had also drawn his pistol. A curtain of smoke and low flame hung between them. The heat haze played tricks, making the horseman waver like a reflection in disturbed water.

Hendrik was aware of another in the field. The Ute, a long rifle raised as he paced steadily. Around his knees the flames still burned, but the sham Indian ignored any pain he felt. He waded through fire towards the stranger.

The horseman whirled around slowly, bringing up his pistol. He sighted on the Ute as the Ute sighted on him. The stranger presented his side to Hendrik.

At the edges of the smoking field, the survivors of the war party stood, silent like a congregation. Even the sorely wounded had hauled themselves to a position where they could watch. Crow Who Mourns held up his hand, keeping everyone else out of the drama. This was between the three of them.

The horseman and the Ute were fixed on each other, like a hawk and a snake. Their guns held steady. Hendrik brought up his Colt and sighted on the horseman. The stranger had a thick moustache and a crinkle of lines around his ice-blue eyes. A straggle of white-blond hair escaped from under his hat.

The three men stood, fingers tight on triggers. The moment extended. Hendrik realised his own hand was shaking. He saw the stranger in his line of fire but he also saw the whole scene from above. A triangle of men in a back-burned scar on an infinite plain of white. The black patch seemed smaller, the white sands a continent.

He blinked and focused on his gunsight. Beyond was the red-painted face of the Ute, mirror-glasses flashing sunlight. He glanced away at the horseman, who stood like a statue, and back at the Ute.

In the mirror-glasses, Hendrik saw tiny reflections. His own image was held in one lens, the horseman's in the other.

"Thou must make sacrifice, Hendrik," the Ute said.

Hendrik had been made to kill women and children. He had been made to do worse things than that.

The horseman did not avert his eyes from the Ute. The smoke had almost cleared.

If Hendrik shot the Ute, would the slate be wiped clean? Was this the sacrifice that was truly demanded?

"On three," the horseman said. His voice was strong, unwavering. The Ute nodded assent.

"One," the Ute said.

Hendrik sighted on the horseman.

"Two," the stranger said.

Hendrik sighted on the Ute.

"Three," Hendrik said, firing.

XI

THREE SHOTS SOUNDED at the same instant.

The Ute's black hat flew off, a dash of blood appearing at his temple, smearing into his hair. Two wounds flowered in the stranger's chest.

Hendrik had shot the horseman. His choice was made. It had been made for a long time. He had only deluded himself that things were other than they were.

The Ute lowered his rifle. He did not touch a hand to his wound. A tear of blood ran under his unharmed spectacles and dropped from his cheek.

The horseman staggered, arms out. He looked at the gouting holes in his shirt and dropped his gun. His knees gave way and he fell back in the stubble.

Hendrik had no idea who the stranger was.

The Ute did not make a move to reload his rifle. He stood tall, fires dead around him.

The stranger's horse nosed the dead ground.

Hendrik walked across the ashes and looked at the fallen man. Wounds still pumped and eyes still fluttered. He was alive.

"You're fast," the horseman said, through blood. "Faster'n him." He indicated the Ute. "I'd have holed his evil eye, broke his damn mirrors, only you got me fust."

Hendrik cocked his Colt again and took aim on the stranger's left eye. The horseman was unafraid.

"Finish the sacrifice, Hendrik," said the Ute.

Hendrik looked across at the Ute. He was walking away to rejoin the war party. Hendrik had no idea who the Ute was either, but the man with the mirror glasses believed he owned Hendrik Shatner.

That might not be entirely true.

Hendrik pulled the trigger and put a bullet in the ground by the horseman's head. Dirt kicked and the stranger lay still, holding his wounds.

"Done," Hendrik called out.

The horseman, stilled, looked up with clear, shocked eyes. He must be in great pain, but he might live. And the Ute might live to regret his assumptions.

"Mighty fine shooting, pilgrim," the horseman whispered.

Hendrik Shatner holstered his Colt and walked away from the man he had not killed.

Brother Clegg had his horse ready. Hendrik mounted up. The Paiute had left to make their own way home. Hendrik looked at the faces of the elect, smeared with paint and smoke and blood. They were solemn, but held no regret.

The war party rode away from New Canaan, not talking among themselves, not looking back. Someone, not Hendrik, began singing "The Path of Joseph". Soon, all the riders were singing the hymn. The sun crawled higher into the morning sky.

the book of marilyn

I
8 June 2021

TROOPER KIRBY YORKE, United States Road Cavalry, shot a glance at the route indicator on the dash. The red cruiser blip was dead centre of the mapscreen, green-lines scrolling past. The ve-hickle's inboard computer hooked up with Gazetteer, the constantly updated federal map and almanac. Geostationary weather and spy satellites downloaded intelligence into the electronic notice board.

The patrol had just crossed the old state line and was heading up to a ghost place that had once been called Kanab. Through the armaplas sunshade wraparound, the rocks and sand of Kanab, Utah, could as well be the sand and rocks of Boaz, New Mexico, Shawnee, Oklahoma or most anywhere in the Des.

Yorke's own reflected vizz, dreadfully young under his forage cap, hung in the windscreen, superimposed on the roadside panorama.

The Big Empty stretched almost uninterrupted from the foothills of the Appalachians to Washington State. Rocks and sand. Sand and rocks. Even Gazetteer could not keep straight the borderlines of the Great Central Desert, the Colorado Desert, the Mojave Desert, the Mexican Desert and all the others. Pretty soon, they'd have to junk all the local names and call everything the American Desert. By then, they'd all be citizens of the United States of Sand and Rocks.

The two outrider blips held steady. Tyree and Burnside, on their mounts, would be getting hot and sticky. You couldn't air-condition a motocyke like you could the 4x4 canopied transport Yorke shared with Sergeant Quincannon. That would be rough on Tyree and Burnside.

Yorke liked the feel of the wheel in his gauntlets, liked the feel of the cruiser on the hardtop. He appreciated a beautiful machine. The Japcorps could put heavy hardware on the roads and Turner-Harvest-Ramirez were known for impressive rolling stock. But the US Cav had access to state-of-the-art military and civilian tech. On the shadow market, the ve-hickle was worth a cool million gallons of potable water or an unimaginable equivalent sum in cash money.

He thought of the cruiser as a cross between a Stealth Bomber, the Batmobile, Champion the Wonder Horse and Death on Wheels. All plugged in to the informational resources of Fort Valens and, through the Fort, into the inter-agency datanet whose semi-sentient Information Storage and Retrieval Centre was in a secret location somewhere in upstate New York.

Ever since the Enderby Amendment of 2013 opened up, in desperation, the field of law enforcement to private individuals and organisations, Yorke had wanted to be with an agency. Sanctioned Ops were the only non-criminal heroes a kid from the NoGo could have these days. T-H-R's Redd

Harvest, who dressed for effect, got the glam covers on *Road Fighter* and Harry Parfitt of Seattle's Silver Bullet Agency was always being declared Man of the Month by *Guns & Killing*, the nation's best-selling self-sufficiency magazine. It was the Wild West all over again. Heat went down all over the country: card-carrying Agency ops out for the annual arrest record bonus and stone-crazy solos who brought in Maniax for bounty.

But Yorke knew the only agency which guaranteed ops a life expectancy longer than that of the average Mafioso-turned-informer was the Road Cav. Quasi-government status bought better hardware, better software, better road-ware and better uniforms. He'd joined up on his sixteenth birthday and didn't plan on mustering out much before his sixtieth. He wasn't ambitious like Leona Tyree. In a world of chaos, the Cav offered a nice, orderly way of doing things. He liked being a trooper, liked the food, liked the pay, liked the life.

He even liked Sergeant Quincannon.

Yorke reached up to the overhead locker and pulled a pack of high-tars down from the Quince's stash. The flap was broken and wouldn't stick back. The sergeant stopped pretending to be asleep, and commented, "I knew that gum-wad wouldn't last."

The flap fell down again.

"Wonderful," Quincannon commented. "They can whip up a machine so tough it can take out Godzilla and so smart it can play chess with Einstein, but they still can't get one itty-bitty little catch to stay stuck where it damn well ought to be stuck."

The sergeant accepted one of his own Premiers. He used the dash lighter and sucked in a good, healthy lungful. Quincannon held it in for a few seconds, then coughed smoke out through his nose. He hacked for almost a minute, cursing between choked gasps as Yorke lit up.

"You jake, Quince?"

"Yeah, boy, fine," he said, refreshing himself with another drag. His face had gone even redder. "You know, back when I was young, there were damfool eggheads who said cigarettes caused all sorts of disease. Heart trouble, the cancer, emphysema."

"I've never heard that," said Yorke, who'd smoked since he was ten. He dragged on his own Premier. "Dr Nick on ZeeBeeCee says nothing's better for your lungs than a Snout first thing in the ayem."

"It was a big flap, but it died down. Some say it was the tobacco companies bought or scared off the eggheads."

"Dr Nick says nicotine prevents Alzheimer's," Yorke said.

Like a lot of people his age, the Quince was paranoid. He was full of stories about the government and the multinats, and the sneak tricks they'd pulled. Yorke didn't believe a tenth of them. If he had a few snorts of Shochaiku in him, Quincannon would start claiming the President was mixed up in underhand arms deals. Yorke was used to the ridiculous fantasies the Quince picked up from those mystery faxes which spread malicious rumour and gossip.

Quincannon choked again but kept on dragging. Hell, if smoking was dangerous, the sergeant would be mummified in a museum by now.

Yorke stowed the pack of Premiers and shut the locker. The flap fell loose again and he noticed a picture of a girl taped to the inside. It must have been from some old magazine, because it was in black and white and the image was faded. A blonde stood on the street in a billowing dress, showing her legs. They were nice legs, particularly up around the thighs. The print on the other side of the picture was showing through, giving her gangcult-style tattoos.

"Old bunkmate, Quince?"

Quincannon grunted. "No, Yorke, just the fillette who got us all into this."

"Into what?"

"Hell, me boy, hell." The sergeant sounded wistful. "See those legs. They changed the world."

Yorke sucked in a lungful of gritty smoke and held it until his eyes watered. Tyree's blip wavered. Since there was no longer any such thing as a Utah State Government, the road ahead was unmaintained. Tyree was signalling slow-down. Sometimes sand drifted so thick you couldn't see asphalt. Without thinking, Yorke adjusted the speed of the cruiser.

"Who was she, Jesus's mother?"

Quincannon didn't laugh. "No, that girl was Marilyn Monroe."

"Hell, I know who Marilyn Monroe is. She's in that show on the Golden Years net, *I Love Ronnie*. The fat lady who lives next to Ronnie and Nancy. Her feeb husband is always coming over and making trouble."

Scanning again, Yorke saw Marilyn's eyes in the pretty girl's face. They didn't quite fit her now.

"Marilyn Monroe, huh?"

"Yeah, she's the one," the Sergeant said, almost wistfully. "Before you were born – heck, before even I was born – she was a big star. Movies. Back when you saw movies on a screen, boy, not in a box. That pic's from *The Seven Year Itch*. I saw all her pictures when I was a kid. *Bus Stop*, *River of No Return*, *How to Marry a Millionaire*. And the later ones, the lousy ones. *The Sound of Music*. She was no nun, that's for sure, they laughed her off screen in that. *The Graduate*, with Dustin Hoffmann. She was Mrs Robinson. And *Earthquake '75*. Remember, the woman who gets crushed saving the handicapped orphans?"

Yorke had never had Quincannon figured for a movie freak. Still, on patrol, you wound up talking about almost anything. Out here, boredom was your second worst enemy. After the gangcults.

"So, she was your pin-up. I kinda had a crush on Frankie Sandford back when she was with that Sove rock band. And Lindsay Lohan was a knockout in *Lash of Lust*. But that don't make 'em world-changers."

The cruiser beeped a gas alarm at them. Refuel within 150 klicks or face shutdown. Yorke stubbed his butt into the overflowing ashtray. The interior of the car could do with a thorough clean-out at some near future point. It was beginning to smell pretty ripe. Dr Nick said there was nothing a woman liked better than the good, strong stench of tobacco, but Tyree always pulled a face when she got a whiff of the ve-hickle's upholstery.

"Marilyn wasn't like the others, Yorke. You're too young to remember it all. Sometimes I feel like I'm the only one that remembers – the only one who knows it could have been different – and that's 'cos my daddy told me all about it. It was October 1960. That was an election year. Richard M Nixon–"

"I remember *him*. Trickydick."

"Yeah. He was running against a bird called John F Kennedy. A Democrat–"

"What's a Democrat?"

"Hard to tell, Yorke. Anyway, Kennedy was a real golden boy, way ahead in polls. A hero from the Second War. A cinch to win the election. There was a real good feeling in the country. We'd lived through the first Cold War and put up with Dwight D Boring Eisenhower, and here was this kid coming along saying that things could change. He was like the Elvis of politics–"

"Who?"

"I was forgetting. Never mind. Jack Kennedy had a pretty wife, Jackie. Old money. She was in all the papers. Women copied her hats. Back then, everybody wore hats.

In October 1960, a few weeks before the election, Jackie Kennedy opened the wrong door and scanned the freakin' future President of these United States in bed with Marilyn Monroe."

"Sheesh."

"Yeah. And they weren't playing midnight pinochle. It was in the papers for what seemed like years. People fought in the streets about it. I'm serious. The Kennedys were Catholics and the Pope had a big down on divorce back then, not like the new man in Rome, Georgi. But Jackie sued Jack's ass. He took a beating in the court and a bigger one at the polls. The country let itself in for eight years of Richard Milhous Criminal. Remember that scam with the orbital death-rays that wouldn't work? And the way we stayed out of Indochina and let the Chinese walk in? Trickydick was like the first real wrong 'un in the White House. Since then, we've not had a winner."

Sometimes Quincannon had these talking spells. Like a lot of old-timers, he remembered things having been better. That was sumpstuff; the Quince just remembered when he wasn't old and fat and tired, and assumed the rest of the world had been feeling good too.

"I voted for Estevez, and I'm proud of it," Yorke said. "It was important to keep the Right Wingers out of the White House."

Quincannon laughed. Yorke thought he might be missing the joke. His Premier tasted bitter. Maybe Dr Nick was right, and he should switch to mild-tasting Snouts.

"Remember the others, boy. Two terms' worth of Barry Goldwater, two more of Spiro Agnew, and even that idiot Ford stuck around for the full eight years. If they were executin' any of them for havin' a brain, they'd be fryin' an innocent man. When Ollie North was in the White House it looked like things were going to change but he was hamstrung by the Republican majority in the Senate. And then we had to suffer Clinton, Gore and Heston, none of whom I'd piss on if the very fires of hell themselves were consuming them. For all the talk of Clinton being the new Kennedy, all it turned out they had in common was a thing for sticking their dicks where they shouldn't. Gore practically stole the election in 2008 and Heston only got the Republican ticket thanks to those propaganda films that fella Moore was making.

"Now we've got a former actor with sweaty palms and a daddy who used to play the president on TV. All he can do is kiss ass for the multinats and go on freakin' TV gameshows so's he can lower taxes nobody pays anyway. I've a feeling Jack Kennedy might have done something for this goddamned country. And Marilyn started the rot. Without her, things would've been... maybe not better, but *different*."

II
8 June 2021

THE NOONDAY SUN was a circle of white hot iron, burning a hole in the blue canopy of the sky. Heat fell on his face like driving rain, hammering his frozen-open eyes. Slowly, his brain cooked.

Brother Claude Bukowski Hooper would die soon. He hoped. The Knock 'Em Sock 'Em Robots had downed him on the blacktop, then driven over him a bunch of times. Instead of knees, he had treadmarks.

Black scraps circled on high. Carrion birds, waiting for the spark to go so they could get their grits. Something with dark ragged wings dipped across his field of vision, flapping towards Brother Lennart.

As he breathed, Brother Claude felt the ends of snapped bones stabbing inside. He was too broken, crushed or squashed to fix. He'd hoped they'd zotz him outright, but here he was left in merciless sun, congealing into roadkill.

His fluid self seeped through sun-cracks in the road. The hardtop vibrated minimally. A ve-hickle, many klicks off. His nervous system fused with the Interstate. After death, perhaps he would see out of cats' eyes. *Everybody knows, in a second life, we all come back sooner or later,* the Josephite hymn went, *as anything from a pussycat to a man-eating alligator…* His senses would spread throughout the country, north to Alaska, down Mexico way.

If only Brother Claude could sleep now…

Loss of blood would probably get him, or else suffocation. It was almost impossible to draw breath into his collapsed windsacks. That was how Jesus died on the cross. As a kid, snoozing through scripture shows on the educational TV that was all the cable Mama could afford, he hadn't thought much about what being crucified was like.

The Romans pierced Our Lord's hands and feet, just as the bots had zero-zilched Brother Claude's arms and legs. The idea was: exhaustion set in and you just sort of collapsed inside, lungs constricted flat by your ribs. He hadn't learned that from educational TV – "Yes, Davey," a fundamentalist cartoon dog might tell an audience surrogate, "it took three days for Our Pal Jesus to die in hideous agony" – but from his tour with the Knights of the White Magnolia. Whenever the Knights found a *houngan*, they crucified the conjure man and watched him fade to black. After a while, it got mighty tedious.

Elder Seth said that as thou sowed, so should thou reap. Brother Claude had never exactly crucified anyone, but he'd stood about uselessly like the sportsfans who voted for Barabbas while gentlefolk were nail-gunned to garage walls.

Fancy-shmancy bio-implants and replacement doodads of the sort manufactured and licensed by the almighty Gen-Tech Corporation could do zero for him, even if he could have afforded that kind of repair work. Not that he approved of mad scientist stuff.

The Knock 'Em Sock 'Em Robots were cyborgs. Ashamed of their remaining humanity, they wore black all-over suits with cut-away patches to show off sparkling plastic or metal. Some must be more machine than flesh.

The bots had a roadblock in the middle of nowhere. A digital display sign on their largest RV read *STOP, PAY TOLL*. The resettlers' convoy had no way around, and little enough goods to hand over. So little that the bots were irritated enough to cut out a couple of the Brethren and enjoy a bout of mindless ultra-violence.

As he stomped Brother Lennart with seven-league feet, the hulking panzerboy they called Pinocchiocchio sang "I've Got No Strings to Hold Me Up or Tie Me Down". He did a puppet-like dance of strange grace, reminding Brother Claude of the old British series – *Thunderbirds, Stingray, The Forsyte Saga* – that filled out the downmarket cable stations.

Something winged was tugging Brother Claude's boot, rolling the foot both ways. He couldn't feel anything that far down, and he couldn't lift his head to shoo the ugly bird away.

Before they drove on, one of the bots had knelt tenderly by him and spilled a little water into his mouth. He tasted his own blood in the drink.

"Are you alright, bro?" The kneeling water-dispenser asked, concern dripping from every syllable.

Brother Claude had tried to smile, tried to make the woman (if woman she was) feel better. She wore a black tutu, fluffed out to show long, shiny PVC-skinned legs.

"Snazz," she said, black against the sun. As she stood, the bot hummed to herself:

"When a gal's an empty kettle,
She should be on her mettle
Yet I'm torn apaaaa-art…"

Brother Claude remembered *The Wizard of Oz*. His MRA Troop had been shown the film, a scratchy video dupe from some striated celluloid print, blown up and projected on an off-white sheet. Sarah Michelle Gellar as Dorothy, Snoop Dogg as the Tin Man, Christopher Lee as the Wizard.

Satisfied, the bot kicked him again, jamming the point of her pump into his ribs, breaking a few more bones.

"Just because I'm presumin'
That I could be sorta human
If I only had a heart…"

HER LEOTARD WAS cut away over her chest like a fetish suit. Her breasts were hard, clear, plastic bumps. Inside were wheels and pistons. An LED clock flashed numbers. Tiny gears moved like insect-legs. A rounded glasspex stomach sloshed with acids that processed whatever the cyborg needed to keep walking. Batteries?

The bots drove away, leaving the stink of their exhaust in the air. Elder Seth said a few words over Brother Lennart, and repeated them for Brother Claude. He had thought it best not to interrupt his own funeral service with unseemly groans. The survivors moved on.

He understood the concept of sacrifice. By his death, the Path of Joseph would be seeded.

He didn't envy the bot. It was better to die clean than live on with half your guts replaced by vacuum cleaner parts and computer terminals.

Nobody had chanced along the Interstate since the convoy followed its yellow brick road. Brother Claude wasn't surprised. Only a damfool would venture this far sandside. A fool, or a pilgrim…

He was twisted in the middle, face up but skewed at the hips, groin pressed to the asphalt. He couldn't feel anything below his ribs. Considering what he could feel from the rest of him, that was a mercy. He realised he was deaf. One of his eyes was shut, sealed by a rind of dried blood.

Brother Claude, born in the Phoenix NoGo, had lived outside Policed Zones all his short life, and always had to follow someone. His daddy took off early – Mama Hooper tried to make out he was some high mucky-muck in Japcorp, but Claude knew better the types she slung out with and so he found other daddies.

During the Moral Re-Armament Drive of the early '10s, the ten year-old Claude enlisted in President Heston's Youth Corps. Big Chuck looked like a Prezz ought to: a mile wide at the shoulders with a jaw like a horse-shoe and acres of medal-heavy chest. When Pioneer Hooper was cashiered for breaking a kid's nose in a dispute about the superiority of *Battlestar Galactica* over *CSI: Antarctica*, he transferred allegiance to Burtram Fassett, Imperial Grand Wizard of the Knights of the White Magnolia. The IGW told the pledge that he, as a white heterosexual male, was a Prince of the Earth, and that it was the young recruit's duty to stick killing steel into the human vermin who dared rise up against nature's aristo-crats.

If he was a Prince of the Earth, he'd tried not to won-der, how come his mama couldn't afford the Playboy Channel?

Then he was a soldier in the War. Not any of the over-seas Wars, like the ones in Cuba or Nicaragua: the War between the Knights and the Voodoo Brotherhood, when the Knights tried to clear nigras out of Arizona. That'd been a gold-plated bust. He'd had noble ideas about racial purity and Aryan *jihad* drummed into his greymass, then it turned out the Knights were financed by raghead trou-blemakers from the Pan-Islamic Congress.

His life was trickling out before his eyes, or at least ticking through his greymass. Brother Claude guessed that was a bad sign.

When T-H-R broke up the Knights and Fassett decamped for pastures greener, Claude drifted a spell. Didier Brousset, head *houngan* of the Voodoo Bros, put a bounty on the pizzles of ex-Knights, so it wasn't healthy to keep your white hood and red-cross robes. Claude was on the streets of the Phoenix NoGo, running. Ducking away from a couple of rattlesnake necktie Bros, he found himself in a meeting hall. A man was speaking. He wore a damfool black suit and a pilgrim hat, like many of his audience. He wore mirrorshades, also like many of his audience. And he had the Truth in his voice.

Claude had come upon the Word of Joseph and found himself a final daddy in Elder Seth. The elder purred a sermon, not shouting like the TV preachies Mama Hooper watched whenever she wasn't pumping the bunk with squiffed strangers. In him burned a fire of faith that spread wherever he went. Claude was not the only convert made in that hall that night. He had to jostle through a crowd to sign up.

Brother Claude had been Saved, he thought: he didn't miss recaff or co-cola or the Devil's music or carnal relations or fast foods or pockets or any of the things he was required to abjure. He wore his pegged black coat and round black hat with pride.

"We need men like thee," Elder Seth said. "The Brethren must have young blood. These are the last days."

Elder Seth believed the heartlands were not lost. The Des could be reseeded, resettled, reclaimed. Most everybody outside the Brethren said Elder Seth was a damfool but the elder had a way of convincing people. Claude joined up with the Brethren's Resettlement Programme. He sang the hymns – "The Battle Cry of Freedom", "'Tis the Gift to Be Simple", "The Path of Joseph", "Stairway to Heaven" – and enlisted as shotgun on the first convoy out of Phoenix for Salt Lake City; 850 klicks of lawless road and burning desert lay before the resettlers.

If he'd actually been given a shotgun, maybe he wouldn't be where he was, but Elder Seth frowned on needless violence. "Our weapons shall be our faith and fervour," he announced, while Gentiles shook their heads.

Brother Claude had no idea where he was dying. He wondered if they had reached the former state of Utah. He had the idea that they'd crossed the state line. This was his first time outside his native Arizona. And his last. According to Elder Seth, this wasn't even the United States of America. He was dying on the chosen ground.

As the convoy put out of Phoenix, crowds had cheered. Plenty of big names from the PZ came out, shielded by armed goons – natch – and Elder Seth made a speech to the multitudes. It had been a speech of hope and promise. The big public screen played a message from President Estevez, fumbling his way through best wishes. The Prezz's speech boiled down to "Good luck guys, but don't blame me if you don't make it." Then the gates of the city were opened, brushing away NoGo derelicts who were camping outside, and – after minimal escorting to get them through the Filter – the resettlers were on their way and on their own.

And here he was, bleeding himself empty on the Interstate. Flies buzzed and he imagined tall, dark figures standing over him. They had faces he could recognise – President Chuck was there, and ole IGW Fassett, and Elder Seth, and the woman-like gadget who had given him water – but no real shape. Elder Seth talked a lot about angels, and spirits he called the Dark Ones.

These must be the Dark Ones.

Where, Brother Claude wondered, were the others now? Elder Seth, and Brother Baille, and Brother Wiggs, and Sister Consuela, and Brother Akins, and Sister Ciccone, and the Dorsey Twins? If he twisted his head a degree or so, he could see Brother Lennart, a black rag-doll with a bloody head. The carrion birds were closing in. And other things had loped out of the desert.

As gangcults went, the Knock 'Em Sock 'Em Robots weren't so bad. Compared with the Maniax, the Clean or the Bible Belt, they were easy-goers. After all, they'd only killed a few of the resettlers.

Including Brother Claude Bukowski Hooper.

A Dark One stood over him, black shadow-robes whipped by an unfelt wind. A bearded man, with goat-horns sticking out of his long tangle of hair. He stretched out his arms and worms dripped from the palms of his hands. Brother Claude didn't recognise the apparition.

The road vibrated. Several ve-hickles, getting close. If Claude held on…

Something gave in his neck and his head rolled. His cheek pressed to the hot, gritty road, and his field of vision changed. Beyond the asphalt was desert. In the distance were mountains. Nothing else. There wasn't a cloud in the sky, hadn't been for decades.

The sun still shone, reflecting like a new hundred dollar coin in the pool of blood that was spreading across the road.

Blood on the road.

That reminded him of something Elder Seth had said. Something important.

Blood…

…on the road…

Blood…

A fly landed on Brother Claude's eyelash. He didn't blink.

★ ★ ★

III
8 June 2021

THE CITIZENS WERE dead. There were two in the road, both dressed the same, both dead the same. As usual, they'd been overkilled. Trooper Leona Tyree assumed a parade had run over them.

"No wonder the population's declining," she said to Burnside.

For the first time in the recorded history of the world, according to ZeeBeeCee's *Newstrivia*, violence was a bigger killer than disease or starvation.

"This one lived longer than the other," Trooper Washington Burnside observed, a frown crinkling his recaff-toned forehead, "the poor bastard."

He stood up, brushing road-dirt off the knees of his regulation blue pants. After a couple of days on patrol, the yellow side-stripes were almost obscured.

Tyree scanned the startled faces, trying to puzzle out the look in the eyes. She always wondered about corpses. What had it been like at the end? Sometimes, she thought she thought too much. Maybe that was what held her back.

"The cruiser's coming," Burnside said.

Like Tyree, he wore a gunbelt and suspenders, heavy gauntlets, a yellow neckerchief and knee-high boots. With his microcircuit-packed skidlid off, he could have been US Cav, 1875 vintage.

And the desert here had always been the same. There'd never been wheatfields in this part of Utah.

But it was 2021 all right. You could tell by the tread-marks on the deadfellas. And the armoured US Road Cav cruiser bearing down on them. The ve-hickle was shaped like an elongated armadillo, nose to the ground. Its grey carapace was coated with non-reflective paint.

"Here's the Quince."

The cruiser eased to a halt. Sergeant Quincannon pulled himself out, hauling a shotgun with him. For a fat old guy, he was in good shape. His ruddy complexion came from high blood pressure, Irish ancestors and Shochaiku Double-Blend Malt, but he never gave less than 150 per cent on patrol. In his off-hours, he was another guy altogether. Now, the Quince was purposeful. This was a situation and he was going by the book.

Tyree considered the possibility that the deadfellas were ambush bait. It was unlikely: there was no cover within easy distance of the hardtop. Besides, this wasn't a convoy route to anywhere. Still, she'd scoped the Des for possible foxholes. A man could hide in the sand, but stashing a vehickle was another proposition.

Tyree gave the *no trouble* sign and the Quince stowed his laser-sight pump action back in the car. Yorke stayed at the wheel. He got squeamish in the vicinity of deadfellas. Not a useful character trait in the Road Cav, but he was stuck with it.

Quincannon strode up. He had the Cav walk down pat: sort of an easy lope, with lots of shoulder action, belly pulled in. It was just the right side of a swagger.

"What's the situation?" he asked.

"Unidentified casualties, sir," Tyree replied. "We came upon them as they are. There were birds but I shooed them off with a miniscreamer."

"This deadfella's been gone less'n an hour," put in Burnside. "The other bit the cold one three-four ticks earlier."

"Careless driving costs lives."

"This wasn't careless. Whoever roadkilled these hombres made freakin' sure they did a snazz job."

Quincannon wiped his forehead with the back of his hand. A minute out of his air conditioning and he was sweating. Flies swarmed on the corpses. Soon the

atmosphere in these parts wasn't going to be too pleasant.

"What do you reckon, sir? Maniax?"

The Maniax were supposed to be off the big board in
the Western States, but there were enough rogue chapters
of the gangcult rolling around pissed to do a pretty sight
of damage before their file closed.

"Could be, Leona. Or Gaschugggers, KKK, Razorbacks,
Masked Raiders, Psychopomps, Hole-in-the-Wall Gang,
DAR, Voodoo Bros; any one of a dozen others. Hell, the
Mescalero Apache ain't been no trouble for a hundred
years, but this is their country too. Killin' people is the
Great American Sport. Always has been."

The Quince got like that sometimes, mouthy and hard-
bitten. Tyree put up with it because the sergeant was a top
op. After Howling Paul McAuley, probably the best all-
round op in the Cav. If she wanted to advance herself off
her cyke into a cruiser and then up the chain of command, she'd need his recommendation.

She'd been a trooper a month or so too long as it was.
Put a tunic on her and she'd make a dandy lieutenant.
Then captain, colonel. It could happen. Her mother had
told her it was important to have ambition.

"What do you reckon to their outfits?"

The deadfellas were dressed square, in black cloth suits.
No glitter, no frills.

"Don't rightly know, Burnside. Let's take a closer scan."

Tyree had hoped he wouldn't say something like that.

Without too much evident distaste, Quincannon exam-
ined one of the corpses, slipping gauntleted fingers
between material and meat. He unpeeled a section of
jacket from the crushed chest. The dead man wore a simple black suit and a shirt that had been white once but was
now mainly red. The shirt was fastened to the throat but
there was no tie.

"Funny thing," said Quincannon. "No pockets. No belt. And, scan, no buttons…"

The dead man had fastened his coat with wooden pegs.

"We found this." Burnside handed the sergeant a broad-brimmed black hat.

"He wasn't with any of the usual gangcults, that's for sure," the Quince said. "The ratskags who zotzed him might have taken his weapons, but they'd have left holsters or grenade toggles or something. This damfool wasn't even armed."

"Do you reckon he was an undertaker? All in black, like. Or a preacher?"

"Second guess is more likely, Leona. Though what the hell he was doin' this far into the sand is beyond me."

"Preachers these days pack more firepower than Bonnie and Clyde," Burnside put in. "Take the Salvation Survivalists."

"The other is dressed the same," Tyree observed.

"Just a gang of pilgrims, then. Looking for the Promised Land."

"The Amish don't use buttons," she said. "Or the Hittites."

"As far as I know, the last Amish were wiped out in '19. But that's a good thought. Plenty of religions about these days if a man has a fancy to pick a new one. Or an old one."

Quincannon stood up and dropped the hat over the dead man's face. He observed a private moment of silence and made a gesture that could either be the sign of the cross or the hoisting of a last drink.

"What should we do?"

"Bad news, Leona. You found 'em. You gotta scrape 'em up and bury 'em by the roadside. I'll call it in to Valens. Burnside, break out the entrenching tools and give the lady a hand. Then we'll go up the road a ways, following the tracks. There *are* tracks?"

Tyree nodded. After the pilgrim-flattening session, the killers' tires would be bloody enough to paint a trail for three counties. The white strip down the middle of the road was a solid red.

"Thought so. Anyway, we'll see who's at the end of the trail. If we're lucky, we get to kick badguy ass before suppertime. If not, we ride through the night and head 'em off at sunup."

The Quince saluted. Tyree and Burnside returned the salutes, and pulled neckerchiefs up over their mouths and noses. They'd had all the infection lectures about handling suspect deadfolks. At an adjustment, the bandanas shrivelled onto their faces, functioning as filters.

"Remember, disease is your worst enemy," Quincannon said, "so check the seals on your gauntlets before you interfere with these former citizens. Snap to it, men."

IV
8 June 2021

THE GIRLS WERE loitering around the Virtual Death Unlimited Arcade, a roof on stilts raised over a platoon of credit-machines. The games centre was attached to Arizona-Wonderworld, a failing mall out in the Painted Desert. In the stores, all goods were on massive discount. Jazzbeaux had glommed a pair of snazz boots on American Excess, a card she intended to pay off when Dracula got a suntan. She even found a stall specialising in ornamental prostheses and tried on a selection of eyepatches, none of which took her fancy.

Jazzbeaux, *née* Jessamyn Amanda Bonney, was Acting War Chief of the Psychopomps. Mostly girls, the 'Pomps favoured spike heels, fishnets, glam make-up, stormcloud hairdos, Sove sounds, painted nail-implants, Kray-Zee pills and Kar-Tel Kustom Kars. Their turn-offs included law n' order, school, soce workers, white picket fences, Ken Freakin' Dodd, Mom's apple pie, Maniax and anyone over twenty.

She popped a cold can of Pivo, the new Czech beer currently benefiting from major marketing muscle. A mouthful was antidote to the subliminal brainwashing in the jingle. She squirted the vile stuff onto the ground and tossed the can in the air, drawing a killing bead on it with her finger as it arced towards asphalt.

There weren't many other customers kicking around. Solids stayed away from the sand. The mall was covered in dog-piss spray tags that marked the place as Maniax Territory. Since T-H-R took down the Western Maniax in a joint action with the United States Cavalry, the backbone of Ariz-Wonder's custom was kicking around the Reformation-Confinement Environments the newsies elaborately didn't call concentration camps. Without its status as a major Maniak drop, this place was headed for ghostville. Unless some new, hungry faction stepped in and took over the patronage.

Let's face it, girlie-girl, a power vacuum invites initiative. As Acting WC, it was her place to think ahead a month or two. Without the Grand Exalted Bullmoose and his Merry Marching Morons, Utah and Arizona – at least – were up for grabs. A nice piece of territory, and a chunk of change. She'd seen stats; it was a profitable patch, and someone had to provide the services the Maniax had been delivering. Some things might not exactly be legal, which meant corps had to filter products through street execs.

Andrew Jean, her trusted lieutenant, had opened talks with the Winter Corp and even the Mighty GenTech. If the corps had things (like drugs and guns and virtual porno) that solids wanted, why should feebs in government stand in the way? Wasn't the Prezz supposed to support Free Enterprise? The Psychopomps were notionally Communist, if only because the reds had better uniforms and songs. It was better for all concerned if alternative enterprise was handled by a gangcult with broadly commie principles rather than a rabidly capitalist crew like the Daughters of the American Revolution.

Sweetcheeks, plump and adorable in leopard-print leggings and a monumental fakefur jacket, wiggled her butt as she zapped into a wraparound screen, her head insectile under the VR helm. She was playing *Mambo Massacre*, a game program combining dancercise and combat; kidstuff until Level Nineteen, when the player faced Jennifer Lopez with a chainsaw. Some of the others fooled with games but most just sat on out-of-order consoles and looked out at the sand. Varoomschka was triple-coating her nails with a hammer-and-sickle motif, working as meticulously as if she were putting the final touches to a Fabergé Easter egg.

So Long Suin's shower radio hung from the frame of one of the cars, tuned to Radio Moscow. Petya Tcherkassoff put his tormented soul into "The Girl in Gorky Park". Jazzbeaux was over her queensize crush on the Soviet musickie but still found it hard not to sway when she heard this song. It was about the singer's beautifully pale ex-lover; in the last verse, it turned out she was pale because she was dead. When Petya threw her over, she lay herself naked in the snow and willingly hypothermed. According to *Moscow Beat* magazine, the girl was based on a real person, Natalia Ludmila Someonova, but Jazzbeaux felt the song was just for her. She resented sharing it with the rest of creation.

Her life had not presented unlimited opportunities. She'd bought the gangcult package early and worked her way up from Shrimp to Acting WC. In her early teens, when Papa Bruno was alive and kicking, she did time as a warehouse gladiatrix, racking enough brownie points to

make her a chapter leaderine. She lost her left eye in a
rumble with the Gaschuggers, and Ms Dazzle, her sponsor,
personally paid Doc Threadneedle for the augmentation
surgery. The Psychopomps were more a family to her than
her late, lamented daddy and long-gone mama ever were.
No 'Pomp had ever tried to sell her; well, not lately…

Jazzbeaux knew the ganggirl scene was stupo, but hey,
what else did she have to do? She could read and type, so
her basic education was taken care of. No way was she
going out for indenture to a Japcorp; she didn't want to
turn tricks for scuzz like her daddy, thank you very much;
and there weren't many other career opportunities for a fillette from the Denver NoGo in These Here United States,
so she'd taken a vacation and was opting to hang out for
the rest of her life.

She'd be seventeen in November. If she made it, maybe
she'd take a look at her life-pattern and change it. Or not.
Nichevo, as they said. It didn't matter, much. Everything was
going to end one day. Probably soon. Five years from now,
when the odometer ticked over all those zeroes, there'd be
a big bang. Everybody said so.

She didn't pay tax but according to Andrew Jean her cut
of last anno's yield put her on a salary par with a mid-level
exec with an American multinat. If today's negotiations
settled favourably, she'd be up there with a fast-track Japcorp software samurai. She wondered if any of the
shoulderpad dolls who strode through offices on business
soaps started out in gangcults. That wouldn't be for her;
she'd never wear a suit.

Sometimes, they'd burn money. Literally. It became a
drag to haul it around in paper or negotiable gems. When
they couldn't jam the trunk shut, they'd scatter stuff for the
sandrats. The 'Pomps were wild like that.

Andrew Jean hunched over a Virtualsex Machine, cockatoo beehive dipping, pretending to interface. The game

was hooked to other locations on the VDU chain; you could virtually rut with anonymes. This model was sneakily altered to function as a terminal for a one-time message. It was part of the II service. Word had been sent to the DAR that the 'Pomps could be reached in the Painted Desert and word had come back that the Daughters were agreeable to one-on-one negotiation.

Jazzbeaux was bored. Until the Daughters approved a site, she was hung up on this spot. The others kept their distance, as always when a negotiation was in the immediate offing. She understood. No one liked to be too close to someone who might shuffle. After, they'd cluster around like amorous octopi and throw her a *party*.

If she shuffled, she hoped Petya Tcherkassoff would sing a song about her. "The Girl in the Ground"?

A dust devil rose out in the Des, coming this way. A heavy machine. Sleek enough not to sound a whisper.

So Long came out of lotus and looked at the silent tornado. She was the kar krazy of the chapter.

"It's a V12," she said. "G-Mek."

Very heavy machine.

Jazzbeaux shut her good eye and lifted her patch. Her optic fed a heat picture to her brain. It was blurry but hot dots told her the V-12 was loaded for bear.

The DAR couldn't know they were here. Virtualsex was guaranteed secure. Both gangcults were laying out a cool ten thou to Irving's Intermediaries, ensuring mutual mystification. The Daughters should be loitering at some other site, waiting for the window to open.

So Long hefted a rocket-launcher and drew sight on the car. She initiated a countdown.

"One pop and bye-bye," she said.

Jazzbeaux shook her head.

"Stand down, *tovarich*. It's just a solo cruising through. We need no hassle today. 'Member, we've an appointment."

Also, from the V12's heat pattern, she doubted So Long's hatpin missile would dent its hide.

"I think it's an old girlfriend."

So Long triggered an abort sequence, pissed off. It wasn't good for deathware to get boiled up but not let off.

The ve-hickle made an elegant curve, dropping rpms, and smoothed to a halt by the porch of the VDU arc. Close up, it hummed like an electric appliance. As dust settled, Jazzbeaux clocked the Turner-Harvest-Ramirez tag. An antique pin-up was stencilled on the fuselage: a girlie in a bathing suit posed on a knobby little bomb with fins, showing one shaved armpit and a Pepsodent gleam. Everyone knew 'Nola Gay. And the machine's owner.

There was an uncomfortable shifting among the 'Pomps. PMS. Pre-Massacre Syndrome. Weapons eased out of sheaths, safeties switched. Andrew Jean remained intent on Virtualsex but 'Cheeks hauled out of cyberdisco and put the helm down.

The V12's door opened silently. A long, long leg slipped out, and touched a dainty boot-toe to the dirt. On the hip was an empty holster. Then the driver got out, holding up a side arm. She wore her naturally red hair long, a rare affectation.

Redd Harvest, the H in T-H-R. Probably the most-profiled Sanctioned Op in the Enforcement Sector, despite her publicity-shyness. The only woman with whatever it takes – sheer guts, colourful psychoses, queen-size deathwish, elephantiasis of the ego – to declare war on the Maniax.

"Hello, Jessamyn," Harvest said. "Still pissing it away with these panzer pussies?"

Jazzbeaux didn't remember Rancid Robyn, her alleged real mother, but Harvest always came on like a mix of Mom, High School Principal and long-suffering Big Sis. They had History back to the '10s.

"Hi, Rachael," Jazzbeaux said. She knew Harvest didn't like to be reminded that she no more used her real name than anyone else. It made her too like the gangbangers who were her prey. "Neat outfit."

Harvest wore a functional one-piece, with a flakjak and a utility belt. Her hair was held back by an Alice band, but frizzed out a lot around her shoulders. It must get in the way in fights.

"And *cool gun*, ma'am. Real *horosho* killing piece."

The Op holstered her side arm. It was something sensuous, with a big kick. She looked over the 'Pomps, probably totalling rewards in her head. Everyone in the krewe had paper hanging over them in some state or other. Most had gone federal and were just wanted.

"Small-timers," Harvest said, snorting. "We'll get down to you someday, but just now we've got a moose to fry."

"Got away, did he, Rachael?"

The Op shrugged.

"If there is a he."

The Grand Exalted Bullmoose of the Maniax was probably a mythical being. No one had ever seen him and lived. Jazzbeaux reckoned it was a revolving office; the Maniax were basically Anarcho-Capitalists, so their hierarchy was about as stable as a lavalamp. That was what made them hard to stamp out; like ticks, cutting off the body wasn't enough, you had to dig the head out of your skin and burn it.

Harvest looked Jazzbeaux up and down, not showing her opinion in her face. If she wore make-up, she'd be a pretty woman. With her legs, she'd even look good in a dress. Once, in previous lives, they'd got close. Too close for mutual comfort.

Jazzbeaux pouted and leaned on a Blood Bowl console. She let her tongue play over her lower lip and fluttered her single eyelash.

"You should have more fun, Rachael," she said, meaning it.

Harvest looked blank.

"Fun is not an early priority."

Before she went into the private sector, Rachael Harvest was a Denver beatcop. She'd rounded up Jazzbeaux back in her gladiatrix days and they'd played Mom-Daught games neither wanted to remember much in the harshness of the '20s. But the Op always made Jazzbeaux feel twelve.

"How's *blat*, Jessamyn?"

Jazzbeaux shrugged. She knew the woman cared (under the armour plate, the Op was a dogoodnik) but she'd never understand. For her, everything was right or wrong and pick-yourself-up. She'd never had a daddy like Bruno Bonney. And she'd never have a daughter like Jessamyn Amanda...

"Must be business openings this anno," Ms Harvest mused. "Especially in pharmaceuticals supply. If I were a smart fillette, I think I'd pass them up. Prospects are strictly short term."

Out of the op's sightline, Sleepy Jane hefted a blowpipe and took aim. She usually packed tranks but she had a variety of interesting psycho-active darts.

"I wouldn't exhale if I were you, Miss Porteous," Harvest said, not turning her head. "If someone were to give that thing a good shove, you'd lose those expensive steel-core teeth."

The blowpipe went down.

"How *do* you do that, Rachael? A pineal peep implant?"

Harvest didn't crack a smile.

"Jessamyn, Jessamyn, what to do about you?"

"Here's a radical concept, how about getting off my back and leaving me the fuck alone?"

Jazzbeaux fancied a wind of disappointment blew across the Op's smooth face. Jazzbeaux would have killed for Harvest's complexion.

"One day, my dear," Harvest said, "there'll be reckoning 'twixt thee and me."

"Won't that be something to see, though?"

Jazzbeaux knew she was flouncing like a lolita, shoving hips against her skirt and blowing bubbles with non-existent gum. It was uncanny how far back the op took her.

"Jessamyn, grow up," the op said, a feeble parting shot. She slipped back into 'Nola Gay and the door descended. The windows were one-way opaque.

The 'Pomps drew fingers and popped off gun-noises at the V12, thumbs recoiling. Sweetcheeks had a bad case of hiccough-giggles, and had to be slapped on the back.

Jazzbeaux wondered why she let Redd Harvest get to her.

"Dance on my finger, ladylove," she said, not loud enough for the car's sensors to pick up.

"Attention," a computer-generated speaker said, "your warrant status and current locale have been downloaded with the nearest node of the Highway Patrol net."

"I'm so scared," So Long said, exaggerating. She'd kept quiet and hung back while Harvest was out of her car.

'Nola Gay did its famous nought-to-ninety trick and zoomed off for the desert horizon.

"Thank Cristo for that," Andrew Jean said. "I've been sitting on the message for minutes. How does Moroni, Utah sound to you? It's up near Silver City and Spanish Fork. Ghost town."

"Snazz."

Moroni? Irving specialised in ghost towns with silly names. II would have scouted the site. The commission was to find absolutely neutral territory for negotiations. Somewhere, the DAR rank equivalent of Andrew Jean would be receiving the same message.

Jazzbeaux gave Andrew Jean the nod.

"I'll tap in an acceptance. *Boyar*, it looks like you're invited to single combat. A duel of honour and business."

Andrew Jean knuckled keys, authorising the transfer of funds to II, accepting the site. As the message was processed, the Virtualsex simulated an affirmative orgasm. The Daughters must have gone with Moroni, too. It used to be form for both sides suspiciously to turn down the first proposal but Irving got offended easily.

'Nola Gay was out of sight. The Psychopomps' ve-hickles were neatly parked in the lot, under armed guard.

"Girlie-girls," Jazzbeaux announced, "we've got klicks to cover 'fore tomorrow night. So let's move out."

V

IN THE OUTER *Darkness, the Old Ones swarmed, awaiting the Summoning. The Dark Ones Who Stand By Themselves. The Summoner felt their immense excitement, their unknown activity, reach through the Planes of Existence, focusing on his own beating heart. The Power of the Crawling Chaos was almost too much to contain in one mere physical body.*

Blood had been spilled on the Path of Joseph. The Channels were opening. Not enough blood yet, but a start was made on the Great Invocation. The ritual, more ancient even than those it was to summon, had been commenced. Again.

The Road to the Shining City must be marked out for the Dark Ones and their Servitors, just as landing lights mark out an airfield runway. The spilled blood would guide the Dark Ones to the Earthly Plane, to the Last City.

More blood, more blood!

The Summoner assessed his work and was well pleased. He had travelled this route before, spilled blood before. Since then, he had had time to wait, time to live. Now the cycle could recommence. Lines came into his head, and he followed them through...

Turning and turning in a widening gyre
The falcon cannot hear the falconer;
Things fall apart; the centre cannot hold;
Mere anarchy is loosed upon the world,
The blood-dimmed tide is loosed, and everywhere
The ceremony of innocence is drowned...

The Irishman had known more than he understood, the Summoner thought, and had died too soon to realise what he was talking of. He was one of the so-called magicians. They had all been fools and children, playing conjuring tricks, never really grasping the cosmic significance of the old rites. He had known them all, and seen them for what they were: the Golden Dawn, Aleister Crowley, A E Waite, Arthur Machen, the Si-Fan, the Illuminati, the Adepts. Fools and children.

The Summoner was happier with his collection of half-mad geniuses: de Sade, Poe, Aspern, Edvard Munch, Bierce, Gustave von Aschenbach, Kafka, Howard Lovecraft, Meyrink, Scott Fitzgerald, Jake Lingwood, Plath, Cobain. Poets and painters and fabulists and freaks. Taken before their times, they had been worthy offerings to the Dark Ones. Nothing so pleased his masters as the waste of human potential. Sometimes he flirted with exposure, allowing the sacrifices to learn a little, letting it seep into their work. He was quite a patron of the Arts. Sometimes, through carelessness, someone doomed to early disgrace and death grew wise and slipped away.

He thought of the singer, Presley, who had so nearly been his toy but who had diverged from the path laid out in blood and gold. The Summoner knew Presley was out there in the world. His was a sacrifice which would be completed some day.

Now the secret societies, the love cults, the freemasonries were gone. The poets and philosophers were dead, the dilettantes and madmen in their graves. But the Summoner breathed still, alone in the knowledge that the Time of Changes was truly imminent.

Fish would sprout from trees and the sun would burn black. But first the blood ritual would be complete, the Dark Ones would walk the face of the Earth, the common mass of humanity would be cast down, the raging chaos would coat the red-soaked land. The battles would be joined, and the fires of ice would burn. The Age of Pettiness would be at an end, and the Great Days, the Last Days, would be upon them. It would be a glorious sunset, and an eternal night.

And the Summoner would have his reward.

zeebeecee's nostalgia newstrivia: the 1960s

Do you remember where you were, what you were wearing, which song you were humming, when Americans touched the moon in 1965? Tonight on Nostalgia Newstrivia, *Luscious Lola Stechkin recalls the decade of Family Value and the British Invasion, of American Harmony and Chaos Abroad… the Solid '60s.*

HI, AMERICA. WOULDN'T you just love to hug me and squeeze me and touch me and feel me?

Slip into your Interactive Rubber Cardigan and enjoy the totality of the Lola Stechkin arm-wraparound experience. For further sensations, turn your dial to 143 and place your mouth to the lip-mallow, selecting the "French Kiss" option. This has been a bonus service from ZeeBeeCee.

Mmmmmmmm-wah! Tonight we drift back to those dreamy idyllic years of your parents' baby-boomette childhood, when Marlon Brando ran the Ponderosa and Richard Nixon ran the country.

It was the decade that began with the promise, made in President Nixon's 1961 inaugural address, that an American would walk on the moon by 1965. That promise, like so many others, was fulfilled.

JOHN GLENN: *One small step for a man, one giant leap for all mankind…*

It was the decade which ended with the escalation of a futile war in South-East Asia. Hostilities between Russian and Chinese ground troops in Indo-China led to a brief, terrifying exchange of tactical atomic weapons along the Sino-Soviet border in the Nine-Minute War of 1970.

FIRST SECRETARY GROMYKO: *The People's Government of South Vietnam cannot be allowed to fall to the barbarians of the North, behind whose depredations we sense the insidious hands of the barbarians of the East.*

MONTAGE: *Soviet troops marching, parachuting, driving tanks, smiling at the camera, smoking kif. Vietnamese villages burning. A running firefight. A Kremlin official reading off casualty figures. Mao Zedong ranting. Long-haired protesters thronging Red Square. Mushroom clouds rising. Gromyko resigning. A KGB officer holding up a severed head.*

Tonight, on *Nostalgia Newstrivia*, we remember the moods and the music, the triumphs and tragedies, the faces and factoids, the prices and the crises, the fashions and the food…

PRESIDENT NIXON: *My fellow Americans, we must survey each situation, national and international, and ask one simple question, not "what's in it for us?" but "what's in it for the US?"*

★ ★ ★

For America, these were years of achievement as President Nixon seemingly conquered the universe. After the calamitous failure of the first manned Soviet orbital flight, we surged ahead in the race thanks to massive US investment in the space programme and the diversion of Russian initiative into its ruinous land war. Mercury begat Gemini begat Apollo begat Hercules begat Pegasus.

Everyone remembers the first men on the Moon, John Glenn and Wally Schirra, but spare a thought for the casualties of mankind's first steps to the stars. Yuri Gagarin, Virgil Grissom, Richard Rusoff, Garrett Breedlove and so many others. A sombre rollcall of heroism.

It was once suggested by General West Moreland of NASA that the moon be granted statehood, though the question of who exactly might represent the new state in Congress and the Senate was never satisfactorily answered.

MONTAGE: *Rockets rising from Cape Canaveral. Rockets exploding on the gantry. Funerals for dead astronauts. Mass oblations before smiling, blown-up ID cards. Americans walking in space. Americans on the moon. Americans beset by tickertape. Countdowns, Touchdowns, Splashdowns. Animated diagrams of weapons satellites. John Glenn in a plaid suit, grinning on the bridge of the* USS Enterprise.

In music, the decade saw the withering of American dominance in the wake of the rock 'n' roll riots of 1961. Followers of evangelist Jimmy Swaggart clashed with those of DJ Alan Freed at Madison Square Gardens, New York. Among the thousands left dead by morning were Chuck Berry, Jackie Wilson, Little Richard and Freed himself. A family footnote was the tragic, permanent crippling of the Reverand Swaggart's cousin, Jerry Lee Lewis.

In the wake of the Tin Pan Alley Self-Regulation Codes, names like Elvis Presley and Carl Perkins disappeared from the jukeboxes, remembered only by a rising generation of Russian children who, energised by the anti-war movement of the late '60s, would transform the American rhythms of the '50s into the all-powerful Sove Sounds of the '70s and beyond.

These were the years of the British Invasion. The Liverpool Sound came to America, represented by Ken Dodd's first international million-seller, "Tears (for Souvenirs)". American artists were fast to react and soon Fabian Forte, Jan and Dean and Gracie Wing were covering the hits of Matt Monro, Mrs Mills and Valerie Singleton.

America's teenagers embraced the Brits but found a place for their own idols. The President, admitting he owned every disc Pat Boone ever cut, commended the music industry for championing decent young citizens whose example in moderate behaviour, modest dress and fetching hairstyles was eagerly copied by adoring fans. The President even confessed one or two "race records" had caught his fancy, reserving especial praise for Diana Ross's interpretation of Rolf Harris's "Sun-a-Rise".

SIZZLING SIXTIES TOP TEN: 1961: "(I Love, I Love, I Love, My Little) Calendar Girl", Neil Sedaka; 1962: "Love Letters (Straight From Your Heart)", Marilyn Monroe; 1963: "Happiness, Happiness (The Greatest Gift That I Possess)", Ken Dodd; 1964: "Shout", Valerie Singleton; 1965: "It's Not Unusual", Norman Wisdom; 1966: "Theme From *Star Trek*", The Billy Cotton Band; 1967: "(It's a Treat To Beat Your Feet on the) Mississippi Mud", James M Hendrix and the Merry Minstrels; 1968: "White Horses", Jacky; 1969: "Hooray for Nixon", Cherilyn LaPierre; 1970: "(I Did It) My Way", Ken Dodd.

At this point, should you wish to further your intimate relationship with the lovely Lola, please press the PAY button on your remote, and attach the milking sleeve as shown in the diagram provided. ZeeBeeCee takes no responsibility for coronary ill-effect or electrical discharges caused by faulty wiring or overuse of this consumer function. If in doubt, consult your family doctor.

While the '10s were marked by War and Revolution, the '20s by racketeering and bathtub gin, the '30s by Depression and the New Deal, the '40s by World Conflict and Swing, and the '50s by the dread shadow of the unleashed atom, no decade before or since has seemed so uncomplicated and peaceful to the great mass of the people of America as the 1960s. There were overseas wars, but America was merely a mournful, helpful observer, consistently intervening in futile attempts to find common ground between combatants.

After 1961, there were no more riots among the young, the happy racial minorities, or the working man. The year 1969 saw the great Peace March – led by the Reverend Martin Luther King, Senator Lyndon Johnson and John Wayne – which gathered outside the Washington consulates of the Soviet Union and the Republic of China. Similar marches in Moscow and Peking were not as peaceful; the death toll of that day will probably never be known.

Employment held steady, rates of divorce and suicide plunged, American industry launched countless successful products – typified perhaps by the most popular car of the 1960s, the Ford Edsel – and the nation's position in the world was paramount.

ALFRED E NEUMAN: *What, me worry? I drive an Edsel!*

★ ★ ★

Truly, the 1960s were the American Decade, and the Man of the Solid '60s was Richard Nixon, the only First Executive ever to have co-hosted *Your Show of Shows* with Milton Berle and Chevy Chase. President Nixon, that wise old bird, resisted calls that he share with FDR the opportunity of running for a third term. With typical good humour, he claimed he could make far more money from books and lectures after his retirement than he ever could in the White House.

PRESIDENT NIXON: *Pat deserves a new coat and Checkers II is looking forward to the California sunshine.*

Who can forget the spontaneous demonstrations of loyalty that erupted throughout the country in 1968, as the presidential campaign took on the good-humoured air of a festival? In Chicago, the Democratic Convention was invaded by pranksters of the "Why Bother?" faction, encouraging delegates not to tinker with success and admit that the party of opposition could not hope to compete with the Administration.

Even losing candidate Hubert Humphrey, polling proportionately fewer votes than any second-placer in history, was able to laugh off defeat with an admission that he didn't envy Barry Goldwater the job of following a fighting Quaker saint in the White House.

That year, John Kennedy, the forgotten man of American politics, remarried, not to the blonde goddess whose wiles had ruined his chance for the presidency in 1960, but to Mia Farrow, youthful star of the summer's heartwarming hit motion picture, *And Rosemary's Baby Makes Three*.

Amid the hilarity and fellow-feeling, one should remember Nixon the Statesman. The triumphs of the Nixon Presidency were epitomised by his swift intervention in

Cuba in 1962, providing air support for democratic rebels who overthrew the short-lived regime of the mad tyrant, Fidel Castro. Here we see American offshore interests triumphant in 1963 as businessman Samuel Giancana reopens the Club Whoopee, Havana. That noise you hear has been identified as the happy popping of champagne corks.

Also, Secretary of State Hoffa presided over the removal of many restrictions which threatened to impede the progress of American industry, granting rich government contracts to the technocrats who steadfastly worked in the space programme. Here, reactionary Ralph Nader slinks away from a congressional committee after the decisive defeat of his Slow Down Emissions recommendations, which would have cut American output by up to fifty per cent.

After deliberating the findings of a committee chaired by Governor George Wallace, the president adopted the policy of Separate But Equal Development in education, housing and employment, ensuring unprecedented racial harmony in the south. The amusing shoeshine boy seen here "accidentally" spilling polish over Governor George's white pants cuffs has been identified as a Mr Malcolm Little, who seems, quite sensibly to judge by that grumpy look on George's face, to have disappeared from history soon after this candid footage was shot.

In 1961, everyone went to the movies and saw Richard Beymer and Natalie Wood in *West Side Story*, Dolores Hart in *Where the Boys Are* and Kirk Douglas in *Spartacus*; in 1970, it was Richard Beymer and Katharine Houghton in *Love Story*, Julie Andrews and Rock Hudson in *Darling Lili* and John Wayne as John Glenn and Clinton Eastwood Jr as Wally Schirra in *The Right Stuff*. In 1961, the top TV shows were *Bonanza*, *The Lawrence Welk Show* and *Dragnet*; in 1970, they were *Bonanza*, *The Ken Dodd Show* and *Star*

Trek. Hair went up and skirts came down. The biggest hit show on Broadway throughout the '60s, so closely identified with the Nixon Era that Pat Nixon took to calling her husband's cabinet "the Twilight of the Gods", was Lerner and Lowe's *Ragnarok*, adapted from Wagner's *Ring* cycle. Here's Rex Harrison as Wotan, to sing us out of our moist-eyed nostalgia with the song President Nixon was reputedly humming throughout his eight years in office...

> "*The darkness is descending all around us*
> *The world, they say, is ending on this spot*
> *Those monsters from the underworld have found us*
> *...It's Ragnarok...*"

Thank you, Lola. We'll look forward to seeing more of your past in the future. Those who took advantage of our full interactive function are advised by ZeeBeeCee's Dr Nick to light up a Snout, the high-tar cigarette that tastes like tobacco and smells like smoke.

Now, it's back to the '20s for an all-new episode of that show that started in the '60s and was featured in our nostalgia binge; Star Trek: The Golden Generation. William Shatner returns as Captain James T Kirk, with Don Ameche as Mr Spock, George Burns as Bones McCoy and Jessica Tandy as Lieutenant O'Hara. In tonight's episode, "The Syndrome Factor", the USS Enterprise visits a parallel universe in which Richard Nixon was assassinated by Klingons in 1963 and the future has become a living hell...

the book of meat

I
8 June 2021

CANYON DE CHELLY stuck its stone finger up at the dusk like a stretched taffy Stonehenge megalith. The free-standing rock tower was a defiant sport. In a million years, wind had created the majestic feature. In a mere minute, the Knock 'Em Sock 'Em Robots would bring the untidy thing down. It was an anomaly and anomalies were intolerable.

Franken Steinberg stood by the bus, recharging as Olympia busied herself with Blastite. Jump leads connected his neck-bolts with the generator. Kochineel monitored, triple-belled cap nodding over the dials. Juice flowed into the capacitors under Franken's clavicles. He could function for a day on less than five cents' worth of electricity.

Considering Canyon de Chelly, Franken found himself questioning the dictum that nature was random and chaotic. The column was so contrived, so perfect that, like his own mainly mechanical body, it bespoke the existence of a creator.

It might be God's colophon, a declaration of copyright and ownership.

The thought was a surplus to the cybermind. He made an effort to burn it from his greymass. When his meatmind consciousness transferred to a more efficient storage vessel, unfruitful byways would be shut off. He longed to achieve true machine state.

He had abraded the GenTech logo from his plaskin face but the symbols persisted inside, a sub-microscopic rash on the robo-bits scattered through his altered body. Retaining memory of his half-life before BioDiv got to work on him, he did not (like more superstitious cyborgs) regard Dr Zarathustra as a god. He had been created equal with meatkind; GenTech BioDiv, for its own reasons, helped him evolve towards perfection.

Towards perfection. That was the path of the bots.

He was not personally involved in Olympia's special project, but he observed her preparations with interest and admiration. Olympia was a good machine, if over-inclined to special effects. Having run calculations through the chipped portion of her greymass, she had determined the exact charge necessary to fell the pillar. Flitting around the pillar on her points, she chattered instructions to Pinocchiocchio, who hulked along after her like a drone, placing the Blastite as ordered.

Olympia hated inefficiency and freaks of nature. It was not enough that meatfolks become machine; the Earth must be covered over with plastic and durium. Gaia, the sentimental personification of the living planet, must become a cyborg, in symbiosis with its machines. That was how machinekind should greet the future.

This current demolition was undertaken aesthetically. The cybermind could create art. It was empirically provable.

Robbie the Robotman and Hymie the Android knelt facing each other over an imaginary chessboard, indicating moves. Their chess programs were so advanced no game could progress beyond three moves without one or the other conceding that stalemate was inevitable. Andromeda watched, amazonian body entirely covered by black cloth, ironically like a good Muslim girl. She laid her marble-white hand on Robbie's shoulder, trying to follow the game with only her unaugmented meatmind.

Darkness gathered as the sun slipped below the horizon. Franken blinked and his eyes infrareddened. Bored, he accessed the time code. LED numbers gave him a time check, flashing alternates in successive population centres. A master reading told him his eyes had been functional for four years, two months, three weeks, six days, nine hours, ten minutes and forty-eight seconds. He watched seconds tick off towards the expiry of his five-year warranty, whereupon he would be advised to seek an upgrade. It was important that the cybermind remain state of the art.

That meant going back to BioDiv. Eventually, the bots would have to resubmit to Zarathustra. There were independents – Simon Threadneedle, most obviously – but only GenTech had the R&D capital. Between meat and metal was the barrier of money.

In the bus, Rosie the Maid and Talos the Bronze Giant made crackling love, wires stretched between plugboards, currents passing between them in rhythmic flow. Most bots eschewed meat sex. Their pleasure sensors were adapted to capabilities beyond human organs.

Olympia returned, a grin obvious under the black scarves that wrapped her head. Her crystal chest sparkled.

"At dawn, as the sun rises, we shall detonate."

"That is nice, dear."

She did a few steps, balancing perfectly. Kochineel inclined his sad clown's face and watched her, active eyes intent. Penny-sized red highlights were painted on his china cheeks and blue-diamond tears etched under his eyes. He never spoke; his mouth was a cupid's bow around a tiny inlet.

"Then, we should give thought to the Grand Canyon," Olympia continued. "Concrete would be impractical, but fast-expanding synthetics are achieving spectacular results. At the current progress rate, the operation will be feasible within two annos. Our gift to the 21st century shall be to smooth over that nasty crack and restore proper feature-lessness to the globe."

"You still have blood on your face, dear. Organic matter from this morning."

Olympia cringed disgust and wiped her forehead with the heel of her hand. Most of her skin was playtex but she had yet to replace her hands or face. Inside, as her superb balance demonstrated, she was all doodads and robo-bits.

Franken was furthest along the road to complete mech-anisation. Only his brain and a few unaugmented bones were original to him. When it became possible to down-load the information that constituted consciousness into silicon, he would willingly abandon physical greymass. He scorned the Donovan Treatment: vulgar brains brooding in bottles had little in common with his improved, aug-mented, demonstrably superior form.

At the other extreme was Andromeda, whose uncannily mobile prosthetic hand barely qualified her for the Knock 'Em Sock 'Em Robots. When funds were amassed, she would have more alterations. Her human body, now in its brief peak of perfection, would customise superbly.

Andromeda walked over, graceful as a panther. She had taken a Pentathlon Gold for the Pan-Islamic Federation at the St Petersburg Olympics in '16, but – a Greek Christ-ian and a persecuted minority within the PIF – had defected. She had been through steroids and longevity programmes, and concluded cyberneticisation was the way to preserve and enhance herself against time.

Olympia watched Andromeda, her body language easy to read. Contempt, jealousy, fear, dislike. Olympia strangely retained much of her meatmind. Eventually, she believed, such irritants would cease to be a part of the cybermind.

Andromeda had sought out the Knock 'Em Sock 'Em Robots, crushing her own meathand to demonstrate commitment. Dr Threadneedle, contracted for the job, was enthusiastic about the possibilities of perfecting the woman. Her hand benefited, like Kochineel's body, from developments in ceramics. It was imitation marble. She would ultimately be a goddess of living stone.

When remodelling was complete, Andromeda would be a better machine than Olympia. There was static between the cyberwomen. Now, Olympia could best Andromeda at any contest of skill or strength; but Andromeda's mentality would eventually prevail. Her greymass was closer to the cybermind than Olympia's part-silicon brain. Trained from infancy to treat meat as if it were durium, she was programmed as a Gold Medal winner.

Andromeda looked up at Canyon de Chelly.

"It is very beautiful," she said. "In this light, almost magical."

"Tchah!" Olympia spat. "You have too much meat in you, madame. Sentimental juices squirt from your heart, poisoning your mind…"

Olympia's heart had been her first replacement. A necessity; the meat organ was defective at birth. That had taught her not to trust nature, and to put faith in the machine.

"Meat is weak," she told Andromeda. "That damfool pilgrim this afternoon. He was pure meat. Look how he burst when squashed. Like a bug."

Olympia was being unkind.

"I would wager your warranty does not cover the treatment you gave that Josephite," Franken told her. "If Pinocchiocchio drove the bus over your chest, your components would fail as surely as the meat of that poor, strange man."

Franken was perturbed by the way the Josephite had accepted his death. As if he were certain of a future.

"My cybermind is of a better quality, Franken. I would not find myself in such a situation. He died for no reason."

Olympia had not acted dispassionately. In killing the man, she had demonstrated something about herself.

"Your brain is still greymass, still mostly meatmind."

"An information storage unit," she said, tapping her skull. "And a reasoning function. Few human brains have reasoning functions. That is why they are obsolete."

"Why did that man defy us?" Andromeda asked. She disapproved of Olympia's treatment of the Josephites. Only interested in the road ahead, she saw no point in the cruelty. Meatfolks were left behind; to Andromeda, that was harsh enough.

Olympia shrugged.

"The rational thing was to pay the toll," Andromeda reasoned. "If they had paid, they would not have died. Why did they not follow that course?"

"Their experience was misleading," Franken explained. "They believed us a common gangcult. The Maniax would have taken tithe and still killed several or all of them."

"We were frustrated in our purpose," Andromeda said, trying to follow the reasoning. "We set out to achieve money by extortion, money we need to pursue our own aims, but gained nothing from the exchange. In a logical sense, we lost."

"We put meat in the ground," Olympia snapped. "Do not underestimate that."

"Frankly, I am still perplexed."

"Catch up, meatdoll."

Andromeda assumed a posture indicating emotional hurt. Olympia did a triumphant pirouette. Kochineel might be sighing, Franken calculated.

"Metal must always master meat," Olympia said, quoting the Knock 'Em Sock 'Em Robots' slogan.

Andromeda said nothing but her hand flexed. Metal might always master meat, Franken considered, but perhaps marble would outlast metal. Nothing was settled.

II
8 June 2021

HE HAD BEEN at the wheel of the Edsel since midday services. Perhaps six hours, with the joyous voices of the Brethren coming over the shortwave joined in song. Like all Josephites, W Bond Wiggs abjured godless radio stations. Those that pretended to be religious were worst of all, polluting airwaves with so-called Christian Heavy Metal, ceaselessly soliciting donations. The Elect had no need of Golden Oldies or Soviet Sounds when they had hymns and a limited band communion.

"Follow the fold, and stra-aaa-ay no more…"

Elder Seth sat beside him, mouth set in a straight line. Another man in mirrorshades might be thought asleep, lulled by the lilting chorus, but Brother Wiggs knew the elder was eternally vigilant. No sin escaped his eye.

After the drive, the flat plastic flask strapped to Wiggs's inner thigh was full and sloshing. Since his voluntary amendment, he ceased to notice the needs of his urinogenital arrangement. Many long-haul drivers without his special consideration adopted such contraptions to cut down on pit-stops.

When the Inner Council of the Brethren of Joseph gathered to plan the first convoy of resettlement, none had foreseen that the demands of nearly a hundred bladders would require more stoppages than equipment failure or skirmishes with hostiles. After two days on the remains of the Interstate up into Utah, that had proved the case. Discipline had to be imposed, especially on children. The theme of the elder's evening address had been Christian Continence.

Today was an improvement over the first spell on the road. The only major stoppage had been that business with the Knock 'Em Sock 'Em Robots. Only two lost.

The road was pitted and going was slow. Though it was the place of the mighty Edsel to lead the resettlers to the Promised Land, Wiggs had to keep the speedometer sacrilegiously at thirty so as not to outpace the earth-movers. There was enough sandside traffic to ensure all roads were passable, but only to a Westmoreland tank or a dune buggy. It was years since federal government had maintained the Interstates. It wasn't a question of money, but a matter of personnel: you couldn't pay enough to make road men risk their lives out in the Des.

These were godless, violent times. The roads were aswarm with predators, intent upon the unwary. Elder Seth insisted the convoy travel without weapons, as a sign they were a threat to no man. Even Wiggs felt that was carrying the Josephite ideal a touch too far, but the will of the elder was ferocious when he had right on his side.

The dead brown country crawled by as the faithful made their way towards predestined salvation.

At about seven in the evening, Elder Seth decreed the convoy should pull over and make camp for the night. Wiggs looked for a suitably sheltered area. Up ahead, stranded in the desert, was the Landsdale, an abandoned drive-in movie theatre.

A tattered stretch billboard advertised Hilary Duff in *Curly Sue*, a motion picture about a godless harlot to judge from the length of tan thigh on the poster. Before his conversion, Wiggs had consumed many such abominated movies. For him, abjuration had been painful. Even after the amendment to his lower region, he felt a stirring in his water at the sight of the sinful Hilary's shorts. She should be severely chastised for putting temptation in the path of a pious man.

Wiggs eased the wheel over and the Edsel cruised into the drive-in, ploughing through a barbed-wire tangle of tumbleweed. The convoy followed, crushing dried-up scrub into cracked asphalt. A small forest of hooked speaker poles, long stripped of their burdens, stood on the lot. Those that hadn't been broken off altogether listed in all directions.

"Ideal, Brother Wiggs," commented the elder. "The Lord has put this place in our path for good reason."

The convoy lined up, facing the bare scaffold where the screen had been hung, as if waiting for the show to start. This must have been a real passion pit. Wiggs could almost smell popcorn, hear piped muzak (Sove Sounds re-recorded by synthestrings), quiver at the moans and sighs from surrounding automobiles.

In sinning days, Wiggs would often-times share a back seat with a godless harlot who deported herself much as Devil's Daughter Duff did in her poster. Soft flesh, warm folds, moist mouth. Hungry suckings and grindings. All such things were now abjured by Brother W Bond Wiggs.

These days, his flesh was iron. He could not be tempted.

Elder Seth unbent from the Edsel and stretched like a cougar. He was a tall, thin man and gave the impression of wiry strength. Wiggs had seen him preach for five hours without so much as breaking sweat. Other evangelists went through shirts like an allergy-sufferer through a box of tissues. A man had to be strong in spirit and body to lead a party into unknown desert, certain that safety and salvation lay at the end of the road.

In the Brethren of Joseph, Wiggs had found strength to best his demons. He would sin no more. He pounded his thighs with fists, reminding himself of his abandoned sins, taking the opportunity to chastise his unworthy flesh.

The Brethren worked like a Marine platoon, fixing up lean-tos and shelters. Brother Baille, who had seen combat in Mexico and the Central American Confederation, posted look-outs and inspected facilities. There was already a line by the rest rooms. Sisters held the hands of antsy children. More than a few youngers had had "accidents", a backsliding against Christian Continence sure to earn many a chastisement.

He walked away from the Edsel towards the skeleton screen. It had to be one hundred feet long and fifty high. Sinful harlots would have filled the view, vast close-up lips swallowing an entire audience at a gulp. Twenty yards from the scaffolding, asphalt gave out to dunes. A low wall was overwhelmed by the sand. Wiggs put his foot up on the wall, pleasurably popping his cramped thigh, and hitched his black pantsleg to the knee. The outflow tube was taped down his leg to his ankle, where a plastic spigot faucet tied off the system.

Wiggs turned the faucet and emptied a day's water into the sand. He felt not so much as a twinge from what wasn't there. Before the amendment, he had worried about stories he had heard of amputees with phantom pains in missing limbs. He had no such experiences. He hadn't put on weight, his voice hadn't climbed an octave and the fire hadn't gone out of his faith; he just didn't feel like being a sinner any more. He had found salvation in the Brethren of Joseph.

A nearby wall, covered in pasted-over and torn-away posters for long-gone coming attractions, was a collage of faces, breasts and legs. Wiggs recognised godless harlots of the silver screen and DVD machine.

Before his amendment, Wiggs had held a special place in his lustful, sinful heart for Jenna Jameson. There were disembodied segments of Jenna on the wall. And Katie Holmes's libidinous eyes, Uma Thurman's mile-long limbs, Reese Witherspoon's welcoming mouth, Voluptua Whoopee's pillow chest. They did not call to him now.

He turned his back on sin and walked back to the vehickles, righteous pride rising. Tonight, if called, he would testify. He must abjure his former ways in public.

Carnal excess had been his abiding drive. Through adulterous fornication, he had lost two wives and three children. Directed by the white throb of his urges, his body was consumed by lust. No woman was safe with him. He would lie, wheedle, cheat, cajole and coerce. Nothing was too low if it enticed some godless slut into his bed or automobile and loosed her from her drawers.

He shook his head with sorrow. Sister Maureen smiled at him and, mercifully, he felt no desire to fall upon her.

As a young man, he had been promising. In Macon County, Georgia, where his daddy was sheriff, he had been a deputy in the early '90s. Law enforcement offered opportunities for sin. Solitary female motorists were persuaded to give of their favours to avoid speeding tickets. The wives and daughters of men he locked in the hoosegow would often yield up virtue in the hope of expediting the release of loved ones. Best of all, many was the loose woman who found herself in an overnight cell when W Bond Wiggs was sole turnkey and custodian. There was a separate section, round the back, for coloured prisoners. Many a night Deputy W B Wiggs would saunter there with a jug of cone liquor, and cut out some little ole gal for a taste of dark meat. He had cleaved to sinning as a fly to sticky paper and tasted the bitter gall of self-degradation.

As the Josephites prepared their simple evening meal in a bank of microwaves, Elder Seth stood a little apart and a little elevated, looking down on his flock. The dying sun flashed in his mirrorshades. He was still as a figurehead. The mere sight of the elder gave Wiggs strength to continue remembering the dark days.

Finally, mere carnality was not enough to excite his depraved tastes, and Wiggs had availed himself of the handcuffs and nightsticks easily accessible in the lock-up. His pursuit of lechery cost him families and his job. His daddy passed on in '08, the day Al Gore was elected. Sheriff Wiggs had been turning an uppity nigra away from the polling booth with a cattle-prod when an aneurysm had burst in his greymass. The new sheriff had immediately kicked Wiggs off the force. In the unholy spirit of vengeance, Wiggs forced attentions on the sheriff's daughters and found it necessary to leave his native county and state.

Now he fervently hoped Sheriff Pullinger could find it in his heart to forgive him for his undoubted sins. He wondered if it were not too late to make reparation.

By the earth-mover, Brother Kenneth and Sister Barbara held hands, and read from *The Path of Joseph*. There was no carnality between the young Josephites, simply shared, untarnished faith. Brother Wiggs regretted his squandered youth.

For eleven years, Wiggs had drifted and sinned. He picked up spells of work as a security Op, but most of his hours were consumed by the pursuit of harlots. He travelled from town to town and state to state, sinning all the way. He had been a notable imbiber of the Devil's alcohol, a habitual drinker of Satan's caffeine and a not-infrequent dependant on proscribed chemicals.

W Bond Wiggs must have stank of his sins. Stank to high heaven.

Trestle tables were erected and food laid out upon them. The Brethren gathered and took their places. Wiggs sat at the elder's right hand, as was fit. Elder Seth read the blessing and the Brethren ate in prayerful silence. Josephites abjured stimulants and spices, so the fare was plain and unflavoured, sustenance for the body not distraction for the palate. Wiggs happily spooned into his mouth a mush which contained all essentials for the prolongation of life but no harmful additives.

After a meal, Wiggs's tastebuds occasionally yearned for coffee, the most reviled of all stimulants. But the only coffee legally available in the United States was recaff, which hardly counted. All in all, he did not miss any of the things the Brethren were required to put behind them. He certainly did not miss the sins of the flesh. These days, he rarely even thought of them.

Young women, old women, illegally young women, indecently old women. Fat women, thin women, short women, tall women. Dark women, fair women, black women, white women. All of them he had used and cast away until Elder Seth showed him how to escape the coils of his desires.

He had been in Tombstone, Arizona, in a pornobooth at the virtual mall, hips bucking as the milking sleeve simulated the skilled orifice of some faceless harlot. The Revelation was a Fiery Coming. It screeched through the sensory inputs and blanked out the sinful loop. Tearing out of the mall, the weight of Sin crushing him like a falling safe, he found his way to a revival staged in the historic OK Corrall. In a Battle of the Brothers, a succession of evangelists mounted the stand, preaching until the audience gonged them off.

"Come one, come all," announced barkers. Anyone could take the lectern.

Staggering into the crowd, self-disgust coursing through his greymass like electricity, Wiggs heard four or five preachers booed off the altar. A hooded pastor of the Church of Jesus Christ, Caucasian, was passed over heads by a multitude of hands and tossed squealing into the street. It was a tough congregation, perpetually on the edge of an ugly mood. A singing nun didn't get into the second "-nique" of "Dominique-nique-nique" before she was stripped of her penguin cowl and dumped in the horse trough. It seemed no one could satisfy this crowd's thirst for a sermon. They had come to hear the Word and weren't taking any tin dollars.

Then, striding to the podium as Wyatt Earp had strode over the same dirt to face the Clanton Boys, came a tall man with a wide black hat and simple mirrored sunglasses.

From that day to this, Wiggs had never seen the elder without his shades. He wondered if the man suffered from some disease of the eyes.

Elder Seth had talked all evening and well into the night, holding the rowdy audience rapt. The Word spilled from him like milk from a pitcher, and the crowd lapped it up like babies.

Looking now at the elder, Wiggs remembered the force of that first experience. Again and again, he thanked the Lord that he had been saved before perdition was unavoidable. Faith had come upon him like a fever.

At the time, he was confused in his feelings, even hostile. He found himself near the front of the crowd, in the company of loose women. The initial fire of his conviction was already petering out, and he was drawn as if by magnetic attraction to painted women. No more than NoGo girls, they wore cutaway plastic minidresses, check shirts tied in tantalising knots above tiny navels and tinselled pseudoleather cowgirl hats. Tags shaped like sheriff stars confirmed their status as registered, disease-free Arizona Harlots.

As Elder Seth preached, the whores inflamed Wiggs's hateful lusts with duplicitous strokes of tongue and hand. He found himself calling out for the gong, a lone voice in the grateful multitude. After that night, two of the lost girls turned away from sin; Rancho Rita was now Sister Rosalie and Chihuahua Chicken was Sister Consuela.

Now, Sister Consuela was beloved of the children. In the Shining City, she would teach the Truth of Joseph and lead the choir. But back then she was an alley-cat who would have rutted with the Tasmanian Devil for a squeezer of smacksynth. In the OK Corrall, she went for Wiggs's sex pistol and almost squeezed off a couple of shots before Elder Seth turned his attention to their corner of the crowd.

Clearly, a certain part of his body ruled the rest of him. It outranked his greymass, his heart and his spirit. Turgid with lascivious blood, it compelled him to cry against the good man who extended the hand of salvation to him.

"Brother," the elder said, fixing Wiggs with his mirror glare, "in the Good Book it is written, in the Gospel of St Matthew, that Our Redeemer said, 'If thine eye offend thee, pluck it out…'"

Wiggs, realisation coming into his head like a bomb-burst, knew Elder Seth had shown him the Way, the only path to his salvation.

III

THE ROADKILLERS HAD made better than average time, which meant the Quince ordered a night ride. They roughly followed the old state line, dipping in and out of Arizona. For safety, they kept their speed down to seventy. Tyree felt as if her mount was hobbled.

She listened to Quincannon make cockpit talk with Yorke, fixing on the buzz as a talisman against the fingers of sleep clawing her mind. She was used to thirty-six and forty-eight hour stretches on the road but bone deep weariness descended with the dark. She felt the force, if not the chill, of wind against her padded arms. After hours in the saddle, stiffness set in from her coccyx to her shoulders. She rode with her knees close to the mount, britches warmed by engine heat, and moved her helmeted head back and forth like a darting snake's to fight the ache in her neck.

The patrol was in close formation, outriders at the corners of the cruiser's headlight throw. Darkness rushed around, the odd roadside sign or abandoned building looming as high-intensity beams briefly lit them up like bright white ghosts.

The unknown pilgrim-flatteners had taken an underused route and left clear tracks even after the blood ran out. Tiremarks cut through drifting sand and patches of heat-melted asphalt, hardened in the night's chill, even showed what brand of rubber the quarry was burning. GenTech, natch. The main ve-hickle was an armoured bus. High speed.

Burnside had popped a couple of pills to keep alert and unconsciously hummed "She Wore a Yellow Ribbon" into his intercom. The tune settled in around the back of Tyree's brain and stayed there.

"Round her neck; she wore a yellow ribbon.
She wore it for her lover who was far, far away…"

Tyree thought of Trooper Nathan Stack. He was far, far away all right, back at Fort Valens, if not exactly her lover. That time in Nicaragua, when their leave coincided and a rare foreign travel permit came along, there'd been a moment when wedding chapels were open and it would have been easy on an impulse to tie a knot. Back in the States, things scanned very different. There were things about Nathan that didn't square with her ideas for the next few years.

"When I asked her why the yellow ribbon.
She said it was for her lover in the US Cavalry…"

She'd set the buzzer in her skidlid to deliver a subaudial jolt every thirty seconds. That kept her awake and alert and there was no risk of developing a dependency. Burnside had popped a few too many pills this tour and she should report him to the Quince. It was in the regulations; but the Cav had regs and rules, and it was a Rule that one trooper not snitch on another, even if she was angling for a promotion.

"Caval-reee, Caval-reee.
She said it was for her lover in the US Cavalry…"

She'd talk to Burnside, suggest he take counselling. His best bet would be Quincannon. The Quince had been through it all and come out the other side. He'd been on these roads forever.

They rode into the night.

Nathan was the recruiting poster image of the Cav. Tree tall, broad-shouldered, strong-chinned. But he looked down at the ground, not up at the skies. Every time Tyree won a commendation or earned a qualification, he found it necessary to throw a major drunk. In the sand, there was no one better as backup, but in everything else Nathan was never there for her. His priorities were hard to figure.

In their next rotation, to Fort Apache in Arizona, Tyree would be riding with Trooper Stack. She didn't know how she was going to feel about that. The worst thing would be if he came over masculine and protective and got himself crippled or killed trying to cover her ass.

Something birdlike with white hair froze in the light-funnel, red eyes staring. Tyree and Burnside swerved in formation to avoid the beast (a mew-tater of some species) but the cruiser ground it under.

Yorke blathered about racking up another score and the Quince told him it was Des etiquette to eat whatever you killed. Yorke suggested that Ms Redd Harvest of T-H-R must get mighty tired of tucking into a roasted Maniak every suppertime.

The Association of Women in Law Enforcement, of which Tyree was Fort Valens chapel boss, had invited Redd Harvest to address them; she had sent back their invitational fax with a scrawled comment, "I'm not a woman, I'm an op". Tyree planned to resign. It was important she advance herself on merit, not by soliciting positive discrimination. She knew how she'd feel if anyone she knew got killed because an inferior woman occupied a position of power and made a mistake. Captain Julie Brittles, to whom the Quince reported, was a hard-ass of the old school and had never been in the AWLE.

"Leona," Quincannon said, "the bus's heat patterns are scrambled up ahead."

"Are we losing the trail?"

"It's still clear, but someone crossed the path."

"Could the quarry have made us? Is someone waiting to give us a surprise?"

The Quince considered.

"Nope, this is too recent. The heat signature suggests something big and alive, now off the road a ways to the north."

"Tyree scanned and saw nothing but the dark.

"An animal?"

"Could be, but it's heading where there's nothing to drink. Only people are stupo enough for that, or smart enough to pack a canteen."

The sand was thin on the road, a light white brushing in which wheeltracks were black lines. Quincannon's phantom trail crossed. It was behind them in an instant, but the image imprinted in Tyree's visor, faded slowly.

"Man on a horse," she guessed. "Weird."

★ ★ ★

IV
9 June 2021

WAITING FOR DAWN was the quixotic act of a unit too close to the meatmind to realise day and night were mere conveniences for those lacking infrared sight. Olympia's aesthetic decision should be outweighed by wastage of time. Once recharged, Franken conceived no reason why they should remain at Canyon de Chelly waiting for an illusory apt moment.

They should blow the column and move on. There were many more anomalies waiting to be tidied up. To pass the time, Olympia danced with Kochineel, her face set in a razor smile.

The resettlers might have notified the authorities. Canyon de Chelly was a National Monument and thus conspicuous. The Knock 'Em Sock 'Em Robots could best any number of individual patrols but if the US Cavalry were to mount a campaign like the one that shattered the Western Maniax, the cyborg future would die a-borning. War must eventually be carried against meat, but now the bots were too few to make large-scale hostilities pursuable.

Besides, strategy decreed the cybermind take complete control of the processes of perfectibility before meatfolks were rendered entirely obsolete. Dr Zarathustra, so amused by the symbolic face he had given Franken Steinberg, must yield BioDiv to his creation.

After Franken, Kochineel was the most complete machine among them. He wore only black scarves to cover meat forearms and skin shins. The rest of him was perfect automaton. His jester's cowl was metallic pseudoleather. Most of his external body was a ceramic carapace.

Andromeda watched Kochineel with interest. His form was what she could expect of her forthcoming alterations. When Franken had been reshaped, durium was state-of-the-art; now, molecule-locked ceramics were proven superior to any alloy. Kochineel's warranty was good up to and including tactical nukes, though he was not inclined to test it. Suppliers only guaranteed robo-bits; they did not extend insurance cover to the greymass where consciousness lived or any original parts required if you were to remain legally and psychologically yourself.

The dance was deliberate and measured. Through his chest-organ, Talos played the "Barcarole" from *Tales of Hoffmann*. It was the wrong tale for the dance, but Franken let it pass.

Kochineel lifted Olympia and morphed her through the air. Their moves were perfect, unwavering. No meat could match the precision. Every step and pose was calculated, computer animation in solid matter. If required, the dancers could encore, replaying their routine exactly to the micromillimetre. Digital dancers would render obsolete stubborn fools who insisted on remaining trapped in steadily rotting carcasses.

Kochineel stumbled.

An ALARM! display lit up in Franken's vision. Something was seriously awry.

Olympia screamed, more in surprise than fear. Somersaulting, she landed on her points. She backed away in horror from her suddenly-imperfect companion, long legs like scissor-blades.

Pinocchiocchio stepped forward but Kochineel waved him away. His cowl-bells sounded, desperately. Kochineel's scarves were wet. He gingerly unpicked the scarf from his left forearm, unwinding cloth away from skin. Much of the skin, and a layer of meat, came away with the scarf. Kochineel's painted doll face could not register shock but the set of his ceramic shoulders, as if he were trying to distance himself from his own arm, gave away his feelings.

The meat of the arm was melting like wax, revealing the clean piston inside. Kochineel's hand clasped and unclasped, then, without the meatmuscles, seized up. It was as dead as alabaster. The Zarathustra rods that threaded through Kochineel's muscles were exposed. The effect was general. All organic matter in Kochineel's body was rotting away.

A splash of thick blood fell around him and dwindled into dead scum, leaving only the microscopic ticks of the nanomachines that had coursed through the cyborg's system. He fell to his knees, molten meat squelching, and looked up. His imploring eyes shrank and fell into his mask.

In the blackness of Kochineel's empty eye-holes, Franken read a bleak future. He signalled the others to stay away. There was a 76.83 per cent probability the effect was viral. Contact could be fatal. Olympia had already made the calculation and scrubbed herself. Franken shut down his ventilation system and systematically expelled air from inside the spaces of his body. The little of his meat that remained was not exposed.

Talos's organ still played. Offenbach drifted across the desert, accompanied by the rasps of Kochineel's exposed gears grinding uselessly against each other.

A diagonal crack shot across Kochineel's face, running from forehead to eye to mouth to neck. Liquid seeped through the fissure and flooded across his face. The grey-mass was gone. Kochineel pitched into the sand, inanimate as a store mannequin. Purely mechanical parts still functioned inside him and would do until his solar batteries perished, but there was no controlling intelligence. Insofar as he could die, Kochineel was dead.

"Most interesting," Franken concluded.

"Look," Olympia said, pointing.

Franken wheeled. Andromeda held up her ceramic hand, staring at it, gripping it with her meat hand. The robo-bit worked perfectly but Andromeda deliquesced. The athlete's stricken face ran behind her veil, soaking through. She assumed a position of traditional prayer, whimpering.

It was a waste of human potential.

Andromeda huddled into herself. Fluids gushed through her robes, splashing across sand and rock. She was the size of a dwarf, and shrinking. Her head withdrew like a tortoise's, sheltering in her fragile ribcage. Noisily, Andromeda melted away.

Her white hand, perfect and shining, lay at the edge of a putrescent pool.

"It would appear we are being betrayed by our meat," Franken said.

The sun rose behind Canyon de Chelly and his IR function automatically cut out. Silver dawnlight flooded the area. The remains of Andromeda and Kochineel looked less real.

In the light patterns the sun made around the stone column, it was impossible not to see the figure of a bearded man, hands outstretched, dressed in a long robe bearing an eight-pointed star. It would have seemed a conventional representation of Jesus, the Christ, were it not for the curly horns sprouting from his forehead.

Franken made calculations but no explanation was forthcoming. There were precedents for such things but the files were still open, awaiting convincing analysis. At some point, miracles had been reclassified as Unknown Events.

Olympia, distraction blanked out, squatted by the console of her detonator. She had reordered her priorities and focused on the task. She flicked all the switches.

The charges around the base of Canyon de Chelly did not explode, but every scrap of meat in Olympia's body did. She was a red hurricane, swirling away from her mechanical parts. In the cloud of flesh, blood and bone, a shadow-woman of durium and plastic was torn apart. Franken's thought processes were scrambled by phenomena they were forced to regard as supernatural, and several of his chips burned out in a sizzling flash. He fought his headache and tried to think through the crisis.

Other bots emitted automatic distress signals as the effect took hold. Pinocchiocchio, Robbie the Robotman, Tetsuo, Hymie the Android, Rosie the Maid, Talos the Bronze, Mecha-Gojira, Tobor the Great, Maelzel. All exhibited symptoms. Franken calculated a 00.00 per cent possibility of saving any of his comrades.

Jesus Goat smiled broadly, his crown of horns bobbing.

Franken, calm under the circumstances, downloaded from greymass into the chips that constituted over half his brain. Memory bytes and personality traits might be lost, but he could survive without the trace elements of his meatmind. The probability was better than sixty-five per cent.

Pinocchiocchio jerked as if manipulated by a mad puppeteer, spare parts flying away from his spasming bulk. He blundered against one of the cars, leaving a substantial dent, and crashed down, breaking apart on the rocks.

This was the crisis of evolution.

Hymie transmitted a cry for help as organs dribbled through the suppurating wound in his lower abdomen. Franken did not have surplus greymass to consider further how assistance might be delivered. In the past, he had faced 00.00 per cent problems and developed solutions that expanded the parameters of the original programming. But he had not then been distracted by threats to his own survival.

Hymie switched himself to auto-euthanasing. His doo-dads were smart parts; when they calculated termination was a certainty, they overruled their owner's greymass and simply ceased to function. Wastage of energy in a hopeless cause was criminally irrational.

Later, when he had survived, Franken Steinberg would calculate what had happened to the Knock 'Em Sock 'Em Robots. There were solutions alternative to belief in forces beyond the natural.

A lesson was learned. The evolution of the Next Gener-ation must not be supervised by the meatmind. If perfection was to come, it must come from the cyber-mind.

V
9 June 2021

FIFTY MILES PAST sun-up city, Varoomschka reported back that she had scoped a party of motorwagons pulled over in the Lansdale Ozoner. Jazzbeaux knew it wasn't worth a detour to the abandoned drive-in. A regiment of raggedyass resettlers could hardly offer serious scav.

The Psychopomp war convoy was spruce-goosed to make an impression, proceeding at speed and in forma-tion. Jazzbeaux was in the front passenger seat of the lead ve-hickle, a salmon-pink Tucker Tomorrow, with Sleepy Jane Porteous at the wheel. She usually drove herself, but had to rest up for the evening's social appointment. Besides, her licence outside the city was provisional and L-plates looked sissy. The Tucker was air-conditioned to a pleasant perfumed breeze. The in-car sound system was tuned to Radio Moscow; Andrei Tarkovsky sang "Twenty-Four Hours to Byelozersk".

Three cars back, Andrew Jean drove a life-size version of Barbie's Dream Motor Home. The gangcult's mobile HQ had hilly curtains on all the windows, sparkly swirls of stars on the bodywork and enough deathware to fight a border war for three months.

The skeleton of the drive-in screen was visible from a long way off. Sleepy Jane, an old-timer at twenty-one, remembered the place from her wild youth.

"Back then." she reminisced, leaning over but keeping her eyes on the road, "before the 'Pomps took me on, I was so numb-dumb I'd spread-eagle in the back of a flat-bed, putting out for popcorn kish or a jolt of zonk. I reckon I could juice off fifteen or sixteen grungy guys and still not miss any good parts of *The Texas Chainsaw Massacre* triple bill. You know the type, girlfriend: cowboy hats, whiskey breaths, room temperature IQs, noodle dicks. 'Tis a pure wonder I ain't falling apart from the Pork Poisoning. I guess I'm just lucky."

"Real lucky, fillette," Jazzbeaux commented.

Sleepy Jane got her name when one of the grunges, a specimen named Buddy Wayne Meeker, thought it'd be hilarious to cut her eyelids with a razor-blade. His performance was so uninspiring she'd fallen asleep before the end titles rolled. Though interrupted by the Lansdale's security op, Buddy Wayne managed to sever a few tiny muscles, giving the ganggirl a permanently dozy look.

Nine months back, Sleepy Jane finally tracked down her amateur plastic surgeon and the 'Pomps had paid him a visit at his place of drinking. Pleased with his shaky night's work, he liked to tell the story to his beer buds, working up a fair old head of laughter as he embroidered details. When Sleepy Jane faced Buddy Wayne down, he recognised her straight off and sprouted a shit-eating grin that was practically a deformity. In the parking lot Jazzbeaux, who'd paid attention to human bio lessons, cut a few of *his* tiny muscles and made the grin a permanent fixture. Then they'd taken turns and cut a few more of his muscles. None of his beer buds were inclined to intervene, perhaps because Sweetcheeks was dancing semi-nude along the bar, pointing her titties and a pumpaction shotgun at a roomful of rednecks. Though good value as a table dancer, Cheeks sometimes got carried away and lost a customer.

When Buddy Wayne told the Sleepy Jane story these days, he'd still grin but he wouldn't be laughing. That was one score evened. Jazzbeaux was making a career of settling scores. It was one of the many character traits she could backtrace to the influence of her father. Though Bruno Bonney was dead, she kept running into him.

Varoomschka called in a detailed report.

"They're pilgrims, *suestra*. Josephites, *en route* to Salt Lake to reseed the Des."

"*Mishkins,*" Jazzbeaux commented.

Without needing an order, Sleepy Jane slowed down. The Tucker crawled up to the Lansdale turn-off. Jazzbeaux saw Varoomschka standing by her cyke, the butt of her Kalashnikov perched on one hip, keeping an eye on a sober crowd of men in rough black suits. Their womenfolk and kids held back, eyeballing Varoomschka with suspicion and alarm. The 'Pomp wore a see-through jump suit over a red bikini with a yellow hammer-and-sickle motif. Spike heel go-go boots and a white fur hat made her nearly seven feet tall. She had unslung her Kalashnikov and put a hole or two in the dirt by the Josephites' feet.

Jazzbeaux watched her own back because Varoomschka sometimes gave the impression that she wondered if she could get ahead by making an opening for Acting War Chief.

The negotiation with the Daughters of the American Revolution was colossally important. Jazzbeaux shouldn't be conce with petty pickings. With two good-sized states to worry about, she should pass on by without rumbling the Josephites or just give them a light pasting to get their food and fuel. She had other *blat* to cover, major league *blat*. There was no need to take the time to beat up on the new pioneers.

But there was a man among them who was unafraid. That was a personal challenge.

"Vroomsh, who's the preachie with the shades?"

Varoomschka pressed a Red Star throat-mic cameo to her larynx and sub-vocalised. The shortwave radio translated her swallowed words into a metallic Hawking voice.

"Elder Seth, he says. Leader of the pack."

Sleepy Jane pulled over and the convoy slid smoothly to a halt. As she got out of the Tucker, Jazzbeaux was pleased to see the 'Pomps were still in formation as if for a parade. The chapter would make the late, genuinely lamented Ms Dazzle proud.

Elder Seth stood tall by Varoomschka, smiling just like her old man. On sight, Jazzbeaux knew she would have to take him down.

"Good ayem, preacher-man," she said, looking at her face in his mirrorshades. Even with the eyepatch, she was doubly cute. "My associate, Miss Porteous," she nodded at Sleepy Jane, "is the *commandante* of this desirable camping area, and we figure you owe her a kopeck or two stop-over fee."

The elder showed empty hands and said, "The Brethren of Joseph are poor. We have little money."

"*Nichevo,* we'll garner the fee in goods. Vroomsh, So Long, take around the collecting plate."

"Foul hagwitch of slutdom," protested a black-hatted pilgrim with a red face, starting forward.

Elder Seth held his arm out, preventing his follower from flying at Jazzbeaux, probably saving his life.

"Stay calm, Brother Wiggs. The sister will find her reward in Heaven."

"Darlin' dearest," she said, dimpling the underside of the elder's chin with the sharpened point of her forefingernail extension, "I'd best find my reward in your pockets, else you'll be waiting for me by the time I get to Heaven."

"We have abjured pockets," Elder Seth said, calmly lecturing as if she weren't an eighth of an inch away from puncturing his carotid artery. "Pockets encourage possessions and we have abjured ownership of worldly things."

"You can vocalise that again, preachie."

Varoomschka and So Long Suin went among the resettlers and their ve-hickles, dropping scav into wire baskets as if spreeing down at X-Mart. The haul was pathetic. Josephites abjured rings, necklaces and earrings, so there was no jewellery. Their clothes didn't even have buttons. Only about one in ten had a watch, mainly cheap American Century dialfaces. The Brother who handed over a five thousand dollar Swiss Chronex was almost relieved, as if he no longer had to worry his fellow pilgrims would find out about his hoard. The *mishkin* even thanked Varoomschka for teaching him a valuable lesson.

"I could teach you a more valuable one if you'd let me, Studley," Varoomschka said, wriggling inside her cellophane-like wrapping, tongue touching the tip of the Josephite's nose. From the man's crawling reaction, Jazzbeaux gathered these people abjured more than pockets.

She opened the elder's jacket and found a wallet hanging on tags. It had a few meagre cashplastics and cards, but she kept it anyway.

"I don't parse you *cheloviks*," she told him. "Life has few enough pleasures. Why turn away from them?"

"One day, daughter, you will understand."

He had pushed the wrong button.

"*I'm not, not, not your daughter, old man!*" she spat.

She looked at his face. It could be a half-mask under the shades for all the expression he showed.

But there was something in his voice. Soothing and threatening, sad and strange. When he called her "daughter", there was an echo of Bruno Bonney, RIP. The word was a lash.

She had to see his eyes. She had to make him human and taste his fear.

"I'll require these," she told him, reaching up and slipping the mirrorshades from his face.

He didn't even blink, though sun poured into his eyes. There was no fear. She couldn't read anything from the colourless ice-chips looking back at her single eye.

Jazzbeaux found she was the one blinking.

"Jessa-*myn*," Bruno said in her head, "c'mon over here and sit on Daddy's knee."

She looked at the shades. They were ordinary. She was sure they were cheap.

"Daddy won't hurt."

Bruno always lied about that.

The brother by Elder Seth's side – Wiggs, the elder had called him – was burning with fear and rage. Jazzbeaux felt the brother's impotent need to hurt her, and it gave her a thrill. It almost made her feel sexy.

She had not been able to enjoy acts of love until her father was dead. She had needed to outgrow guilt and pain.

Elder Seth didn't show anything. Jazzbeaux could swear he didn't feel anything. She had thought her father was like that, but, in the end, she had made him feel too many things.

If the only way of getting a reaction out of someone was to rip out their throat, then Jazzbeaux was willing to go the distance. She tried the same stunt on Officer Rachael Harvest once and wound up with a cracked wrist.

She had to make the elder's face flicker.

"Andrew Jean," she called out. "They must be hiding *something*. Bread-fruit trees or coffers of gold. Their whole lives are in the motorwagons."

Andrew Jean considered the question and agreed.

"Find the scav," Jazzbeaux ordered. "By any means necessary."

Andrew Jean saluted, shocking pink fingernails tipped to a beehive hairdo.

Jazzbeaux's lieutenant had a mean streak which sometimes went a mile too far. The paper on Andrew Jean listed a couple of murders Jazzbeaux would have been ashamed of. So she was usually careful about tasks she assigned in that direction.

Now Jazzbeaux was being wilful. What happened next would not strictly be her fault – she had issued no specific orders – and, indeed, Elder Seth would be as responsible as anyone else for the blood that was bound to be spilled.

Andrew Jean cut out a couple of the pioneers and jostled them into a bunch. Three men, youngish, anonymous, good-looking. Andrew Jean always had good taste in men. One was the *cheloviek* Varoomschka had shaken down for his watch.

"These pilgrims have names, preacher?"

Elder Seth nodded.

"Brother Akins, Brother Finnegan, Brother Dzundza."

"Cosy."

The Josephite's face was stone over a skull.

"Do you feel like divulging the whereabouts of your fabled stash? A fabulous treasure must lie hidden in your transports. Think not that you can dupe the Psychopomps."

Without pleading, he told her, "There is no treasure."

She drew her Magnum LadyKill and hefted the pistol, resting the sight against the elder's throat apple. The gun

was a Christmas present from the ganggirls, with a senti-
ment inscribed on the grip.

"If wishing makes it so, tell yourself there's no
ScumStopper in the chamber."

The LadyKill was a single-action weapon; it cocked and
fired with one pull. A light touch and Elder Seth's head
would vanish. Also, considering recoil, Jazzbeaux would
crack her wrist again, but nothing ventured, nothing
gained.

Andrew Jean prowled around the three Josephites,
inspecting them, feeling up butts, flicking ears, tugging
sleeves. Akins, the youngest, muttered a prayer.

One of the sisters struggled forwards to plead for the
elder's life. She was pushing forty and abjuring make-up
was not a good policy decision for her.

"Sister Ciccone." Elder Seth said, silencing her, "take
comfort. The Lord will know His own."

The sister sniffled but got back in line. There was something about her squinty eyes that didn't fit with the God
Squad.

"Any final thoughts?" Jazzbeaux asked.

Elder Seth did not even pop sweatbeads. He looked as if
he were sure his throat was bullet-proof.

With three precise stamps, Andrew Jean broke three
knees, stepping down on legs as if breaking sticks for kin-
dling. The brothers screamed and fell to the blacktop.

"Vroomsh," Andrew Jean said, "the K'lash."

Varoomschka tossed the Kalashnikov over. The gun
fell into Andrew Jean's hands and discharged almost by
itself.

A stitching of bullet-holes raked across the asphalt and
opened bloody cat's eyes in the Josephites' backs. Akins
screamed painful prayer. Dzundza of Swiss-watch fame
was shocked instantly dead. Finnegan, modelling himself
on the elder, held in his yelps.

Jazzbeaux did not know how she felt. Years ago, Officer Harvest had tried to brainwash a conscience cop into her skull. Sometimes the dumb bitch wouldn't shut up. Bruno Bonney and Buddy Wayne Meeker, OK; but what about these three pilgrims? They had done her and hers no harm. Jazzbeaux shook her head and swallowed the thought. She would have to squelch Redd Harvest one day, then maybe she'd get some peace. If only people wouldn't stick things in her head that screwed up her thoughts.

Andrew Jean levelled the rifle and pantomimed a massacre, making bang-bang sounds as the barrel raked across the flinching crowd. Sweetcheeks cheerled with a few killercalls and a couple of bump 'n' grind steps. So Long, uncomfortable with this sort of action against civilians, kept her opinions to herself.

It had gone further than Jazzbeaux intended.

Elder Seth watched without even showing interest. It would be easy to shove the LadyKill past his teeth. If she shot a ScumStopper through the roof of his mouth, she'd explode his greymass. *Then* she'd see a reaction.

Andrew Jean switched the Kalashnikov from automatic, and shot Akins in the foot, the ankle, the calf, the knee, the thigh, the hip…

A woman in the crowd was sobbing. Sister Ciccone.

"Leave them be," Jazzbeaux said, finally. "Trash their chariots."

Andrew Jean, taking a broad interpretation of orders, shot Akins and Finnegan in the heads, finishing their business. A party of 'Pomps filtered – attacked the Josephites' ve-hickles. If she were thinking straight, Jazzbeaux would have ordered the girls to scav usable spare parts.

"Akins, Finnegan, Dzundza," Elder Seth said. "Remember their names, daughter."

"I told you," Jazzbeaux shouted, whipping the barrel of the LadyKill across the man's face. "You're not my daddy."

He spun away from her but did not fall. Wiggs held him up. She should have crushed a cheekbone, but only raised a bruise which sweated red droplets.

He had not needed to remind her. She never forgot the names of her dead.

She holstered her gun unfired, and unhooked the elder's shades from her chain-link garter.

His eyes fell on her.

"People like you have been looking at me like that all my annos," she said, twirling the sunglasses. "I can hear you thinking, 'one-eyed skank', 'lowlife panzergirl', 'cock-sucking slut'. I've beard a lot of names."

She put on the shades. Strangely, they didn't make things darker. They must cut out glare or something. Maybe if she had two eyes, she could see a difference. No one could blame her for her anti-social attitudes; she was mono-scopic, *handicapped*. Society was piled up against her. Of course, she'd had two good, green eyes back when she'd done for Daddy. But Daddy was another sort of handicap.

The Psychopomps weren't just a gangcult; they were a Support Group for Survivors of Severe Abuse.

The 'Pomps were finished with the convoy now and back in formation. Varoomschka straddled her cyke like a cover girl, an outstretched boot-toe near Akins's head. To move out, Sleepy Jane would have to pizza-plough over the deadfellas. Fine. It would underline the point.

So Long Suin hunched impatient on her cyke. Her lips were pursed and her eyes were slits. She had a determined look that told Jazzbeaux she'd be filing an official complaint with the Den Mother about this. That was another hassle she'd have to deal with.

Elder Seth still looked at her. He wiped blood from his cheek with a kerchief and seemed to wipe the bruise off his face. It was quite a trick; one she'd have loved to learn.

Surely a Josephite wasn't likely to have bio-amendments. Most of these revivalists expended a lot of energy condemning ungodly tinkering with the divinely ordained human form. There were always scandals when televangelists raised money they sneakily used to have the Zarathustra treatment. But Elder Seth struck her as a very different stripe of preachie from the likes of Reverend Reggie Jackson or Harry Powell. It must be a trick of the eye.

Jazzbeaux took off the shades but found herself blinking and put them back on.

"Cool as snazz," she said. "I think they set off my outfit."

She rejoined Sleepy Jane in the Tucker, feeling headachy and unsatisfied. Suddenly she *wanted* to be in a nice, clean gangfight, biting and scratching and stabbing and gouging until the insect buzz in the back of her head was blotted away.

Petya Tcherkassoff sang "Purging My Love" on the radio. It always struck her as deeply chilling.

Through the windscreen, Jazzbeaux saw the Josephites standing like trees in the Petrified Forest. Elder Seth was the tallest tree in the pack. His hat-brim shaded his eyes with darkness.

"This was his lucky day," Jazzbeaux said.

She had let him live. She had taken his dark glasses and let him live. Two mistakes, she thought.

Bad ones, her phantom father whispered.

"Wagons roll," she said.

VI
9 June 2021

MORE DAMFOOL DEADFOLKS, Tyree thought, surveying wreckage, Well, arguably folks. And, until, bagged and tagged, only arguably dead.

Burnside, always a backdrop buff, was struck silent by Canyon de Chelly. No matter how many times he patrolled Monument Valley or the Painted Desert or the Petrified Forest, the trooper was compelled to waste valuable minutes staring. He should buy a book of postcards and get it over with. He kept on his skidlid, glareproof visor down, as he looked up at the free-standing column. Despite the technology wrapped around his head, he shaded his eyes with his hand.

As Burnside gazed up at the wonders of nature, Tyree rooted down in the dirt for the detritus of man.

"The place scans like an amnesty point for robo-bits," she said into her intercom. The Quince, a few miles back in the cruiser and gaining, grunted at her commentary.

Turning over a durium arm with her boot, she continued her report.

"We've got brand-new prostheses scattered like seashells. I'm no expert, but I think some of the smaller contrivaptions are doodad hearts and kidneys and the like."

She picked up a glass eye. Its pupil dilated suddenly and she dropped it as if it were a slug.

"And we have abandoned ve-hickles, some with trace blood in their treads. Plus what looks to me like explosive charges wired around the base of a national monument!"

The cruiser was in sight now, growling up an ill-maintained access road. Few tourists ventured this way nowadays. Out in the Des, you were more likely to pick up a permanent disability than a novelty hologram. Besides, once you've seen one acre of sand...

"Looks like a bird of prey," Burnside said, pointing out a circling black bird. "A hawk or something."

"Probably a vulture," Tyree said. "A disappointed vulture. There's no meat around here, just metal."

Burnside tore himself away from the grandeur and started poking around amongst the robo-junk. Some remains were almost complete, like empty suits of armour.

Dried smears of oily substance were all over the show, coating the abandoned doodads but also streaking the sand and rock. It had a faintly nauseating odour. Tyree had no idea what the stuff might be, but didn't care for it.

Quincannon ambled over from the cruiser, Yorke trotting behind like a faithful terrier. They looked like a father-and-son team; the young trooper trying to copy the older, bulkier sergeant's Cav swagger. Yorke was OK for a kid.

"Have you pulled wires on the infernal devices?" the sergeant asked.

"We thought you'd like to take a scan, Quince."

Quincannon raised a disapproving eyebrow at the arrangement of detonators and charges.

"It's just demolition equipment;" he said. "You couldn't even call it a *bomb.*"

Tyree agreed, but it was never a good idea to perform surgery on Blastite without a second opinion.

"Burnside, disable and collect the fireworks."

Burnside saluted and snapped to, scurrying around the base of the column to unfasten the packages.

"We'll put 'em under Captain Brittles desk for the Fourth of July," Quincannon said.

The Sergeant squinted at a decal on one of the abandoned cykes. It showed Pinocchio making obscene use of his liar's nose.

"Knock 'Em Sock 'Em Robots," Quincannon said.

Tyree agreed. Yorke needed the full explanation.

"A cyborg fraternity. Renegades from GenTech Bio-Div's New Flesh programme. They aren't really even a gangcult. There's a semi-official Hands Off note posted on them. BioDiv wants to observe them in the wild, see how they survive the environment."

"Not too snazz, I guess," Tyree said.

"Good call, Leona. Scans like a back-to-the-old-drawingboard situation to me."

Canyon de Chelly was an android graveyard. Maybe the bots always crawled here to die. In the future, poachers would recover a fabulous fortune in circuit boards and brainchips from the shifting sands. All they had to do was cripple a toaster and follow the tracks.

"What happened?" Yorke asked. "They all go bughouse and tear out their robo-bits?"

Tyree imagined a religious frenzy falling upon the bots. Her daddy had been a small-time preachie, specialising in Biblical excoriations like "If thine glass eye offend thee…" But theory didn't fit the picture.

"No, they're still here," said the Quince. "Scan those stains. I've seen sludge like that before. When the Virus Vigilantes launched a bioweapon against the Road Runners back in '17, that was the kind of stuff left behind. It's human compost. They tagged the effect the Meltdown Measles."

Yorke did a little dance, scraping black goo off his boot-soles. Tyree couldn't believe that human flesh and bone deconstituted to such an extent, but Quincannon knew best.

"The air tests clean," Burnside put in, a satchel of Blastite and fuse equipment under his arm. "I ran the check first thing. No out-of-the-way bugs."

"This doesn't feel viral to me," Quincannon said. "Scan the way the works are scattered around…"

There were robo-bits strewn in a wide circle, as if they had been wrenched apart and thrown to all points of the compass.

"This feels violent to me. Cold. Brutal."

"Very brutal," Burnside said.

"Should we call it in to Fort Valens?" Yorke asked.

Quincannon nodded. "Trail runs out here. The way I picture it, the perps ran into natural justice. The bots zotzed the pilgrims then something bigger came along and totalled them. Case closed, and we should get back to our route."

There was a distant whup-whup-whup. Tyree saw a sleek shape in the sky, some sort of mutant helicopter. The thing did a circle of the rock column and she tagged it as Private Sector. There was a discreet Japanese GenTech logo.

"Visitors," Burnside commented.

"Best behaviour, boys," Quincannon said, heavily depressing the irony pedal. "We don't want a diplomatic incident."

There was bad blood between the Quince and the Jap-corps, Tyree knew. There was a dead girl in the story.

The spidercopter made a neat landing and withdrew its blades. It was gleaming white and had no obvious windows.

"You expect them to troop out behind a robot and say 'we come in peace'," Yorke said.

"They don't need that," Quincannon said. "They're the new owners."

An aperture appeared and steps unfolded. Two figures stepped down precisely. They did look like aliens. Their Self-Contained Environment suits were sexless and slimline, with filter-mask helmets that resembled samurai armour. They bowed formally and advanced.

"This equipment is the property of GenTech," a computer-generated voice advised the patrol. "Thank you for protecting it. Your welcome assistance is now surplus to requirements."

It was impossible to judge whether the voice came from either of the SCE figures or the spidercopter.

"With all respect," Quincannon said, not bowing, "serious crimes have been committed. We're not rightly sure whether this junk is evidence or the perpetrators."

The figures froze and inclined heads towards each other. A tiny buzz indicated a conversation.

"The air's clean," Burnside said, helpfully. He held up his test print-out.

The SCEs took a moment. One raised an arm and punched buttons on a wrist-band. Tyree guessed the equipment was several generations in advance of the wheezy old contrivaptions Burnside had to lug around. There was a ping which, she assumed, confirmed Burnside's tests. As one, the figures touched buttons at their necks and hoods were sucked into their collars, rolling back like foreskins. Anonymous faces emerged, a Caucasian man and a Japanese woman.

"You will please help Dr McFall-Nagai and Engineer Huff gather the GenTech property," the helicopter said. Tyree didn't quite like its tone.

"It's just junk," Yorke said, kicking a stray leg. The Japanese — Dr Shimako McFall-Nagai, her breastplate read — cringed. In that moment, Tyree found some sort of fellowship with her; it was irrational to think a prosthesis felt pain, suggesting a welcome streak of human idiocy.

"If you will kindly have care," Dr McFall-Nagai said. "Delicate recording instruments are concealed."

"You're looking for the black boxes?" Quincannon asked.

"Indeed," the woman confirmed.

Tyree didn't understand.

"The company has been letting its experiments loose," Quincannon explained. "The bots must have imagined they were renegade, but they've been monitored all along."

The GenTech officials methodically went through the detritus, retrieving specific doodads.

"Why didn't they use the OFF switch when it scanned like they were killing people?"

"There is no OFF switch," the helicopter said.

"Don't be so sure of that," said Quincannon, raising his voice unnecessarily. "Something sure found a way to pull the plug on the bots"

Tree got the impression the helicopter was sulking. She noticed Dr McFall-Nagai shudder when the sergeant shouted at it. Whoever generated the voice was a high-level suit. Also, a high-level creep.

Engineer Huff found something and signalled urgently. The Japanese bowed to the Cav and hurried over.

"This one still functions," Huff said.

The woman knelt like a paramedic and started working on an opened chestplate with chopstick-like implements. She was attending to what looked like a complete android. Its soft, green plastic face was a Boris Karloff mask. It even had bolts in its neck.

As Dr McFall-Nagai worked, sparks flew. She muttered in Japanese.

Tyree cautiously approached, careful not to get in the scientist's light. The Frankenstein monster's eyes opened and closed like goldfish mouths. The scientist left the bots' chest alone and. shifted attention to the head. She found a seam and pressed, opening the flat skull. A glittery crystal ball was exposed, sludged with what the Quince called "human compost". Lights fluctuated inside.

The scientist whistled.

"Ambitious," she said, "but unsuccessful."

"Can it still think?" Huff asked.

She slipped her tool into a hole in the ball. A light in the implement's butt flashed.

"Point debatable. It can calculate but it cannot intuit. Therefore it cannot be classed sentient. It may retain limited motion controls and be programmed for repetitive functions, but this is at best a robot. As a human being, he is dead."

Suddenly, the Frankenstein monster sat bolt upright, hinging at the waist, arms outstretched like a sleepwalker.

The scientists were pushed aside.

The bot's chin dropped and it rasped, "I live!"

Its heavily lidded eyes were half-alive.

"That's not possible," Dr McFall-Nagai said, not unkindly. "You have no brain, merely storage cells."

An arm lashed out, tossing the woman away. She yelped surprise.

Tyree had her sidearm out. So did the rest of the patrol.

"Be warned it is an offence to damage GenTech property," the helicopter shouted.

The Frankenstein monster stood, a giant-sized Glow-in-the-Dark hobby kit. It wore shredded black coveralls. Its body was metallic. Offence or not, it scanned as if it couldn't be damaged.

"Does this thing have civil rights?" Quincannon asked Dr McFall-Nagai, who was scrambling upright.

She thought a moment, "I would have to say no."

Quincannon spanged a bullet off the Frankenstein monster's face, shredding plastic over its forehead. Undented metal gleamed.

The robot, no longer organic in any sense, looked up at the sky and reached out, grasping for the sunlight. It might have been smiling, it might have been worshipping.

"What's it doing now?" Tyree asked.

Dr McFall-Nagai shrugged but made a suggestion. "Having a religious experience?"

The Frankenstein monster staggered towards the spider-copter. The aperture nervously contracted shut.

"Did I request thee, Maker, from my clay
To mould me man? Did I solicit thee

From darkness to promote me?"

The creature was imploring. The spidercopter was silent.

Tyree was baffled, but Dr McFall-Nagai told her, "Milton, *Paradise Lost*. The epigraph to *Frankenstein*. All cyborgs revere the book, and the films *Pinocchio* and *The Wizard of* Oz. For obvious reasons."

With a Karloffian roar, the Frankenstein monster attacked the spidercopter. Its large, ungainly hands found no purchase on the smooth machine surface.

"It's molecule-locked ceramic," Huff explained. "Three times as resilient as durium alloy."

"That thing's a pot?" Tyree exclaimed.

The Frankenstein monster's fingers scrabbled and broke. An arm extruded from the spidercopter and a needle-beam sliced through the bot's neck, shearing away the head.

The thing fell dead.

"That shouldn't have happened," Dr McFall-Nagai said. "With no greymass, it could only follow programs. It could not act independently. It could not quote Milton."

"It did a pretty snazz job, missy," Quincannon said.

"Dr Zarathustra acted prematurely," the Japanese woman said. "The specimen should have been maintained in its state until a thorough examination could be conducted."

Tyree looked again at the featureless spidercopter, impressed. Zarathustra was a household name, a force in GenTech's BioDiv. If anyone born of woman lived forever, it would be his fault.

The Japanese was politely puzzled.

"This has been an Unknown Event," she concluded.

"I've heard that expression before," Tyree said. "I've seen it in reports."

The scientist looked almost afraid.

"There have been many UEs. Things that should not be have been and continue to be."

"Didn't we used to call them miracles?" Quincannon asked.

The scientist nodded vigorously, fringe shaking.

"The world is coming apart. Immutable laws have been broken. Laws of physics."

"Other laws have been broken," Quincannon said. "Laws of America. Against murder, for instance. The bots killed a couple of pilgrims just over the Utah border."

The sergeant was looking at Dr McFall-Nagai, but was speaking to Zarathustra inside the spidercopter.

"There's a case that anyone claiming ownership of the robo-remains could be classed an accessory. Like a dog-owner who lets his pitbull savage kids. If BioDiv were monitoring the Knock 'Em Sock 'Em Robots' actions and didn't intervene, there could be hefty charges."

The aperture reappeared, wordlessly summoning the scientists. Huff had collected a string of egg-shaped devices in a clear plastic suitcase. Dr McFall-Nagai bowed rapidly and apologetically, then retreated with her assistant into the spidercopter. The machine snapped shut, extruded blades and rose vertically in parallel with the stone column.

"That woman was worried, Quince," Tyree said.

All around them, left-over robo-bits ticked. A wind seemed to pass through. Valves still functioned, pistons clicked, joints locked and unlocked, cables contracted.

"So she should be, Leona."

Yorke picked up the Frankenstein monster's head, holding it as Hamlet held the skull. Dr Almighty God Zarathustra had left the anomalous thing behind. He wanted only evidence that conformed to expectations and would suppress anything that didn't fit in with the rigidly maintained scientific world image of consensus.

"This'd look fine in the mess hall trophy case," Yorke said.

The mouth opened, dropped, and a voiceless buzzsaw whine came out. Yorke dropped the head fast and kicked it away, shivering.

"Very funny, Yorke," Quincannon said.

Burnside scanned the painfully blue sky until the spidercopter was gone in the haze.

"Remember clouds" the trooper said. "It's been a long time since you saw a cloud."

Quincannon took a last recce of the site and ordered everyone back to their ve-hickles.

"We should backtrack from the original incident," he said. "Pilgrims don't just come in pairs. There'll be a whole load of folks, probably in trouble."

Trouble, Tyree thought: our job.

VII
9 June 2021

WITHOUT THE SPECTACLES, the Summoner boiled with anger. The surface of his mind was still as glass but great rages tore and shrieked in the depths. He wished to bathe in blood.

As the half-human, half-machine abominations were smitten, the Path was blooded. Another move in the ancient rite. The one-eyed girl had disrupted the ritual. The Summoner saw something in her. She was young and foolish, but behind her face was something struggling to be born, something with row upon row of shiny teeth. There was a moment when he could have killed her, but he had let it pass. After so long a wait and so close to the culmination, he needed to leave loopholes. Or else where was the challenge, where the enterprise? He could regain the spectacles. He would wipe away the one-eyed girl. But first he would be tested and proved.

He felt her tugging at the corner of his mind. Jessamyn Bonney was not yet aware she had impinged upon his consciousness. Doubts bothered her like butterflies, but she had not yet troubled herself to think too much of her prize. If she continued to wear the spectacles, she would of course be forced to think more deeply.

At a swallow, he learned the girl's history, probed her flaws, knew where she would bend, where she would break. Her years were so few, so brief, so banal. When they met again, he would know which points to pressure.

In the Outer Darkness, the Masters stood still and silent, regarding the tiny bauble of the Earth with ferocious interest. The Summoner knew the Dark Ones would soon stir. The entities had many names, earthly and otherwise: Nyarlathotep, Tzeentch, Sathanas, Ba'alberith, Klesh, Tsathoggua. Princes of Darkness and Blood and Fear, dimly perceived by every human culture that ever was. No man but the Summoner had any but the faintest idea of their true nature.

Sacrifices must be made. Elsewhere, the Nullifiers were intent. For there was a balance to the darkness, a concentrated dot of light that would grow as the Last Days proceeded. The great game of infinite universes would be played out one more time, one last time.

He felt the weight of years lifting from his mind as he developed the strength he would need to survive the few remaining moments of history. Sometimes he wondered if he could remotely be considered a human being. The shape he wore was transient and deceptive; the labyrinth of memory that was his mind was beyond human imagining. Even geniuses and madmen had been unable to share his visions. His other selves, from the other continua – the masked sorcerer in his castle, the information-bloated leech in his pyramid – overlapped his mind briefly, flaring with their own purpose.

Would the one-eyed girl come to appreciate the gift she had taken? She could no more use the spectacles than an ant could conceive of a whale, but she might discern a certain curvature of the landscape, a certain quality of shadow…

In the near future, his hands would be red with her blood. His mind would be his own again. In the meantime, the ritual continued…

VIII
9 June 2021

THE PATROL MADE good time on the pilgrim trail before making camp, returning to where they had buried the roadkill. The cruiser had a microwave for reheat-rations and an in-built recaffolator, but Quincannon liked to get a real fire going. He said the desert night didn't sound right without crackling. Also, flames kept unwelcome critters away. Every month, some straying patrol logged a sighting of something that shouldn't be alive.

Yorke and Tyree spent half an hour rounding up scrubby weeds and wooden jetsam for the fire while the Quince and Burnside raised the wind-wall and the pup tents. With the sun falling rapidly, the task had some urgency. Under starlight, it was impossible to find anything.

Half-buried by the road was a bookcase, complete with paperbacks. There was a set of Margaret Thatcher's "Grantham" romances, which had been popular back in the '90s just before the publishing industry went into its final death throes, and a few pulps by David Icke, who turned out to be a bad Brit science fiction writer.

The bookcase and books were all the troopers needed to get a good fire going. Yorke stamped the furniture into fragments and made a pile. Tyree was nervy about putting books into the blaze, which Yorke couldn't understand. They were just dead old words on paper.

While Quincannon boiled up a pot of recaff, hoping that real fire might improve the taste, Tyree hauled herself off to one side with a paperback called *Newtworld* and started reading. Yorke eyed her. She was like that in off-hours, withdrawn and a tad nose-in-the-air. She was seeing Nathan Stack, another trooper out of Valens, but the affair seemed on the wane. Yorke, who hadn't had himself a woman since his last leave in Tucson, would have liked a chance, but Tyree had a good five years on him, and he knew she didn't take him seriously. She had tiny lines around her mouth and eyes, but was in shape. A man could do a sight worse...

"March over, Leona." the Quince said. "Get your reheated taco and grits."

Tyree scrambled nearer the fire and took a plate. With her helmet off, she had honeyish hair that cleared her shoulders by a couple of inches.

"What's the book about?"

"So far as I can scan, it's set in the future when intelligent swamp creatures rule the planet and the Brit government are amphibians. Except the prime minister, who's a jellyfish. The first couple of pages are torn."

Quincannon looked at the faded book cover. It showed a man-sized lizard with a big gun and a British policeman's helmet.

"I've heard enough strange stories not to be bothered with this stuff..."

Yorke could tell the Quince was in a vocal mood. They'd be lucky to get to sleep before three, by which time the sergeant would have done his best to pack them off to dreamland on the nightmare express. If it was scary, it had happened to someone Quincannon knew.

"Wasn't today strange enough for you?" Tyree asked. "You met the Frankenstein monster. And Dr Zarathustra."

"Hell, Leona, today didn't even go off the Odd scale into Weird."

Yorke bit into his taco. It was standard Cav rations, meat in one end and fruit in the other. You ate your way through to dessert. He washed down protein-intensive chunks with swallows of hot, muddy coffee-derivative. Everyone who remembered what they called "real coffee" bitched and pissed about recaff, but it tasted OK to his buds.

Quincannon poured himself half a mug, then fished a flask out of his britches' pocket and sloshed in enough Shochaiku Double-Blend to fill the mug to the brim.

"The way I scan it," he said, "we're off duty. And off duty, our gullets and guts are no business of the United States Road Cavalry."

He offered the flask around. Burnside and Tyree waved it away, but Yorke took a hefty gulp. Battery acid sloshed against his sinuses and seeped out of his tear-ducts. Fire spread into his stomach.

"Ah, but it has a powerful kick to it," Quincannon said, smiling like a proud father. The more whiskey he had in his blood, the more Irish crept into his accent.

Burnside, having wolfed his rations down, untelescoped his travelling flute and began to blow scales. He liked to get his hour's practice in every day, even on patrol. Scales became a mournful improvisation, low and unobtrusive. Wash Burnside had a melancholy, wondering streak. He didn't talk much about his past.

"Quince, did you follow what that Japanese woman was saying about UEs?" Tyree asked.

Quincannon shrugged.

"Scientists don't like to admit the Lord has them foxed. Recently, they've run up against too many things they can't explain. And explanations that have done good service for centuries have been wiped off the blackboard."

"I don't see how that can be," Yorke put in. "Up's still up, and down's down."

"Mostly," the sergeant agreed.

Above, the desert stars were jewel chips scattered on thick black velvet. The universe was vast and coherent; endlessly changing, yet endlessly the same.

"That UE stuff sounds like blowback roadgrit to me." Yorke admitted.

The Quince was quiet for a moment. Yorke thought his words were echoing out into the big empty.

"Give me your gauntlet, trooper," Quincannon said.

Yorke was reluctant.

"I won't hurt it."

Yorke tugged one of the heavy pseudokid gauntlets from his belt and passed it over. Quincannon exposed the digital read-out and scrolled through the functions – time, compass, blood pressure, geiger counter, atmospheric pressure – until he found the thermometer.

"Now, which of you bright souls can tell your ol' Quince what are the extremes o' the Celsius scale?"

"Zero degrees and a hundred degrees," Tyree said. "The boiling and freezing points of water."

"Take a gold star and go to the head of the class, Leona m'love. For hundreds o' years, we used Fahrenheit which no one could figure. The idea of Celsius is that the scale stretches between the two easiest-to-remember temperatures."

Actually, the gauntlet thermometer could read off in Celsius or Fahrenheit.

"Now, you watch that pot o' cursed God recaff."

Quincannon squeezed his meaty hand into Yorke's gauntlet and picked up the hot pot. The glove was proof against anything short of an oxy-acetylene torch. Flipping open the lid, Quincannon shifted the pot from embers to a still-burning patch. Flames licked up around it, soot streaks clawing the sides.

The Quince dipped a finger into the brown liquid and stirred, making a disgusted face. Burnside played variations on "Vodka in the Jar", an Andrei Tarkovsky hit from the '10s. Within a minute, the recaff was bubbling and spitting.

"You'll stain my glove," Yorke protested.

Quincannon waved him back with his free hand.

"Worry not, the bounty of the United States is unlimited. Now, you'll agree that this foul brew is boiling?"

"Yes."

"Literally, boiling?"

Steam soaked the gauntlet. Angry bubbles burst on the surface. Liquid slopped over the side and dried to cracked paint.

"Sure."

"Then, me bright boy, take a look at yer man, the thermometer."

It read ninety-two degrees. Yorke tried to figure out the trick.

"That's not water. That's recaff."

"Good lad, well thought. The boiling point o' water polluted with this rotted poison should be slightly *above* one hundred degrees Celsius."

Yorke's head hurt. Tyree huddled over the fire, flame-shadows on her face, red light in her eyes, peering in fascination at the experiment.

"Last time I tried this little stunt, boiling point was ninety-four degrees Celsius."

"Well," Yorke said, "ninety-two is still plenty hot enough."

"Did you find this out yourself?" Tyree asked.

The Quince laughed. "No, it was one o' those funny items at the ass-end of Lola Stechkin's *Newstrivia* bulletins one night a couple o' months back. I just put it to the test."

"Is freezing point affected?"

"Now how would I be knowing that?"

Quincannon pulled his hand out of the pot and gave Yorke back the gauntlet. The index finger was thoroughly browned.

"I'm sorry, me boy. It looks like a cesspit dipstick."

"What does it mean?" Tyree asked, brow furrowed.

Quincannon shrugged again. "Lower fuel bills? The end o' the world?"

Out in the desert, something began whining in answer to Burnside's tune. Yorke found himself shivering.

zeebeecee's nostalgia newstrivia: the 1970s

TONIGHT, GIVING HIS *first major tele-interview in ten long annos, we have one of the seminal voices, faces and butts of the 1970s. Ask your grandparents, and they'll be sure to recall that droopy tache, that craggy grin and that battered balalaika. Nobody embodied the ideals and failings of the dream decade more than the style-setting, chart-topping, Soviet singer-songwriter, Andrei Tarkovsky.*

Born in Moscow on 4 April 1932 – he's a moody Aries, fillettes – Andrei studied at the Institute of Oriental Languages and the All-Union State Jazz and Blues School before taking his first gig in 1954, as a geological prospector in Siberia. Two long, cold annos rooting through frozen ground provided him with the material for his autobiographical first album, There Will Be No Leave Today, *in 1959. In the '60s, he was in the mainstream of Soviet pop music, receiving official approval and Union-wide acclaim for the seminal beetroot beat platters* Ivan's Childhood *and* Ikons. *It was only as the wave of the Sove Sound hit big in the '70s that Andrei became the irrepressible and outrageous rebel he remains into the twenty-first century.*

No matter how grey that moustache, wrinkly those crags or out-of-tune that balaidika, An-drei is still the genius of gloom, internationally hailed by his nickname "the Purge". Each new departure, new religion or new marriage hits headlines. Before Andrei sits in the Moscow Mud Pit with our chirrupy inter active diva, Lynne Cramer, let's listen to his first international colossus, from that atomic year of 1972, "Solaris"…

> *"Sooo-laris, oh-oh,*
> *Po-laris, oh-oh, oh-oh,*
> *Watch the mushrooming clouds*
> *Blot out the vanishing crowds…"*

LYNNE: For poprock fans too young to remember the dim and distant pre-wrinkle days of 1972, "Solaris" and "Polaris" were the first nuclear weapons used in battle since 1945, deployed by First Secretary Leonid Brezhnev, who was the Kremlin Top Kat, in answer to the use of scurvy bioweapons by Mao Zedong, head honcho of the Peep's Republic of China. Andrei-Babe, at the time you wrote and recorded the song, you were a Red Army reservist. Did this inspire your strong and, at the time, unusual anti-war stance?

ANDREI: Oh yes, Lynne. Moscow in those days was a wild and crazy city and the young were pleasure-seekers trailing in the wake of the idols of the day. Kanya Tcherkassoff, who I'm sure your viewers know as the grandfather of current teen heartthrob Petya, was starting his so-called career and his fans ran riot, spraying his name all over the metro and committing colourful suicide in the streets. There were those of us who thought them *mishkins*, but the lotus eaters didn't listen to us. There was faction-fighting between the fans of trivial pop and those of us who yearned for a more serious, philosophical approach. They called us the "Glums" and we called them the "Glits". On Soviet Tankmen's Day we would all head to the shores of the Black Sea for an open-air concert and always there would be clashes between Glums and Glits. It came to a head in the year 1972, with the mass suicide of the Kamchatka Chapter of Tcherkassoff's fan club. As the war in Vietnam turned nuke, the cloud of death really did hang over us all. We Glums were proved correct. There was more to worry about than pimples and hollow cheeks.

Tragically, many boys who thronged to my concerts did not live out the year. Over a million died on both sides of the Sino-Soviet border, rendering vast land-tracts uninhabitable for the next century. It was time to be out on the streets, protesting. We chanted slogans like "Ivan, Come Home", "Hell *Niet,* Don't Go to Viet" and "War is Bloody Bad". I first sang "Solaris" at a rally in Red Square and the next day Comrade Brezhnev, with typical good humour, ordered I be called up and packed off to the killing zone. He specified that my duties involve searching irradiated areas for dog-tags. A few short annos before, I was awarded the Tchaikovsky Medal and the Order of Dizzy Gillespie for *Ikons* and Brezhnev hummed my tunes when drunk in public. Now I was a dissident, on the dreaded Shit List. I was inspired to write my great hit song, "The Tunes, They are A-Stinking".

LYNNE: You never went to the war, though?

ANDREI: There was a well-established underground rail-road for those who resisted militarisation. Like so many other evaders, I was smuggled into Finland. Since I was a public figure, moves were made for my extradition but I kept moving. I visited the West, though I found it grey and poor and not to my taste. It was a great tragedy to me to come to America, land of my musical heroes, to find nobody remembered Chuck Berry or Little Richard or Elvis Presley. All the kids in Detroit and Baltimore were buying Kanya Tcherkassoff records.

I continued to record and release material. I played concerts, for those in exile. When Poland withdrew from the Warsaw Pact, I shared the stage, for the only time in my life, with the dreary Kanya. He insisted he top the bill, but I showed him up by delivering a twenty-minute encore of "Solaris" that finished as I set fire to my balalaika and did a cossack dance in the flames. He was too busy crying with shame to best that. My discs were *samizdat*, circulated underground in the Soviet Union, but I understand kids would pass them from hand to hand and listen in defiance of official rulings. Many were executed by the KGB for crimes no worse than owning a proscribed "Solaris" single. Of course, execution might be thought to be too lenient for those who wasted their roubles on Kanya Tcherkassoff platters…

LYNNE: About this time, you had a great following. Russian kids copied the way you dressed…

ANDREI: We all wore those flared blouses and tight, shiny boots. Tie-dyed kaftans were the uniform of protest. And the beards, of course. My beard was bigger than all the others, my moustache droopier and more luxurious. In Helsinki, I found I had lice, picked up in the boxcars I had hidden in during my escape. I shaved the lot off, all my hair, and the kids copied that too. I was amazed. Everyone trooped around as if they had already been shipped off to Siberia. The Labour Camp Look was huge. Tcherkassoff, who had to have artificial hair implants to fit in with the previous style, was so livid he developed a multiple personality disorder.

LYNNE: Those were hard times?

ANDREI: Intolerable. Everybody thought the Chins had long-range missiles which could strike at Moscow, Kiev, Leningrad. The end of the world was coming. That was why the kids were rebellious. They felt their parents had gambled away their future. There was no reason not to sleep around, to smoke *kif,* to play records loud, to defy authorities, to ride tractors through collective farms at the dead of night.

Boys of fourteen and fifteen were packed off to die in Vietnam for a cause they couldn't understand. There were a lot of Russian books and movies about Vietnam during the 1980s and '90s, trying to make out the suffering was good for the soul. You've seen the Rostov films, about the Stakhanovite veteran who never stops fighting. Or *The Bear Hunter, Dosvidanya, Vietnam, Born on the First of May.* All of them are beetroot mulch.

Back then, we were having to get our real news from the BBC World Service and the Voice of America. When the Chins came in to support the People's Republic of the North against the People's Republic of the South, we did not find out for many months. Those over twenty simply did not believe we were losing. The official Tass line was a succession of easy victories. But if the victories were so decisive, why was the war dragging on? Brezhnev even tried to keep the nuclear exchanges quiet.

Apart from the areas poisoned by bug bombs and nukes, the USSR lost much territory to scavengers. The Japanese reoccupied Sakhalin in '72 and the Shah spearheaded a drive to seize Transcaucasia. The Pan-Islamic Federation got together just as Turkey was invading Greece and armies of the faithful "liberated" Albania and subcontinent-sized swathes of Soviet Central Asia. The crescent still flies over those lands and, though it is always the Greek Christian terrorists who get publicity, tiny guerilla wars fester after over twenty years, as in Serbia and Ireland. Of course, the resources channelled into Vietnam meant Russia had to duck out of the space race, leaving the stars to the Americans, who turned out to have no use for them. In 1973, Mao claimed he had won the war just because Brezhnev had fallen from power. Of course, China was in the middle of its own break-up into semi-feudalism. I deal with all this in my concept album, *The Dragon and the Bear*…

LYNNE: Is it true that Yuri Andropov personally invited you back to the USSR?

ANDREI: That's what I heard. Of course I thought it was a trick. To us, the KGB were pigs. It was rumoured they had death camps for dissidents, deserters and evaders. The Movement was riddled with KGB COINTERPRO spies who would encourage protesters to acts of defiance then turn them in for harsh punishment. But Andropov knew a dead horse when he saw one and engineered the overthrow of Brezhnev in '73. His great slogan was "anti-corruption" and there certainly was a change in the Soviet character in the mid-'70s. It was much later that I returned to Moscow, 2009 to be precise, and, though interviewed extensively, was not arrested or assassinated. At this time, I was a Scientologist. Many fans who came to my first concert in post-Brezhnev Moscow were disappointed that I made the artistic decision not to sing any songs but chose to play an acoustic accompaniment to texts from L Ron Hubbard. I was sincere in my beliefs, just as I was sincere when I converted to Judaism, Catholicism, Sufism, EST and the Brethren of Joseph. Searching for truth has always been a part of the Russian soul.

LYNNE: How had things changed in Moscow?

ANDREI: Other than the country's total embrace of Western capitalism and a coffee shop on every corner? I wasn't so young any more. Fashion had passed me by a little. There was a burst of reactionary music. You remember the *kulak* rock of 1977, all the spitting and slam-dancing and such. The Sex Vostoks, Little Vera, that shower. The youth of the day despised the message of peace my generation wished them to receive. They pierced their noses and cheeks with sharpened vodka bottle caps and wore surplus Red Army uniforms with radiation burns and bullet holes. My records were still popular with those of my old fans who hadn't been killed. It was a relief, actually, not to have to pander to teenagers. I was able to follow artistic impulses, to plough my own furrow.

LYNNE: Those were the years of your *Nostalgia* album and tour. Many viewers will remember the spectacular circus which accompanied that remarkable achievement.

ANDREI: I was looking for a way of expanding my vision into a totality of art, to reach beyond the confines of popular music. I felt my vision demanded the twelve elephants, the banana-shaped dirigible, the cannons, the dead clowns, the hologram mushroom clouds, the mass tractor pull and the dance of the duelling chainsaws. In America, I'm still best known for the songs from *Nostalgia*. I believe that "Looking Back to the Future Unborn" was recently sampled in a television commercial for a psychiatric health drive.

LYNNE: Indeed, then it re-entered the charts.

ANDREI: It's a good cause, and I'm proud to serve it.

LYNNE: Among your contemporaries, who do you most admire?

ANDREI: Vania Vanianova, of course. The Kulture Kossacks were the only indie band of the early '80s worth standing in line for.

LYNNE: You were married to her?

ANDREI: Briefly. Between Sufism and vodka rehab. After the vasectomy but before the cancer ward.

LYNNE: What do you really think of Kanya Tcherkassoff?

ANDREI: I suppose he can't hurt anyone. We had a sort of *detente.* All that Glum and Glit business seems antique these days. He was supposed to appear on the *Offret* album but had one of his nervous breakdowns the day before the recording.

LYNNE: And Premier Abramovich?

ANDREI: He does about as good a job as anybody does. There might not be much left of the Soviet Union but we are fairly prosperous, reasonably democratic and culturally in acceptable shape. He hasn't had to call out the tanks and shell his opponents, unlike your President Estevez, has he? But I'm disappointed by the Soviets of the '20s. When I think of the good people who died, the struggles and sacrifices, I'm saddened to see that we have such a trivial, money-obsessed society. Our heroes are not poets and painters but computer programmers and contraceptive entrepreneurs. Moscow is a plague of Nostalgia Boutiques pushing expensive recreations of *our* fashions from the '70s. I wish I had copyrighted the usage of the word. The blouses are even baggier, the kaftans more tie-dyed, but it's not the same. These clothes are clean, for a start. We Russians have turned our backs on melancholy and brainwashed ourselves into happiness. Happiness is not good for us. We should lead the world; instead we manufacture more and more useless luxuries. Things must change.

LYNNE: Andrei, thank you.

ANDREI: Thank *you*, Lynne.

LYNNE: No, Thank *you*…

ZeeBeeCee is proud to announce the Andrei Tarkovsky Collection, a lifetime of hits available for download right now. Order now to receive your commemorative set of MP7 shades, Andrei Tarkovsky novelty nose and realistic droopy moustache, absolutely free. With a full academic commentary by noted authority Charles Shaar Murray, this definitive Andrei is available only to ZeeBeeCee subscribers who log into the datanet address flashing at the bottom of the screen. We guarantee this set will be complete for years to come, since Andrei has signed an exclusive non-recording contract, vowing not to cut any more discs for the rest of the decade, so you need not live in fear that your Andrei Tarkovsky Collection will be rendered instantly obsolete by ventures into new styles, religions or media. We're paying Andrei not to do anything new, so you can enjoy the great work that lies permanently in his past…

the book of the road

I
10 June 2021

"NINE VE-HICKLES, CAMPED off-road in a box canyon," Burnside reported. "Place used to be a drive-in movie theatre, the Lansdale Ozoner. Maybe thirty, forty citizens. Repeat, citizens, *not* gang personnel. No deathware in sight. All in black, like our flat friends two days back. They don't scan hostile, but they don't scan too healthy either."

Quincannon spoke into the communicator. "We'll be along directly, trooper. Do not establish contact until we're with you. The DAR didn't scan too hostile either, then they slaughtered F Troop with hatpin missiles."

"Check, sergeant."

Yorke had been driving since they broke camp at sunup. They were well into Utah. Quincannon was keeping watch on the scanners as the cruiser took in the view. The roads here wound through canyons and passes. Road Runner country. It was ideal ambush territory and you had to keep a camera-eye on the horizon for sniping

points. There had been no trouble but that didn't mean
there wouldn't be. Up on the roof, swivel-mounted sensors swept the landscape.

"So, what are we doing, Quince, rescuing or policing?"

"Could be either one, Yorke. Either one."

The cruiser blip joined the Tyree and Burnside blips on
the mapscreen. The troopers were off their mounts, waiting for the heavy brigade. With assumed solids, procedure
was to approach as a unit. Only certified gangcults war-
ranted the surprise sneak-up. Quincannon signed for the
troopers to saddle up and follow the cruiser. It was the
regular formation again.

"Just slide 'er into the canyon, Yorke. Don't make too
much of a noise but don't be too stealth-oriented either.
We don't want to provoke any trouble. People in situations
are liable to get panicky. Even decent folks have big guns
and hair-triggers these days. And, believe me, my favourite
song is *not* 'I Love a Massacre'."

Yorke took the cruiser off the road and the suspension
had to do extra work as it bounced over dirt track. The
cruiser was so well-sprung, you could put a shot glass of
whiskey in the cup-cradle and not lose a drop over the
brim.

There was a bunch of wheelmarks in the dust. They
hadn't bothered to cover their trail. Therefore these were
more likely to be victims than violators. The cruiser was
gearing up for a fight, just in case. Yorke was still rattled
from the patrol's brush yesterday with Boris freakin'
Karloff and the Spidercopter of Doom. A row of lights on
the dash went green one by one, and flashed regularly. The
laser cannons were primed, the mortars ready to slide out
of their holes, the directional squirters keyed up for tear
gas, the maxiscreamers humming.

If Custer had had just one of these babies, he would
have come back from the Little Bighorn a live hero.

"You hear that?"

Yorke strained his ears and Quincannon twiddled up the directional mics, homing in on a noise.

"Singing?"

There was a faint, reedy whine. Voices joined, none too professionally, in song.

"A hymn?"

"It's a psalm, Yorke. 'How Amiable are Thy Tabernacles, O Lord of Hosts'. You should have paid more attention in Sunday school."

"My parents are secular humanists, sir."

Quincannon mimed spitting.

Hymns gave Yorke a bad feeling. "What do you reckon, Quince, the Bible Belt?"

"Could be."

Yorke's hands were sweaty on the wheel. He had bad memories of the Bible Belt, a motorised gangcult of Old Testament fundamentalists. They wore spade beards, linen robes, open-toed sandals and "Jesus Kills" tattoos. Their kick was doing the Lord's work, but they were more inclined to Smite the Unrighteous and Put Out the Eye of Thine Enemy than Turn the Other Cheek or Love thy Neighbour. They had moved into a couple of wide-open townships in Arizona, Welcome Springs and Buggered Goat, and renamed them Sodom and Gomorrah. Then they had razed the places to the ground and righteously slaughtered everyone in sight in the name of the Lord. They could easily have moved this far north.

Yorke had been captured by the Bible Belt three patrols back, and was sentenced to die by the sword for having ungodly Avril Lavigne downloads in his MP7 shades. He still owed the Quince for pulling him alive out of Gomorrah, Ariz. And he still owed the Bible Belt for the three plastik and steelspring fingers he was toting on his left hand.

The cruiser quietly approached the drive-in. There was a camp at one end. A group of people stood together as if at a meeting, scanning up at where the screen used to be. They were the ones singing. Someone with a bigger, blacker hat than the rest stood on the hood of a motor-wagon, leading the congregation. The only one who could see the Cav coming, he kept waving his arms, keeping the psalm going.

Yorke let out a breath. The preacher was not Hezekiah Tribulation, messiah of the Bible Belt.

"Time to break up the sing-song," Quincannon said.

He turned on the outside hailers and spoke into the mic.

"Attention. This is the United States Road Cavalry. We mean you no harm."

He was obliged by law to say that before he shot anyone.

"We are here to offer assistance."

Yorke pulled the cruiser over and saw the blips converge as Tyree and Burnside parked by them. He still had the wheel and was supposed to stay at it in case the hymn-singers proved dangerous. It was the spot he liked. It felt a lot less exposed than getting out and talking to strangers in the Des.

The lights stopped flashing and glowed steady. The weapons system was waiting for the touch of a switch to cut loose. Yorke wouldn't even have to aim anything, unless he wanted manual override. The cruiser was ready to put a hole in any moving or stationary blip on its sensors without the photoactive Cav strip down its pantslegs.

The hymn ended and the singers turned to look at the newcomers. One or two went down on their knees and prayed out loud. They were either thankful for the rescuers or making their peace with God before they got killed trying to kill someone else. The Bible Belt went in for praying in a big way. And torture. Somehow, the two always seemed to go together.

"See you later, Yorke."

"Sure thing, Quince."

Quincannon stepped out of the cruiser and walked up to the choir, empty hand outstretched.

II
10 June 2021

THERE WAS SOMETHING strange about the preachie's shades. Jazzbeaux had worn them on and off for nearly a day. They were clearer than regular dark glasses and had a queer effect. She was used to the more-or-less flat, one-third obscured panorama of monocular vision augmented by an optic replacement. Once or twice, she thought she scanned things in the periphery that couldn't be there. Indistinct, but unsettling. Sometimes it was like seeing in 3D again. The disturbing presences hovered in the extreme left field, where she could usually see nothing.

"Whassamatter, Jazzbie," Andrew Jean asked, "you a *loca* ladybug? You're spookola in spades this ayem…"

The Psychopomps were grouped outside Moroni. The convention was that everyone parked neatly like solid citizens and walked into the arena like old-style gladiators.

Jazzbeaux sat on the hood of the Tucker, dangling the shades from her mouth. It occurred to her the glasses might be some new type of "safe" psychoactive. The lenses might convert light rays into optical illusions. It was possible. She'd read such things in magazines.

"No probs, Ay-Jay," she said.

This was important. Some liked a little high before a negotiation. It made them loose, less concerned, more daring. Jazzbeaux preferred going in straight. Back in her warehouse gladiatrix period, she always saved the Kray-Zee pills for after the bout.

Winning still hurts, she had learned.

So Long was running through stats on the DAR. In the chapter they were dealing with, there were a few well-known scrappers but no clear contender. That gave the Daughters the advantage; going in, the rep would know exactly who the 'Pomps would put into the ring. Jazzbeaux was facing some unknown.

"If t'were me picking the negotiator," So Long muttered, "I'd go for this fillette, Valli Forge. She's got more confirmed kills than anyone else in the chapter."

"Bio-amendments?"

So Long made the shaky sign. "None on record. Interesting chemical dependency, but she's not likely to be in withdrawal crisis when you do the dance."

Jazzbeaux liked high-fliers. They didn't know when they were damaged. The whole point of pain was to tell you when to protect yourself. Anyone with smacksynth or zonk in their system would stumble around on two broken legs until it was over.

Impulsively, Jazzbeaux slipped on the shades again. Last night, in the dark, she had scanned too many things. In daylight, they should be safe. The view seemed to ripple and voices whispered in her head. She swore she could hear the preacher man fuming.

"Best of luck, *suestra*," Varoomschka said, lying. If Jazzbeaux came out of this badly, Vroomsh would be the obvious candidate for Acting War Chief.

Jazzbeaux looked briefly at her, and flash-saw a jewelled skeleton wrapped in crinkled plastic. All the 'Pomps looked briefly shrivelled and dead. Then there was a shift and things settled – Varoomschka filled out her see-through jump suit properly.

Sweetcheeks stuck a wet kiss on her face, leaving a lipsticky heart. Jazzbeaux rubbed the girl's back affectionately, taking in a lungful of the scented air around her.

After only seconds in the shades, migraine sprouted. A hot nail drove between her eyebrows. Jazzbeaux took off the glasses and thought of throwing them away. She could drive a cyke over them and the distraction would be over. But she just slung them around her neck.

From inside the Tucker, Sleepy Jane reported the seismograph had picked up ve-hickles on the other side of Moroni.

"Company's here," she said.

The world looked real again but Jazzbeaux found herself wanting to put the glasses back on. It was like when she was eight and Dead Daddy put her on Hero-9 to keep her under control. She'd had to wean herself off the dope over a period of years and still felt the occasional urge for a H-9 hit. She knew a lot of addicts – there were dotted blue bruises behind Sweetcheeks' plump knees and Andrew Jean kept a powder compact filled with zonk – and even more people who were just more comfortable facing the world in an altered state.

It was reversed for her, like a negative picture. As a child, she'd been drugged for annos on end and never had a say. She remembered her first straight hours, when Officer Harvest put her in solitary after a juvie bust; *that* experience had been like the revelation some get the first time they go out of their skulls. Since then, she'd become more and more hung up on her straight spells, taking fewer and fewer drugs, spending longer and longer with only her unaugmented senses. One day soon, she would be hooked on reality.

Unless the shades scrambled her brain.

It was an irrational longing but after minutes it became irresistible. She fought it for as long as she could, but it was such a silly thing. She was Acting War Chief. She wasn't afraid to wear a pair of glasses.

"We don't go into town until nightfall," Andrew Jean said. "That's the arrangement."

"That'll make for a long, dull afternoon," Jazzbeaux replied. "Oh well, *que sera, sera*…"

She fiddled with the shades, tapping her teeth with an arm. She knew she should eat but didn't feel hungry.

Sweetcheeks was absorbed in a tiny game console; she was hung up on a scenario called "Perfect Date", but hadn't yet made it to the senior prom, let alone gone all the way with the class captain. The one time Jazzbeaux played the thing, she wound up being gang-banged by the football team and dismembered by a serial killer.

Varoomschka unshouldered her boom-box and slotted in 'Tasha's *Ancient Mariner Mambo* album. It had never been one of Jazzbeaux's favourites. 'Tasha had been married, at different times, to Petya Tcherkassoff *and* Andrei Tarkovsky. *Moscow Beat* said she represented a fusion of Glit and Glum. Jazzbeaux just thought 'Tasha was a pretentious whiner.

Maybe she was growing up.

Finally, she snapped, and – trying not to look desperate – casually slipped her head into the glasses, shaking back her hair at the same time. As the bridge settled against her nose, she kept her eye shut.

She heard 'Tasha singing:

"It is an Ancient Mariner
Who stoppeth one of three,
And by your hairy tangle beard and that glitter in your eye,
keep his filthy rotten hand off of me…"

Jazzbeaux opened her eye.

This time, the effect was different. Colours were brighter, but less sharp. There were shadows where there shouldn't be. It was a little like a Hero-9 or Method-1 buzz, but without any elation. Somehow, with the glasses on, she felt compelled to look back over her shoulder all the time.

> *"Like one that on a lonesome road*
> *Doth walk in fear and dread,*
> *And having once turned round walks on,*
> *And turns no more his head;*
> *Because he knows a frightful fiend*
> *Doth close behind him tread."*

She couldn't stop herself turning and looking back over the roof of the Tucker. Out in the Des, sands shifted. The sky was featureless, without even any birds.

She couldn't see the frightful fiend but that didn't mean it wasn't there. A strange shadow crept across the sand like a pointing finger. She had to hold herself to suppress a shudder.

Beyond the Des, she imagined a lone figure, advancing steadily with long-legged strides, face in the dark under his hat-brim. The preacherman was coming after her, coming for his property. That shouldn't have scared an Acting War Chief. But it did.

III
10 June 2021

BROTHER WIGGS WATCHED with suspicion as the cavalry-man walked towards the faithful. He logged the sergeant's side arm, but noted the buttoned-down holster flap. The man didn't need to draw his weapon; there was enough rolling death in his machine to level the Lansdale Ozoner and anyone in it.

Why could Gentiles not leave the Brethren of Joseph alone? Must there be nothing but trial and blood along the road to the Shining City?

The cavalryman put his gauntleted hands on his hips and looked the congregation up and down. Under his hat-brim were sharp eyes.

"You folks having a church service?" the sergeant asked.

"A funeral service," Elder Seth replied. "For those lost along the road."

The elder's voice, heavy with sorrow, carried across the drive-in. There was a muttering of amens.

"I think we found a couple of those souls a way south of here," the sergeant said. "Sort of spread out across the road."

Elder Seth bowed his head and stretched out his arms. It was as if he were hanging from a cross of pain.

"Brother Hooper and Brother Lennart."

"This wake for them?"

"Amongst others." The cyke troopers had dismounted and joined the sergeant.

One was a woman, provocatively dressed in indecently tight pants; the other was a black man, the type Wiggs's daddy would never have let onto his police force.

"How many more pilgrims have you lost?"

"Brother Akins, Brother Dzundza, Brother Finnegan."

"Seems to me you've been mighty careless with your brothers."

A spurt of anger shot up from Wiggs's belly. How dare this Gentile address himself so facetiously to Elder Seth? From a dozen yards away, Wiggs recognised the red blossoms of alcohol abuse on the sergeant's face. The cavalryman stank of sin.

The Lord knew, with women and nigras and who-all else knew what, the US Road Cavalry was mightily degraded. Wiggs saw them as no better than the other motorised killers, the resettlers. The girl-witch who had taken the elder's shades had been indecently dressed too.

"Let's scan your dead," the sergeant said.

Elder Seth had laid out the brothers lost to the murderous harlots on the road beyond the drive-in, where their martyr's blood had been spilled. The sergeant glanced over the three, who were concealed by a bloodied sheet.

"Traffic accident?"

"Murder!" Wiggs shouted. "Foul, bloody murder."

A look from Elder Seth stunned him into silence.

"Someone will have to tell me what happened," the sergeant said. "If people are killed, you have to report it. That's the law. We can't catch killers if witnesses don't come forward."

The sergeant was lecturing them as if they were children.

"They were painted women." Sister Ciccone said. "Evil spirits in female form, wallowing in the lustful filth of their fornications, drinking deep of the cup of depravity."

"That pings the timer, Quince," the cavalrywoman said. Her voice rasped through her helmet, like one of the godless cyborgs who slew Hooper and Lennart. "We had a report from T-H-R that the Psychopomps were raising their profile sandside. With the Maniax out of the pool, you expect smaller fish to flood in."

"We'll need to take statements," the sergeant said. "From all of you."

Elder Seth was unconcerned. "Earthly wrongdoers will receive their just reward on Judgement Day. It should be no concern of thine."

"Tell that to your perforated brothers."

Without his dark glasses, Elder Seth looked no different. In most lights, his eyes themselves were mirrors.

"This pilgrim seemed upset earlier," the woman said, indicating Wiggs. "Perhaps we should start with him."

Wiggs bowed his head in shame and silently prayed for guidance along the Path of Joseph. He had journeyed far from his sinning days, but was constantly reminded of the long, rocky road he had yet to travel.

The woman stood close to him. As she breathed, the front of her tunic swelled and shifted her yellow US Cav braces. She was a shapely woman, the Devil's worst temptation. She still wore her helmet, and her faceplate was opaque. Wiggs imagined an angel's eyes and a harlot's mouth, with a length of flaming hair confined in a tight clip.

"Brother…?"

"Wiggs," he admitted.

"Will you give a statement?"

He looked to Elder Seth who did nothing to suggest he should not cooperate. Wiggs knew it would go easier if they tried to help the officers. If some innocent bystander gave him trouble when he was a deputy, he always found a way to slow them down. His daddy had a saying, "Nobody's innocent, but some folks just ain't been found out yet". Cornered by the police, everyone had something to feel guilty about.

Wiggs more than most. Guilt was his constant companion.

"Whatever thou wish," he told the cavalrywoman.

The helmet nodded. Wiggs recalled situations when he would take advantage, pressing unwelcome attentions on a witness, approaching a crime scene with shameful desire in his heart. Was this hussy looking at him with lust?

"Scans like we'll be visiting with you folks a spell," the sergeant said. "Any chance of a meal and a drink?"

"Thou art welcome to share whatever we have," Elder Seth declared.

IV
10 June 2021

TYREE THOUGHT THE Josephites were damfool cracked, but they still seemed confident about their jaunt. Despite the deadfolks they had left along the way. They just took it all, kept singing their hymns and following their damned yellow brick road.

Surprisingly, the Psychopomps had left them with all their food and water. Elder Seth must be a persuasive fellow, to convince a gangcult to leave supplies. And to get this crew out on the road in the first place.

It was just one freaking miracle after another with him.

It was nearly nightfall now; the patrol had spent the afternoon processing statements. Tyree had started to tape and annotate an account of the gangcult incidents from that strange, squeaky little southerner, Wiggs. He was a soul in torment who hadn't quite abjured all he should, to judge from the way his eyes roved up and down her body. He was the type who meets a woman and can describe her bra size but not her eye colour.

The statements told them nothing they couldn't have guessed. When they learned what happened to the Knock 'Em Sock 'Em Robots, the Josephites didn't even gloat. The general mood was sorrowful, that lives were ended before errors were recognised. Tyree couldn't understand that degree of forgiveness and wondered if the dead brothers would have gone along with it. If she got pancaked by bad guys, she'd expect her friends to be angry about it, and maybe even hit the old vengeance trail. It might not make a dead person feel better when their killers were zotzed, but it sure couldn't make them feel any worse.

Quincannon had downloaded a précis to Fort Valens. Apparently, the Psychopomps had been sighted – by Ms Redd Harvest, no less – at some mall and there was a black flag by their file. The gangcult were climbing the hit parade towards the Most Wanted top twenty.

If the Josephites were annoyed with anyone it was the 'Pomp who had stolen Elder Seth's mirrorshades. All the statements tallied on the detail, though they varied on everything else. What sort of a person finds scavved sunglasses more memorable than a triple murder?

The women were preparing an evening meal. Burnside had hoped they'd brew up a couple of pots of coffee –

some rich folks could still get the real stuff brought in from Brazil or Colombia, and the Brethren must be pretty well set up to mount such a damfool expedition – but it turned out that coffee was one of the sinful, worldly things they abjured. Even recaff was off their diet sheet, and that bore about as much relation to good coffee as a flea did to a dog.

Without meaning to, Tyree drifted in with the women-folk and found herself helping out with KP. As she opened packets, Sister Maureen told Tyree all about abjuration and all the things she didn't miss. Tyree thought Sister Maureen was cracked. Hell, without coffee, carnal relations and a good clean gun, life wouldn't be worth living. As the woman ticked off each new thing the Josephites had given up, her sisters sighed with happiness. Sister Ciccone, whose pureness of mind and body suggested a lobotomy, was especially joyful at her abandonment of the pleasures of the flesh. Tyree wondered if the Brethren of Joseph reckoned smugness was a sin. Nobody in the congregation seemed keen on giving *that* up.

The Quince was face-slapped to learn the wagon train was dry. Back in Valens, the Sergeants' Bar would be opening up about now, and Quincannon would normally be in his corner with his bottle of Shochaiku, yarning with Nathan and the others. Tyree preferred to spend her downtime jacked into combat simulators, bringing up her points average to impress the promo board. That was one of the things that was curtailing her on-off relationship with Nathan; come the next round of exams and advancements, she'd outrank him. He was enough of an old man to find that insupportable.

Being around these people, with their fixed smiles and damfool passivity, made Tyree edgy. They didn't display grief for their dead friends, just smiled and said the departed were in a better place. The only thing these

Josephites seemed good for was singing psalms. That might prove useful, though. The way they were headed meant they would be going to a lot of funerals.

The Quince was still talking with Elder Seth, recording notes on his HanHeld. Tyree, bored now her interrogation quota was used up and unable to listen to Maureen and Ciccone any longer, wandered over to the lean-to by the main motorwagon, where the two men were doing their business.

"So," Quincannon said, "let's get this clear, you're... what did you call yourselves?"

"Resettlers, sergeant. We are here to reclaim the promised land."

Quincannon was having trouble with the word. "Resettlers?"

"Like the original pioneers, we are proceeding to the appointed place."

"Salt Lake City?"

"The flower of the desert. The Shining City. It is the Rome of our faith."

Quincannon whistled, not complementarily.

"I know Salt Lake. Used to be a Mormon hang-out. But it's a big ghost town now. The lake dried up when everything else did, and the solids died off or moved out. All there is now is the salt. Maybe a few scumscavengers, a gangcult hideout or two, but that's it. There's nothing for anyone in that hellhole. The Cav don't even bother to patrol the place."

Elder Seth smiled the insufferable smile of someone who knows something he's not telling. Tyree's preachie father had been shaky with doubts all his life, but this God-botherer was certain he knew how the universe was ordered.

"It will be resettled, sergeant. The deserts will bloom again."

"Are you some kind of irrigation expert?"

Elder Seth smiled again. The sunset caught in his eyes, giving him burning pupils like the Devil. Tyree couldn't tell, but she thought the elder's eyes were silvery.

"That too. Mainly, I am a guide. I am just here to show these benighted people the Way…"

"The Way to what? A dusty death out here in Nowhere City, Utah?"

"Forget that name, sergeant. The Brethren of Joseph have changed it. By presidential decree, this territory is called Deseret now."

"Desert?"

"No, *Deseret.* It is an old name. A Mormon name, as you said. The Mormons were, in many ways, a wise sect…"

Tyree knew that was an unusual thing for a Josephite elder to say. They didn't usually have a good word for any other brand of Christian.

"The whole state, and more, is legally the property of the Brethren of Joseph. You will not be surprised to learn no one else wanted it. The purchase price was one dollar. This will be where it all start."

"What?"

"The reseeding of the Americas. The Great Reversal."

Tyree felt tingly up and down her spine when Elder Seth spoke. His calm, even voice carried the unmistakable fire of truth. She didn't understand him but she could understand why people followed him. In some circumstances, she would have considered banging a tambourine in his backing group.

Sister Maureen brought him a cup of some unsweetened chocolate drink, and he smiled upon her. If the Josephites hadn't abjured carnal relations, Tyree would have sworn Sister Maureen had itchy drawers for Elder Seth. The preacher was handsome in a cruel son-of-a-bitch sort of way, and his sombre sobriety suggested the sort of challenge any real

woman would relish. If Gary Cooper had a mean streak a
yard across, he would have been ideal casting for *Dead in the
Des: The Elder Seth Story.*

"We will make a difference, sergeant. We will found
our Shining City."

"That's your right, elder," said Quincannon, turning
off his HanHeld. "But you're certifiably insane to come
out here with no weapons. This is wild country."

There was a move in Washington, championed by Senator Manson, to amend the Constitution; outside the
Policed Zones, the right to bear arms might well
become an *obligation* to bear arms. The reasoning was
that anyone who made easy meat of themselves was
wasting the time and budget allocations of law enforcement agencies.

"We have our arms, sergeant. Faith and righteousness.
Nothing can stand for long against them."

Though she didn't talk about it with Cav personnel,
Tyree had signed a petition against the Manson Amendment. The reasoning that any man not in possession of a
gun was begging to be murdered was too close to the
infuriatingly popular reasoning that any woman in possession of a vulva was begging to be raped.

"You might try explaining the faith and righteousness
deal to the fellas Leona buried klicks back. Hooper and
Lennart, wasn't it?"

"Our brothers understood. They went to glory joyous
in the knowledge of the Lord. They forgave their tor-
mentors."

Quincannon was exasperated. He got up, and walked
away. The elder watched him off; from the rear, Quincannon's manly stride looked uncomfortably like a fatty's
waddle.

"Sister," Elder Seth turned to Tyree, "was there something you desired?"

He was a tall man and must be well-muscled under his preacherman's suit. She could imagine him bending an iron bar into an oval without raising cords in his neck. She had no idea how old he was. His hair was as black as his hat and there were no lines on his face and neck, but a depth to his voice, a tone to his skin, suggested maturity, even venerability. When he smiled, he was careful not to show any teeth.

She had the most peculiar, not unpleasant, squirm inside her abdomen. Indecent ideas came to her.

Follow me, the elder's eyes seemed to say.

She wanted to answer.

Suddenly, she was nervous again, watching the sun go down in Elder Seth's eyes. He drank his chocolate.

"No, sir," she said, "nothing."

V

10 June 2021

THE DAR HAD been racking up a heavy rep in the past few months. They had total-stumped some US Cav patrol in the Painted Desert and some were saying they had scratched a Maniax Chapter in the Rockies. After tonight, their time in the sun was Capital-O Over. And the Psychopomps would *rule!*

Jazzbeaux pushed a wing of hair back out of her eye and clipped it into a topknot-tail. She took off the shades and passed them back to Andrew Jean. A wave of slight sickness passed from her mind and she felt stronger, closer to the edge. Later, she'd think it through; now, she had busy-ness to bother with.

Moroni was a typical Irving's Intermediaries arena, some jerkwater zeroville nobody gave a byte about. They could rumble on Main Street without fear of interruption. The DAR clustered around the bank building, while the 'Pomps hung back by a deserted virtual arcade.

Buildings here were on raised wooden porches, Old West style. Tumbletrash blew through, skipping over the dusted and cracked road like crippled birds.

Jazzbeaux, still feeling the hugs of her girlies, stepped off the porch and into the street. Torches in the broken streetlamps and at points along the roofs cast firelight onto the street arena. After negotiations were over, the town could bum for all anyone cared.

She beckoned the Daughter forward with her razorfingered glove, and gave the traditional high-pitched 'Pomp giggle. The others behind her joined in, and the giggle sounded throughout the ghost town.

The Daughter didn't seem concerned. She came out from her corner daintily and used the bank's front steps.

Jazzbeaux got a first good look at Valli Forge, the girl she would probably have to zotz. She was maybe seventeen, and obviously blooded. There were fightmarks on her flat face and she had a figure that owed more to steroids and implants than nature. Her hair was dyed iron-grey and drawn up in a bun, with two needles crossed through it. She wore a pale blue suit, skirt slit up the thigh for combat and a white blouse. She had a throat-cameo with a hologram of George Washington and sensible shoes with concealed switchblades. Her acne hadn't cleared up yet, but she was trying to look like a dowager.

More than one panzer boy had mistaken the Daughters of the American Revolution for solids, tried the old mug-and-snatch routine, and wound up messily dead. The DAR were very snazz at what they did, which was remembering the founding fathers, upholding the traditional American way of life, and torturing and killing people. Personally, Jazzbeaux wasn't into politics. She called a gangcult a gangcult, but the Daughters tried to sell themselves as a Conservative Pressure Group. They had a male adjunct, the Minutemen, but they were pussies. It was the Daughters you had to be concerned with.

"Come for it, switch-bitch," Jazzbeaux hissed. "Come for my knifey-knives!"

The Daughter walked forward, as calm as you please, and with a samurai movement drew the needles out of her hair. They glinted in the torchlight. They were clearly not ornamental. She grinned. Her teeth had been filed and capped with steel. Expensive dental work.

"Just you and me, babe," Jazzbeaux said. "Just you and me."

The rest of the DAR cadre stood back, humming "America the Beautiful". The Psychopomps kept quiet. This was a formal combat to settle a territorial dispute and shouldn't be queered by kibitzers. No matter what happened here, the 'Pomps could gain something from a quick fight rather than a long war.

This was not a funfight. This was Serious busy-ness. Jazzbeaux heard they did much the same thing in Japcorp boardrooms.

Valli Forge drew signs in the air with her needles. They were dripping something. Psychoactive venom of some sort, Jazzbeaux guessed. Her system had absorbed just about every juju the GenTech labs could leak illegally onto the market, and she was still kicking. And punching, and scratching, and biting.

Still, she meant to keep straight. The shades-shadow in the back of her head was bad enough.

The Daughter was obviously pumped up on something. Conservatives abhorred recreationals but they went in for short-term enhancements the way newstrivia anchors went after facelifts.

"Steroid *suestra*, I hear they're talkin' about settlin' the Miss America pageant like this next anno. You get to do evenin' dress, and swimwear, and combat fatigues."

Valli Forge growled. Her shoulders bulged with boosted meat.

"I wouldn't give much for your chances of winning the crown, Valli Girl. You just plain ain't got the *personality.*"

Behind her eyepatch, the implant buzzed open, and circuitry lit up. She might need her optic's burn function. It made for a grand fight-finisher.

Jazzbeaux held up her ungloved hand, knuckles out, and shimmered the red metal stars implanted in her knucks. Kidstuff. The sign of The Samovar Seven, her fave Russian musickies when she was a kid. She didn't freak much to the Moscow Beat these days, but she knew Sove Stuff really got to the DAR.

"You commie slut," sneered Valli Forge.

"Who preps your dialogue, sister? Tipper Gore?"

Jazzbeaux hummed in the back of her throat. "Unbreakable Union of Soviet Republics…" The 'Pomps caught the tune and joined in. The Daughter's eyes narrowed. She had stars on one cheek, and stripes on the other. The president of their chapter wore a Miss Liberty spiked hat, and carried a killing torch.

"Take the fuckin' slag down, Jazz-babe," shrilled Andrew Jean, always the encouraging soul.

The DAR switched to "My Country 'tis of Thee". The 'Pomps segued to "Long-Haired Lover From Leningrad", popularised by Vania Vanianova and the Kulture Kossacks.

Valli Forge clicked her heels and made a pass, lunging forwards. Jazzbeaux bent to one side, letting the needle slice air over her shoulder, and slammed the Daughter's midriff with her knee. The spiked pad ripped through Valli Forge's blouse and grated on the armoured contour-girdle underneath. The Daughter grabbed Jazzbeaux's neck and pulled her off her feet.

Jazzbeaux recognised the move. Her daddy had tried it on her back in the Denver NoGo when nine year-olds were worth a gallon on the streets. One thing she had to say about Dad, at least he had prepped her for the world she was going to have to live in. Other girls graduated from the Policed-Zone high schools, but she knew she was a woman the day she ripped her old man's throat out. If she was lucky, she might live to see twenty-five. She didn't believe she'd marry Petya Tcherkassoff and move to a *dacha* on the steppes any more.

She bunched her fingers into a sharp cone and stabbed, above Valli Forge's girdle-line, aiming for the throat, but the Daughter was too fast, and chopped her wrist, deflecting the blow.

Just what her dad used to do – "Jessa-*myn*, cain't you be *sociable*?!" The shit-eating dickhead.

She danced round the bigger fillette, getting a few scratches down the back of her suit, even drawing some blood. Valli Forge swung round and Jazzbeaux had to take a fall to avoid the needles.

The 'Pomps were chanting and shouting now, while the DAR had fallen silent. That didn't mean anything.

She was down in the dirt, rolling away from the sharp-toed kicks. The DAR had good intelligence contacts, obviously. The girlie had struck her three times on the right thigh, just where the once-broken bone was, and had taken care to stay out of the field of her optic burner. Of course, she'd also cut Jazzbeaux's forehead below the hairline, making her bleed into her regular eye. Anyone would have done that.

But Jazzbeaux was getting her licks in. Valli Forge's left wrist was either broken or sprained and she couldn't get a proper grip on her needle. There were spots of her own blood on her suit, so some of Jazzbeaux's licks must have missed the armour plate. The hagwitch was tiring, breathing badly, sweating like a sow. That armour must be feeling mighty heavy and mighty confining. Her daintiness was gone, and she was flailing.

Jazzbeaux used her feet, dancing away and flying back, anchoring herself to a broken lamp-post as she launched four rapid kicks to Valli Forge's torso. The fillette was shaken. She had dropped both her needles. Jazzbeaux caught her behind the head with a steelheel, and dropped her to the ground. She reared up but Jazzbeaux was riding her now, knees pressed tight. She got a full nelson and sank her claws into the back of her neck, pressing the Daughter's face to the hardbeaten earth of the street. Blood welled up around her nails. Jazzbeaux touched it with her tongue and caught a thrill from whatever was circulating in Valli Forge's system.

For a wavering moment, she thought the girlie was going to throw her off. A shadow seemed to fall over them, a shadow with silvery mirror-eyes and a fringe of horns.

This was no time for a delirium flash.

Finally, Valli Forge stopped moving and lay still in the dirt, and Jazzbeaux stood up. Andrew Jean rushed out, and grabbed her wrist, holding her hand up in victory.

"The winnnnerrrr!" Andrew Jean shouted, sloppily kissing her. Sweetcheeks was crowding in, and the others. Only Varoomschka, sardonically impressed but certain she could have ended it in half the time, held back.

None of the Daughters made an effort to fetch their champion. They stood before the bank like American Gothic statues.

Jazzbeaux pulled her eyepatch away and scanned the DAR. They were impassive as the optic burner angled across them, glinting red but not yet activated.

"Is it decided?" Jazzbeaux asked, wiping blood out of her eye.

An older Daughter, with a pillbox hat and a grey-speckled veil, came forward and stood over her sister. The girlie on the ground moaned and tried to get up on her elbows.

The veiled Daughter kicked Valli Forge in the side. The poison blade sank in. The fallen Daughter spasmed briefly and slumped again, foam leaking from her mouth.

"It is decided," said the veiled Daughter.

The DAR picked up the deadmeat and faded away into the darkness.

The Psychopomps pressed around her, kissing, hugging, groping, shouting.

"Jazz-beaux! Jazz-*beaux!* Jazz-*beaux!*"

The Psychopomps howled in the desert.

"Come on, let's hit somewhere with intelligent life," Jazzbeaux shouted above the din. "I'm thirsty, and I could use some real party action tonight!"

VI
10 June 2021

"SERGEANT!" SHOUTED YORKE. "Incoming from Fort Valens."

Quincannon jogged back to the cruiser, belly bobbing, between hi suspenders. His placket shirt was undone and his yellow bandana was unfolded into a lobster bib.

Night had come down hard on the drive-in and the Josephites were at a trestle table, singing all forty-eight verses of "The Path of Joseph" before launching into supper. They offered to share their meal with the patrol. The invitation was not mandatory, which Yorke considered a mercy; he'd rather eat K-rations than chow into the grey gruel the sisters were serving up. He could understand why a body would want to think up extra verses of the anthem to put off that first fateful mouthful. Maybe if you wore your mouth out on the hymn, you couldn't taste the gunk.

The sergeant squeezed himself into the cruiser and keyed in his reception sign. The two-way screen irised open and Yorke saw Captain Julie Brittles at her desk, fussing with her waves of hair and the two rows of buttons down the front of her tunic. Brittles was always fidgeting with something.

"Quince," she said, "we've got your report. Good work. Nice and concise. No words surplus to needs."

"Thank you, ma'am. It's all cleared up here. Burnside has done his best with the Josephite mechanics and I reckon the motorwagons will roll out of here come tomorrow. Not much else we can do. Just add the charges to the warrants out on the identified Psychopomps, especially this Bonney fillette."

"Quite. Ms Redd Sainted Harvest has put a bee on our tail about that specific individual. She makes it clear that she doesn't want a lacquered hair on her pointy head hurt in the arrest process."

Quincannon whistled. Brittles gave a captainly shrug.

"My guess is that Ms H wants to do all the hurting in this instance. I understand there is personal business between them…"

Yorke understood. It was not a good idea to interfere in Redd Harvest's personal business. The op was almost as fond of violence as the sort of gangfilth she tracked.

Brittles kind of smiled and said, "Also, Quince, we have polite E-mail from GenTech BioDiv, with regards to an incident in the vicinity of Canyon de Chelly."

"It's in the report, captain. I've made suggestions as to further investigation. Those bots had run into something strange we haven't seen before. We should get a team out there."

Brittles's smile got tight. "GenTech respectfully request we keep our noses out. They'll do the follow-up. The remains of the Knock 'Em Sock 'Em Robots have been officially labelled property of BioDiv. We're soldiers, not scientists. No side issues, sergeant. Remember the Thin Blue Line."

Quincannon didn't argue. He didn't talk a streak about the boiling point of water either. Rule One of the Cav was to bitch down, not up; that wouldn't be affected by alterations in the fundamental nature of the universe.

"My suggestions are in the report already, captain."

"We'll handle the deletions, Quince. No need to bother yourself with keyboard work. We need you in the field, not at a console."

"Yes ma'am."

Brittles wasn't saying something. Yorke saw the shifty look in her eyes. The captain was the kind of old girl who wasn't happy unless she had a long-tongued trooper under her desk working up a shine on her boots. Yorke could tell when she was gearing up to dish out a zeroid assignment nobody in their right mind would accept. Like now.

"Permission to circle back to Valens, ma'am? We've been out for five days now."

"Denied, Quincannon."

Her slight smile had a nasty twist in it. Yorke wondered if there had ever been anything romantic between the sergeant and the captain, and whether that had anything to do with the way Quincannon's troop, of which he was a fully paid-up member, got all the scut details. Like checking out Sodom and Gomorrah, Ariz, or escorting the Dirty Protest Skunx chapter of the Maniax to the Alcatraz Express.

"You have fresh orders coming in," Brittles said. "The cruiser will print them out directly."

Captain Brittles cut out and Quincannon said "Goodbye" to a dead screen. The dashprinter gurgitated a strip of paper. The Quince and Yorke looked at it curling out of its slot. The orders ended and they both sat in the cruiser, putting off the moment. Finally, with a protracted sigh, Quincannon tore the paper free and scanned it, face falling.

He swore, crushed the paper into a ball, dropped it on the floor, swore again, got out of the cruiser, kicked some sand, swore extensively – affrighting a pair of Sisters who happened to be passing – and walked off, muttering thunder and fire.

When the Quince was gone, Yorke picked up the paper, uncrushed it, and got a sneak preview of the troop's orders. He swore too.

VII
10 June 2021

YOU COULD BURN up by day and freeze to death at night in the desert. The Josephites built a cooking fire but let it go out. They kept warm by going to bed early, though Tyree was damned if she could see what for.

"No carnal relations," Yorke kept chuckling. "It hardly seems like living at all."

Back at Valens, Yorke had come on to her a couple of times when Nathan was out on patrol. She hadn't let anything develop as long as they were in the same troop. She didn't want to divide loyalties. Still, once she got her cruiser and had maybe a stripe or three on her shoulder, things might change, especially if Nathan dropped out of the running.

She looked into the fire and thought about the future. Everybody seemed to think it was all used up. Even the Josephites were convinced these were the Last Days.

Kirby Yorke was sort of appealing, with his fair hair and crooked smile. But he kept making remarks about the way she filled her Cav pants, and she was bored with that. Every woman in the service got fed up with cracks about her ass. Tight pants were about the only thing you could wear on a mount without risking a stray fold of cloth getting caught in the workings and causing a flip-up crash. Nobody ever passed remarks about the way sergeants and troopers of the male persuasion strained the seats of their uniforms with that species of elephantiasis of the butt so common in Americans.

Quincannon had detailed Burnside to requisition firewood and get a pot of recaff going. He'd nastily offered a cup to Brother Baille, but the man virtuously resisted the temptation. Tyree could tell Baille missed recaff and probably other things too. You didn't yank out your taste buds and hack off your primary sexual characteristics when you converted to the Path of Joseph, though there were sects which went in for that sort of thing.

And there was that creepy Wiggs weaselling around. From something Sister Maureen had said, she understood he *had* gone for a dick-ectomy. The snip explained a lot. She wouldn't have liked to meet W Bond Wiggs *before* he took the drastic surgical option. He must have been a pedigree hound.

She wondered if it was a good idea to check warrants on the Brethren. Elder Seth quite likely specialised in recruiting former sinners. Poor souls might earn the forgiveness of the Lord before troubling themselves with earthly obligations like prison sentences.

Wiggs would look mighty cute in stripes and she just bet his unusual genital arrangement would be boffo in the showers.

"Are we really stuck with these damfools, Quince?" asked Burnside.

Quincannon swilled the last of his recaff about his tin mug and threw it in the sand. "I'm afraid so, Wash. Orders from on high."

"General Haycox?"

"Higher." Quincannon stuck a Premier in his mouth and swivelled eyes to heaven. "The Prezz himself is behind Elder Seth. Hell, he practically gave away Utah. Can you imagine what'd happen if he tried that with New York?

He thinks resettlement is a jim-dandy idea and is backing up the Brethren of Joseph in their scheme to rebuild Salt Lake City."

"Why didn't he hire the California National Guard to babysit this wagon train instead of letting 'em get cut down like dogs by every fuckin' stray that comes by?"

A match flared and the Quince sucked smoke. "I said Estevez was backing the Josephites, Leona, not that he wanted to spend *money* on them…"

Everybody laughed. The federal government was reputed to be bankrupt after the last round of trade incentives. Ottokar Proctor, the famous free-market economist, had prodded the President into a policy, endlessly announced in TV ads, called the Big Bonus. Its planks seemed to be high public spending, high unemployment and massive tax cuts. Tyree wasn't a genius-level economist, but it sounded like a Brinkof-Doom spree to her and she wasn't surprised now that it had fallen apart. There was something about Dr Ottokar Proctor that made her skin crawl; he had tiny eyes, like a mean cartoon character.

The Cav were still being paid in scrip, redeemable only at the fort's authorised stores. Valens scuttlebutt was that the government even planned withdrawal of its portion of the US Road Cavalry funding next season, and that private individuals and companies were invited to step in. The rumour mill suggested, the best tenders so far had come from GenTech, Winter Corp and Walt Disney Enterprises. They could be wearing Mickey Mouse shoulder insignia next year.

Tyree would be a lot less happy having to do or die for faceless corporate creeps than for John Taxpayer. The corps owned enough of the world as it was. Somebody had to be on the side of people.

"Estevez made a snazz speech about the resettlement drive last week and swore to cash in on any good publicity there might be if Elder Seth doesn't get himself killed. But he hasn't got his neck stuck out so far he'll look a bozo if the Brothers and Sisters disappear in the Des."

"Why are we along for the ride?"

Quincannon exhaled a cloud of smoke. "We're wagonmasters, Yorke. We're protecting the wagon train from injuns and varmints and outlaws. Like in the first pioneer days, when the West was a virgin wilderness waiting for the farmers to cultivate it."

"But that was then…"

"It wasn't so long ago. I was born down in Wyoming. Pretty good country it was before it stopped raining and all the grasses dried up and blew away."

"There weren't never no fuckin' grass in Wyoming, Quince. I been there. It's worse than here. Just sand dunes."

"It wasn't always like that, Yorke. The Midwest used to feed the world. We had enough for ourselves and some over to spare for other country's needy folks. Not now, though."

"More of your UEs, Quince?" Yorke asked, grinning crooked.

"Nope, don't need paranormal phenomena to explain that. We can't blame this on the universe, it's our own sweet fault. It's to do with fuckin' pollution. Back when Trickydick was boosting American industry in the Golden Days of the '60s, Congress squashed a whole raft of laws which regulated where the factories dumped their trash. A man named Ralph Nader poured pollution over himself outside the White House and lit up a match as a protest, but nobody paid any attention. The idea was supposed to keep America competitive with all those hellholes like Poland and Indonesia where eight year-olds with kleenex masks work in sulphuric acid fumes for ten cents a day. The corps pumped their waste sludge into the rivers and the oceans and the water don't evaporate no more. So it don't rain, and we ain't got no grain nor grazing land. That's why there's a big desert filling up the map of the United States. Funny what folks will do for cold money, ain't it?"

Burnside listened intently to the old man. "Is that why the seas are rising?"

"I suppose so. I was in N'Orleans once, when I was a kid. Right pretty city it was too. Now, we all know it's half-underwater and all the houses are on stilts. Crazy. My grandaddy fought in Europe in World War II. When I was a kid he used to tell me he'd taken up arms to make a better world, but I guess this ain't the one he meant."

"They say things are better in Russia."

Quincannon laughed so hard he started coughing, and coughed so hard he brought up a mouthful of brown spit that hissed in the fire.

"Oh yeah, Russia. Boy, that is a good one."

Yorke was hurt. "What did I say?"

Quincannon wouldn't tell him.

"Quince, did you ever see the Mississippi?" asked Burnside. "Back when it was a river, I mean, before the Great Lakes dried up?"

"Yeah, I scanned the Missus-hip, and the Missouri, and Niagara Falls — that's Niagara Muddy Trickle these days — and I remember when you could swim in the sea off Monterey without wearin' a self-contained environment suit and when New York didn't have that damn wall to keep out the stinking water. I remember all those things. But when I die, that'll be it. You can all forget those days and get on with what's here and now. At least Elder Seth is doing that, coon-crazed as he is."

Tyree recalled the sunsets in Elder Seth's eyes and the iron in his voice. She would not have called him crazed. He was too resolute, too *scary* for that. She supposed it took more than a nice guy to lead a wagon train.

"Do you believe in what he's doing, Quince?" she asked. "In the resettling?"

"Hell, Leona, I wish I could. I hauled in a drunken Comanche from that war party who took on the Bible Belt last month. He said his people have returned to the old ways because the buffalo were coming back. They were going to cover the land like a thick rug. That ain't never gonna happen. And the wheat ain't coming back neither. Just sand, like Kirby Yorke here says. That's what America's gonna be. Just sand. Over a hundred years ago there were people in uniforms just like ours helping to build a new nation, to create something. We're here to stand back while it falls to pieces. Not a thankful task, but someone has to be mule-headed enough to do it, and I guess we elected ourselves."

The fire burned low. Out in the Des, something was howling. It might have been the thing from last night, loping along in the hope of mating with Burnside's flute. Tonight, it was louder and hornier and angrier.

"And that," said Quincannon, "sure as hell ain't a goddamned buffalo."

VIII
11 June 2021

QUINCANNON HAD A Sons of the Pioneers MP7 on and hummed along to "Bold Fenian Men". The cruiser was at the head of the motorwagon train as they passed through a place called Moroni. It was just a ghost town. Yorke, out of habit, was about to log it as still unpopulated.

Whenever they scanned signs of new habitation, they were supposed to call in so Valens would schedule a check-out sometime soon. It wasn't exactly illegal to move into a ghost town, but most of the people who thought that sounded like a good idea were into practices that were.

"See up there, Yorke, the roofs."

On Main Street, the frontages were topped with soot, where fires had once been. There was still a little smoke. Some of the charred boards were rimmed with glowing edges.

"Looks like we missed a party."

There had been torches in the streetlamps. Yorke scanned the buildings with the cruiser's sensors. There were no bodyheat blips.

"Whoever it was, they're long gone, Quince. Want to stop and do a recce?"

The sergeant pondered.

"Nope, just log a note. It's another information bit. You never know, maybe it's the piece someone somewhere is looking for to complete his puzzle."

Yorke made the notation and transmitted it into Gazetteer. Anyone on the system would be forewarned upon entering Moroni.

"This patrol is dragging on, Quince. Do you reckon we'll ever get back to Valens?"

Quincannon grunted and shrugged. None of the troop were happy with this detail. Playing nursemaid to the Josephites seemed too much like walking through downtown Detroit or Pittsburgh with a "Shoot Me" sign picked out on the back of your jacket.

The Prezz might have given Elder Seth Utah to play with, but he hadn't guaranteed to clear out the former owners or any gun-toting vermin that might be left behind. The truth was that the President of the United States of America was only something like one hundred and twelfth Most Powerful Individual in the World these days. He ranked somewhere below most GenTech or NeoTech mid-management execs and could probably put less soldiers in the field of combat than Didier Brousset or the fabled Exalted Bullmoose. Corporate smoothies and psychotic punks ran the world and the Cav was one of the few hold-outs against any and all factions.

Admittedly, it had been quiet so far today. Quincannon pretended to be asleep in the passenger seat, but kept stirring to check the scanners and change the music. Burnside and Tyree were talking back-and-forth on open channels and Yorke was getting just a little jealous listening in. Guys in cruisers were supposed to pull all the tail, not guys on the mounts. It was a Cav tradition. Yorke felt he was letting the troop down by allowing Burnside to make time with Leona. She had cold-shouldered him so far, but he knew he was well in there. Nathan Stack was more or less definitively out of the picture. After this patrol was over, he would be making some definitive moves, and then he would have some stories for the bunkhouse. If this patrol was ever over.

Tyree was telling Burnside about a vacation she'd taken in Nicaragua with Nathan Stack. She was full of praise for the Central American Confederation, and said the people were less personally hostile to *Norteamericanos* than you'd think. And they had the real stuff, coffee. Yorke worked up a little jealous glitch, imagining Stack sharing a pot of coffee with Leona Tyree. He couldn't remember ever seeing her out of uniform. In Managua, she might even have worn a dress. It was hard to imagine, but pleasant...

The Josephite convoy moved slow and steady out of Moroni like an old-time wagon train, ve-hickles piled high with personal possessions, the furnishings of lives soon to be recommenced in the promised land. The motorwagons even looked like prairie schooners, with their tented canvas covers and roped-on barrels.

In the rearview dashscreen, Yorke saw the elder sitting in the Edsel next to his driver, Wiggs. Elder Seth's shaded eyes fixed on the road ahead as if he could see destiny on the horizon. He didn't move much, like the figurehead of a ship, or one of those wooden Indians you once saw outside small town stores. The heat didn't bother him any more than the cold had done last night.

"What do you think of that Elder Seth, Quince?"

Quincannon grunted. "That's a man who certainly seems sure of himself, Yorke. Scans like he's never had a doubt in all his years. There's a name for religious folks like that. Folks who never doubt. Fanatic."

"But he's church folks, like a priest or the Pope…"

Quincannon mumbled "Secular humanist" disparagingly.

Suddenly, with the sun overhead, there was a commotion back in the convoy. Burnside and Tyree left off crosstalk and simultaneously signalled halt. Quincannon pushed his hat back and sat up. Yorke stopped the cruiser and Elder Seth's Edsel braked, lurching a few metres closer to the cruiser than suggested by any highway code. Elder Seth was out of the cab and back with his people, who congregated in the middle of the convoy.

As usual, Yorke got left in the cruiser while Quincannon went to see what the trouble was.

IX
11 June 2021

SISTER MAUREEN WAS nearly dead and Brother Baffle was hysterical.

"She fell… fell…"

Tyree held the woman, trying to stop her shaking. Her right hand was a bloody smear on the road and most of her face was gone. There was no hope.

"I didn't mean…"

Burnside grabbed Baille and took him away. The Quince had his medpack out and was squirting the bubble out of the hypo.

"Morph-plus," he said. "It'll stop her kicking long enough for us to see if there's anything can be done. Give me her arm, Leona."

Tyree grabbed the flailing left arm by the elbow and held it fast as Quincannon tore Sister Maureen's sleeve open. He swabbed the patch over the vein with a dampragette and took aim. Tyree gripped the elbow fast, and cooed soothing platitudes into the woman's ear.

"No," said Elder Seth, calmly, taking Quincannon's wrist. "No drugs. She has abjured them."

The Quince stood up and turned angrily on the elder. "I ain't about to hop her up full of juju. I'm just tryin' to save her pain. Ain't that what your god would want us to do?"

Elder Seth didn't back down. He took the syringe away and laid it down on the hood of Baille's Lada. Tyree briefly wondered what a Josephite was doing with an expensive imported automobile. There was a red splatter across the bodywork and the hubcap was still dripping.

"My god is merciful, Mr Quincannon."

The elder knelt down and took the woman from Tyree. She was unwilling to give the wounded sister up, but she sensed Elder Seth's touch and struggled to press herself to him.

Tyree was pushed back.

Sister Maureen moaned as she was shifted but settled in Elder Seth's arms. Incredibly, given that she barely had cheek muscles left, she smiled and seemed to sleep. She was still breathing. Her hoodlike bonnet had been scraped away by the wheel and her hair was free. It was long, blonde and must have been beautiful once.

Tyree pulled away and stood up. Her shirt and pants were bloody. Quincannon was still angry but kept quiet.

Elder Seth brushed Sister Maureen's hair away from the ruin of her face and wiped some of the blood off with his hand. More welled. Tyree scanned bone shards, and was sure the oozing pulp was greymass, brain tissue. She had never seen anyone hurt this bad yet still alive. Elder Seth was praying silently, lips working, tears coursing from his reflecting eyes.

The other Brethren gathered around and joined in prayer. Baille was back under control, praying hard with the rest. Sister Ciccone supported him.

Elder Seth finally shook his head. Sister Maureen's breathing stopped. He laid her on the roadway and stood. The deadlady continued to leak, rivulets of red following the cracks in the neglected asphalt, spreading out from her head in a spiderweb pattern.

Elder Seth gave Quincannon back his hypo and the sergeant looked as if he wanted to use it. On the elder or on himself. It didn't matter.

Tyree realised she had been praying hard with the best of them. Somehow, she knew the words.

X

THE SUMMONER REJOICED, as more blood was spilled, soaking into the stony ground.

It had been easily accomplished, leading the sister to the asphalt altar and allowing the sacrificial wheel to break her. There was little pleasure in the killing part of it, little novelty.

The blood spread, sinking in. Each drop was a beacon, lighting the way to the achievement of the dark purpose. The ritual progressed well. The Dark Ones were imminent.

zeebeecee's nostalgia newstrivia: the 2010s

THE 2010S WAS the decade when America woke up and smelled the coffee… only to find you couldn't get coffee any more. It was a time of crisis and change. In these bloody years, armed criminal factions known as gangcults carved out fiefdoms, fought wars, levied taxes. Weakened law enforcement agencies struggled ineffectually with groupings like the Maniax. Emerging from an unholy marriage between the Unione Siciliane and the Hell's Angels, the Maniax combined the high organisation of an established nationwide crime syndicate with the savage brutality of the worst motorcycle gangs.

The government recognised a wholesale breakdown of law and order and took measures to check the tide of anarchy and violence raging throughout cities and towns. After the Enderby Amendment to the United States Constitution of 2013, the field of law enforcement was opened to certain private individuals and institutions, bringing new firepower to the war against crime and a new expression to the language, the Sanctioned Operative, or Op.

In tonight's Newstrivia seminar, ZeeBeeCee's Brunt Hardacre, co-host of *Snitchwatch USA* reminisces about the lawless days of the so-called Death Wish Decade with Mr Tad Turner of the nationwide Turner-Harvest-Ramirez Agency, Mr Elvis Presley, an independent op whose Hound Dog Agency is based in Memphis, Tennessee, and Senator Sean Penn of California, recently a stern critic of the Enderby system.

HARDACRE: Hi guys, this is a manly news show for manly men, so kick that goddamn bitch into the kitchen where she belongs and pop a tube of ice-cold Pivo. Pull up your Lay-Zee-Boy lounger and open the front of your pants if that belt buckle is cutting into your gut. Feel free to scratch that itch. Go on, get your nails into it until your balls feel good. I know the bitch says it's disgusting, but she don't understand the itchy balls phenomenon on account of because she's a chick, right? Anyway, it's not like you got the preacher or the goddamn bank manager coming round to save your soul. Just get comfortable. You finished that first brewski? Hey, have another. I bet you're drinkin' Pivo, the high quality beer brewed from artificial hops by authentic Czechs in the Minneapolis vats of GenTech BevDiv.

You know what would go great with that Pivo? A big plate of Meskin Tortilla Chips slathered in guacamite. Remember, unless it has the GenTech ChowDiv logo, it's not real Meskin food. Sounds good? Well, give that troublesome female a yell and clout her until she dang well brings you a plate. Remember, to the moon, Alice! You're a guy, you work hard all day so she can put her feet up and watch all the ZeeBeeCee soaps, so the least she can do is bring you some dang chips when you're havin' a brewski or eight. Am I right or am I righteous? You surely, purely know I am.

Tonight's rap session is going to incite controversy, so feel free to yell at the TV if what someone says riles the bejesus out of you. Direct your aggression at the rubberised punching patch to the side of your screen. Of course, for a monthly surcharge of only thirty dollars fifty at fourteen per cent interest, you could order the new GenTech non-shatter screen. Made of high-quality porous plastic, this scans like your regular boob tube but gives like a punchbag. No longer need you restrain yourself when a whingeing geek comes on to whine that layabouts on welfare need to be re-educated rather than cattle-prodded. You can let fly with a good old guy-style haymaker and have the satisfaction of feeling face crunch under your fist without fear of damaging your knucks or your TV set. Maybe you've always had a hankering to stick a couple of good right hooks onto one of those stuck-up Miss Priss newstrivia babes who you just know would spread 'em for some guy in a thousand-buck suit with a faggy haircut but would ignore a real man like you as if you were scumdirt in the sewer. Now you can bebop a Lola on that expensive nose without fear of personal bankruptcy. Call the toll-free number flashing on the vid right now for three months' free trial period of an abusable screen. If feelings of hostility last for more than forty-eight hours after you've hit the TV, consult your family psychiatrist.

Hell, that's the goddang plugmercials out the way, let's get on with the freakin' show. We got three real guy-type guys up here today. If the boom mic gets in close, you'll be able to hear their balls clack even when they're sitting down. First up is Mr Thaddeus Turner, a founding director of the Turner-Harvest-Ramirez Agency, the best known and probably most effective Sanctioned Agency in the United States. And soon to become international, Tad?

TURNER: Yes, indeed. We're opening T-H-R depots in London, Karachi, Tokyo, Moscow, Paris and the Antarctic.

HARDACRE: So, foreign felons will soon fear the Scum-Stoppers of your legendary partner, Redd Harvest?

TURNER: Yes, indeed. Ms Harvest intends, once she's cleared up outstanding business in the States, to do a tour of duty supervising the establishment of justice T-H-R style throughout the globe. Incidentally, Brunt, she sends regrets that she couldn't be here tonight, but she's out tracking down the last few stragglers of the south-western Maniax.

HARDACRE: That's the feared gangcult you and the United States Cavalry just totally decimated?

TURNER: Yes, indeed. We were proud, as Senator Penn will note, to work closely with federal agencies on this large-scale, supremely successful action.

PENN: Hrrmph grrmph frrmph.

HARDACRE: I'm sure the senator has a deal to say on that point later. But not all ops work for Agencies like T-H-R, with their luxury expense accounts, top-of-the-line equipment, vast infonet resources and a huge staff of back-up personnel. Many ops have one- or two-man companies and go it alone against crime and criminals, like the gunfighters of the Old West or the private eyes of the 1930s. One such is our next guest, Colonel Elvis Presley.

PRESLEY: It's a pleasure to be here, suh.

HARDACRE: Thank you, colonel. Some of us have parents who remember your name in a different context, that of a popular entertainer way back when. How did you get from there to here?

PRESLEY: I figure no one really recollects the old days, Mr Hardacre. It was a world of time ago. I went in the army and turned my thinking around, came out after my hitch was up, didn't like what I saw back in civvies, and went in again for a forty-year spell. I saw action in Central America, Bosnia, Afghanistan, Iraq and a bunch of other countries that needed protecting. When I retired, I started up ma Hound Dog Agency. I figured things had changed a whole bunch more, not for the better, but one man could make a difference. That's what I see as the job of the sanctioned op, making a difference.

TURNER: Yes, indeed. I'd like to put in that I agree with Colonel Presley. In troubled times, Joe Citizen rests easier knowing sanctioned ops are out there, guarding the walls of civilisation against gangcults at the gates.

HARDACRE: The client list of the T-H-R Agency is a mite different from the sort of folks who go to Hound Dog. You mainly represent multinats for fat fees or go after fugitives with big bounties on their heads, while Hound Dog advertises its services to folks with no other resources, widows and orphans and such.

PRESLEY: I'd like to bet a dollar Mr Turner is going to say "Yes, indeed".

TURNER: Yes, in… ulp. Actually, it's true we service a different sector of the market. Diversity is what caring capitalism is about, Brunt.

HARDACRE: And our third debater is Senator Sean Penn of California, the Golden Boy from the Golden State.

PENN: Good evening, Brunt.

HARDACRE: I hope the camera crew remembered to take the glare off that grin, senator. I've a nasty feeling your teeth just blinded a fourth of our viewers.

PENN: Very amusing. I was led to believe this would be a serious debate.

HARDACRE: That's how we are at ZeeBeeCee, Sean. We're funny as all get-out on a Tuesday afternoon, but we get to the heart of the issues and dig around until we're comfortable. Since this is supposed to be *Nostalgia Newstrivia,* we should start by reminding ourselves what all the fuss was about back in the '10s. I think it's fair to say the first four or five years of the decade just saw everything in America going all out to hell in a steam-powered handcart.

TURNER: Yes, indeed.

HARDACRE: I knew you'd say that, Tad. We hit 2010 with Al Gore in the White House and the beginnings of heavy environmental problems. For reasons no one has got around to explaining, the whole of Middle America was seriously turning into the blighted desert we have these days. Some loons say it's all uncontrolled emissions from industry and toxic wastes from polluting plants, but that seems mainly to be anti-corp propaganda spread by dissatisfied eggheads. Others are suggesting that perhaps the climatic changes are more likely to be caused by uncontrollable cosmic forces. UFOs or whatever. Maybe even a sneaky plot by the Pan-Islamic Congress or the Central American Confederation to wreck our glorious ecosystem by pumping in desert germs. A lot of folks at the grassroots believe things like that, though there are less grassroots around these days.

At the same time, our country's law enforcement infra-structure was showing all the gumption of a dried-up cow turd. Tribalism became a force in American society and gangcults sprang up all over the place, at first mostly founded on religious or political splinter groups or simple style decisions. Old gangcults – like the Ku Klux Klan, Satan's Stormtroopers, the Sons of the Desert, the Los Angeles Crips, and the Amboy Dukes – became street-corner superpowers and began to run communities for their own profit and amusement. In 2011, gangcult-related violence was a bigger killer in America than lung cancer. New names blazed into the headlines in bursts of semi-automatic gunfire: the Virus Vigilantes, the Psychopomps, the Frat Boys, the Flying Circus. And the Maniax, a loose confederation of motorsickle crazies who rapidly absorbed lesser groups and became a bigger, bet-ter-equipped, more dangerous outfit than any other armed force based in the Americas. In 2012, it was estimated the average family spent as much on self-defence as on food, either by purchasing more of the weaponry that flooded the market or by subscribing to one of many protection-insurance schemes.

When Al Gore left office in '12, it was obvious the Prezz no longer ran the country. Big Charlton Heston, who took up the reins, announced recovery programmes and moral drives and vowed in his inauguration address to retake Washington State from the Maniax. We all remember how the Navy SEALS got whupped by the Grand Exalted Bullmoose in the Battle of Seattle, the most humiliating defeat suffered by American troops on American soil since the Brits burned the White House in the War of 1812. At this time, history called. A true hero emerged from the dust of disgrace to make this country a place you could again be proud to call your own.

TURNER: Yes, indeed.

PENN: Hrrmpph grrmpph.

HARDACRE: I mean, of course, Senator Thomas J Enderby. A man of vision, a man of courage, a man of spirit...

PENN: A man serving twenty years in a re-education programme for gross corruption.

HARDACRE: Still a controversial issue, senator.

TURNER: Yes, indeed. I firmly believe Senator Enderby was the victim of a liberal-anarchist conspiracy to discredit the Enderby System. The Filipino houseboys who brought the accusations against Tom were never proved–

HARDACRE: That case is still under appeal, Tad. We really can't allow you to comment further.

PENN: The only real discredit to the so-called Enderby System is the bloodthirsty kill-crazies, who call themselves sanctioned ops. Let's face it, most agencies are licensed gangcults. Take the Good Ole Boys of the South, whose affiliation to the outlawed Knights of the White Magnolia has been proved by independent investigation–

HARDACRE: Mighty controversial there, Sean. You're getting ahead of yourself. I reckon from the feedback in my ear that a fair portion of viewers just bounced a Pivo can off abusable TV monitors. Our Death Threat Switchboard is jammed.

PENN: Believe me, I'm trembling with fear. The agencies are so used to gutlessness they always resort to facile intimidation like this. It underlines my point about the interchangeability of the average op and the average gangcultist.

HARDACRE: You've made your point, I reckon. Tad, could you tell us a bit about how T-H-R got into the sanctioned op business?

TURNER: Yes, indeed.

PENN: Yes, indeed. Yes, indeed. Yes, indeed. It's like a broken doll.

TURNER: ...Yes, indeed... To answer your question, Brunt, we were aware the Enderby Amendment was on its way to becoming law. We sought financing from insurance companies, pension funds and other conservative investment groups. Our reasoning was that most agencies would specialise in local and specific problems, so we should look at the macropicture and be an interstate, even international, organisation. Mr Ramirez and I both had a background in law enforcement; when I was its financial comptroller, the Cincinnati Police Department showed a profit for the first time in fifteen years, and Mr Ramirez supervised the re-establishment of the penal colony on Alcatraz Island. We were fortunate, of course, to land Redd Harvest so early in her career. She was a solo, very much like Colonel Presley, but we persuaded her of the benefits which would accrue if she worked with a big outfit. She was on the board almost from the first.

HARDACRE: Some say she's just a glamour figurehead. She gets on the cover of *Guns & Killing* every month. Since Jessica Alba played her in that miniseries *Redd Dust,* she has been the most sought-after op of all.

TURNER: Yes, indeed. Though I know for a fact that she's not personally a fan of this publicity flack, it's certainly raised the profile of T-H-R in, uh, unexpected ways.

HARDACRE: Actually, Ms Harvest doesn't seem keen on the fuss at all. She's been getting snazz at shooting the lenses out of those flying spy newscams. Homer Hegarty, the gorenews commentator, has brought a personal injury suit against her after a recent injury, has he not?

TURNER: Yes, indeed. I have to accept Ms Harvest is certainly more, uh, newsgenic than Mr Ramirez or myself.

HARDACRE: You guys, you're basically desk ops?

TURNER: Yes, indeed. I'm sorry… what I mean is that it's vital T-H-R have a strategic force. Ms Harvest is a hands-on op, which means she gets photographed for magazine covers or sound-bitten for newstrivia bulletins. Her skills are certainly as valued in the boardroom and on the field. But you shouldn't forget the importance of such unglamorous number-crunching aspects of the job as accountancy.

PRESLEY: Man, I wish I made enough to be able to afford an accountant. I just have to help people and hope to get paid off in home-grown produce. Say, anyone here wanna buy a truckload of powdered rutabaga?

HARDACRE: Do you admire Redd Harvest, colonel?

PRESLEY: We've met. She's a right purty lady. And a mighty competent op. Can't say much for her taste in company though.

TURNER: Yes, indeed. While she's out there, ordinary people are safer. That's what woolly headed politicians never understand—

PENN: At this point, I feel I have to state that I have never brought specific charges against the individual under discussion. I understand cases are pending with regard to some of her actions, but no conclusions have been reached.

TURNER: Yes, indeed. That's because the scumbags Redd zotzes are usually too dead to complain to mommy.

PENN: I hope viewers paid attention to the last comment from Mr Turner, because I think they'll find it revealing about the attitudes of the agencies. As a breed, sanctioned ops take to fighting fire with fire so enthusiastically that we may not have an unburned inch of America left by the turn of the century. Faced with a genuine problem, the gangcults, we chose not to examine our society to find out why people allowed gangcults their power but to create a bunch of semi-legal vigilantes and turn them loose. Naturally, the results have resembled all-out war rather than social reform.

HARDACRE: Sean, you say we should send nuns and social workers against Maniax and Psychopomps?

PENN: No, I say we should send nuns and social workers, as you put it, into the NoGos to reach the kids before they join the Maniax or the Psychopomps. The Policed Zones of our cities have shrunk and comfortable people have built higher, thicker walls. Things have got unbelievably rough out there. I say we should extend the basic rights and protections our country used to offer to all its current citizens. We have to make our own society a thing people want to be a part of because it is fine and just. We cannot terrorise the people into wanting to be with us. We cannot make the children of the NoGo solid citizens by pointing guns. Eventually, the "innocent bystander" may go the way of the dodo and America will be one huge warzone with an entire population of combatants.

HARDACRE: And you blame the ops?

PENN: No, I blame money-minded munitions manufacturers who, deprived of international markets during the so-called 'War on Terror', flooded America with cheap weaponry, then set about creating stresses in society which increased the demand for deathware. Now I blame the media, the agencies and the multinats who keep this intolerable situation running, as the kill-count gets up there with a World War, simply so they can keep showing a profit. Every corp on the big board has semi-legal subsidiaries which filter product through to the big customers in the black economy. So-called commentators like Homer Hegarty and, with the utmost respect, you yourself Mr Hardacre, actually encourage gangcult depredations simply so you can fill up airtime and shove photogenic explosions between the ads.

HARDACRE: Harsh words, Sean. Colonel, do you have anything to say to refute the senator?

PRESLEY: Gosh, um, uh, a lot of what he says makes sense. If he can make a decent world, I'd be the first to turn in my gun. I'm getting on in annos and I'd appreciate sittin' on a porch in peace, strummin' a guitar for the rest of my days. But till then, there's people who need help and can't afford the fancy fees Mr Turner levies. I'm an independent op, and I'll stay that way.

PENN: Colonel, you have my word you are not one of the villains I'm aiming to bring down.

HARDACRE: That's touching. What about Mr Turner?

PENN: Brunt, as I'm sure you are aware, there are laws of slander.

TURNER: They'll only take my guns away from me by prising them from my cold, dead hands. Yes, indeed.

PENN: The only things your fingers ever touch are computer keys, salary-man. My guess is you've never been shot at in your air-conditioned office.

TURNER: Umph grumph–

HARDACRE: Hold on guys, let's keep our sleeves down. There you have it, a regular rough-house debate just like in the old days. Mr Turner thinks the ops are doing a fine job keeping the filth in their place; Senator Penn thinks Mr Turner is full of shit; and Colonel Presley is just trying to keep his customers satisfied. Me, I sleep better knowing my blonde-haired little nine year-old is protected by Burton and McGhee, who have a one hundred per cent kill-rate in kidnap cases. If this debate has worried, disturbed or upset you, get that bitch to haul another six-pack out of the icebox and suck down a couple more Pivos until the pain goes away.

Next week on Nostalgia Newstrivia, *in our "Living Memory" slot, we look back with misty eyes to last year, 2020. Liz-Beth Hickling, the look of last year, brings back the people, the places, the faces, the fashions, the music, the massacres. You haven't yet had time to forget, but we'll remind you all the same.*

the book of blood

12 June 2021

IN THE QUIET of the morning, Judge Thomas Longhorne Colpepper uprolled the blinds and took a look at the peacability. From the window of his study, on the top storey of the clapboard courthouse-cum-town-hall, he could survey the main street of Spanish Fork, Utah, and be satisfied with the world he had made.

Everything was still except the creaky sign of the Feelgood Saloon, which was electronically jiggered to waver as if in a breeze even when the wind was down. The town slowly came to life. The scissor-legged shadow of Christopher Carnadyne skittered across the street like a stick insect as the undertaker took his morning constitutional. Carnadyne doffed his creperinged top hat to Mrs Dolley Magruder as they met in the street and exchanged pleasantries. Cash crop farmhands with bellies full of big bean breakfasts broke out of the Chow Trough and headed off to the fields for a hard day cultivating the Whoopee Weed. Small children played with dogs. Honest traders opened for business. O'Rourke's Security Goods offered a special summer price on kevlar.

The judge was proud of the town. His town. He liked to think of Spanish Fork that way. It was certainly the way most folks had come to think of the old place. The judge was a contented man. Spanish Fork was a peaceful community, a friendly town like they weren't supposed to be any more. They had some laws, but not so many a man couldn't cut loose a little. They had a deep-water well which still ran pure and was under twenty-four hour guard. Murder wasn't necessarily a capital offence in Spanish Fork, but stealing from the well was.

The town had a few deputies who had made names for themselves and decided to settle down. Job Fiske had been with T-H-R until they'd parted company over his disrespectful treatment of a Japcorp *oyabun,* and Matthieu Larroquette had made the cover of *Guns & Killing* when he'd brought in the serial killer Hector "Chainsaw" Childress in Albuquerque, New Mexico.

Nice, regular, deputy-type guys, they made sure the peace was kept, or at least as much of it as the town decreed desirable.

The sun was high already and Main Street baked. Without the well, Spanish Fork would have parched up and blown away like all the other towns hereabouts. The place had once been called New Canaan – it was in the county records – and the sand had flowered through the miraculous agency of that deep water. Then, the fruitfulness had excited envy and a parcel of no-good Josephites and Indians had fallen upon New Canaan, massacred everybody and razed the place to the ground. There was an ugly memorial by the old corn exchange. Judge Colpepper had learned the lesson of history. This time,

Spanish Fork was ready for whatever varmints came out of the Des, sniffing after the precious nectar.

From one end of the street, a figure strode on powerful legs. It was Matthieu Larroquette. In town, he walked everywhere, tireless. The first biker who thought the pedestrian deputy would be easy meat soon learned about the kick Larroquette packed in his amended arm. Things were so quiet, the judge could almost hear the jingling of Larroquette's spurs. Carnadyne raised his hat and stepped aside, letting the Deputy past; the undertaker's toothy grin suggested Larroquette was good for his business.

You could tell it was a civilised community. Colum Whittaker had a twenty-five-foot polished wood bar in the Feelgood Saloon, the Reverend Boote kept a nice little church nobody shot up too much, Chollie Jenevein ran a world-class auto repair shop with spare parts for everything from a '55 Chevrolet to an orbital shuttle, Dolley Magruder's sporting gents and ladies entertained nightly at reasonable rates at the Pussycat Palace on Maple Street, and Judge Thomas Longhorne Colpepper was in charge of a picturesque gallows with facilities to handle five customers simultaneously.

Just now, Colpepper only had one set of guests to be bothered with and he had a sense that they could be handled.

When the Psychopomps hit Spanish Fork late the night before and headed for Colum's twenty-five-foot bar, Job Fiske had made a personal call to inform the judge. Colpepper considered things a moment and looked up the rap-sheets on the interagency datanets. He didn't consider crimes committed outside the city limits much to do with him, but he liked to keep abreast of things. There was a girl with the 'Pomps, Jessamyn Bonney, who was earning herself a rep. Twenty-three semi-confirmed kills, starting with her own father, and some interesting black-market surgical amendments. She would be a *Guns & Killing* pin-up within the year.

The judge told Fiske to keep a watch for a girl with one eye, and make sure her lieutenant Andrew Jean wasn't too enthusiastic with the beehive hairdo-concealed slipknife. A solo op in Montana had got a nasty surprise from ignoring the orange-haired 'Pomp with the eye make-up and there hadn't been much left to bury afterwards. Otherwise, if the 'Pomps were content to be good customers, and pay for their food, drink, gas, auto repairs and party favours, the judge was content to let them be. The secret of the town's survival was that folks that other communities saw as threats, Spanish Fork treated as customers.

By now, Colum's bartender down at the Feelgood would have told the ganggirls all about him, and maybe, if they were lucky, they'd respect his rep. It had been a while since he'd officiated at one of his special quintuple necktie parties.

Things were pretty quiet. A recorded note from Fiske on his oak desk reported that the Psychopomps had enthusiastically partaken of the fare at the Feelgood and broken a little furniture. Nothing indispensable. Then they'd rented cabins over at the Katz Motel and broken some of Herman Katz's ugly tables and chairs while passing round the glojo Ferd Sunderland mixed up in the back of the drug store. A couple of the hardier boys and nancier girls from the Pussycat Palace had gone back to the Katz for a little Strenuous Recreation with the ganggirls.

The judge had a warm glow as he imagined the fun the boys and girls must have had and must still be having in and around the shower units, hot tubs and waterbeds of Herman's Party Cabins. They wouldn't be too competent at trouble-making, at least until suppertime.

Judge Colpepper fastened his bootlace tie and put his big silver-banded black hat on his flowing silver locks. He felt his inside vest pocket for the derringer dartgun he habitually carried and slipped polished Colt .45 Pythons into his hip holsters. The guns were satisfyingly heavy, fully loaded with ScumStopper explosive rounds. The weight dragged his pelvis down and back, inspiring him to puff out his chest and walk tall. He settled into his long black frock coat, ensuring the skirts hung properly over his guns. Scanning himself in the mirror, he was well pleased.

Descending from his study to the courthouse steps like God from heaven, he was ready when Larroquette came by to accompany him on his regular tour of the town.

"Good mornin', judge," the deputy said, taking off his datafeed Stetson. The sockets on his shaven head stood out raw. He had been scratching them again.

"Good morning, Matthieu. Thank you for the report on the Psychopomp situation."

"Weren't nothin', judge. Just keepin' tabs, like you always say."

The judge joined Matthieu in the street. Job Fiske, quiet and compact, ambled out of the shadows to join them. Fiske hefted a robobit arm, replacing the one he lost in action against the Clean, and clacked his claws encouragingly. Behind his back, some of the Feelgood boys called him Deputy Lobster, but a nip from that doo-dad discouraged disrespect.

"Any strangers to report, Job?"

Fiske stood straight. "There's some old cowpoke, judge. On a horse, if you can credit it. He's been seen a couple of times on the outlying spreads. Nowhere near town though."

"Not messing with our weed?"

"Not as far as I can tell."

"There's no trouble from one lone ranger, then. Still, if you can find anything out about him, do so. A man on a horse is unusual round these parts. A man without wheels under him has got to be some sort of weirdo."

"Herman Katz says he passed by the motel two, three days back. Herman says he thought the cowpoke had been out on the trail a long, long time. Covered in white dust, like a ghost."

Colpepper grinned. "Well now, Herman's been a mite touched since that sad business with his mother. It's a shame, but you shouldn't take much account of what he says."

The judge looked up and down Main Street. Ferd was sweeping up out front of the drugstore. Colpepper returned the druggist's wave. The man was a world-class pharmaceutical whiz but he had opted to retire to Spanish Fork for his health and tinker away with his chemistry set. His special Candy Z mixes attracted a lot of customers.

Accompanied by his deputies, the judge walked his rounds. Every day, this gave him a sense of his power, his stability. He knew the solids could set their clocks by him. If they saw him about, they knew the town was still safe.

Kids played by the gallows, throwing stones at the head of the car thief the judge had sentenced yesterday. Damfool had been caught with electronic keys lodged in the shock alarm of the Magruder station wagon. He'd been too stunned and shaken to say anything during trial or execution. They never did find out his right name, though he looked a bit like Ryan Reynolds. The Judge hated the way the remakes of the *Smokey and the Bandit* movies made rural law-enforcement officials out to be even more pompous and ineffective than the originals; probably been a contributing factor in the severity of the sentence.

Colpepper smiled as the children ran up to him, hands open. He found the bag of Ferd's jujubes he always kept for the little 'uns and passed them out. They ran off again, jubes popping as they pressed them to their tiny, happy nostrils.

"You see, Matthieu, Job," he declaimed. "You see what this is all about; what we're standing up for here in Spanish Fork?"

Larroquette pulled his datafeed down over his head and drew in his breath sharply as its terminal plugs slid into his sockets. The Stetson hummed and the deputy held up his amended arm. Electricity crackled between his fingers and he primed the pump action. He saluted, ready for work.

As they walked down Main Street, the judge bid good morning to various citizens who passed by. Carnadyne lurked by his coffin shop, nodding in thanks for the county fee on the car thief; he'd have the whelp off the gallows and into a lime-pit by nightfall with no ceremony at all. Colpepper bowed to Miss Dolley and told her to report any undue wear and tear on her folks before the 'Pomps left town.

Larroquette's Stetson downloaded information.

"Anything new, Matthieu?"

"We got some Josephites coming into town, with a United States Road Cavalry escort. It's a motorwagon convoy. They'll be passin' through on the road to Salt Lake City."

The judge pondered and his hand just happened to end up resting on the pearl-inlaid handle of a Colt Python.

"Josephites, huh? This town's got good cause to care very little for Josephites, Matthieu. Too much like Mormons for my taste. All that hymn-singin' and holiness. Mormons used to think they owned the State of Utah, Matthieu. I hear tell that damfool in Washington DC says these Josephites can have it now."

They were passing the Corn Exchange Video Arcade. A wind-worn cross stood, its base bearing a plaque that listed the names of the settlers killed by Josephites and Indians in the Massacre of 1854. You could hardly read the names any more and one arm of the cross was bent since some unwise Maniak used it for target practice. A mangy cat, nesting under the monument, took fright at the approach of the law and slank off towards some shadows.

Colpepper looked at the monument and thought back. Utah folks didn't need to go as far back as 1854 to have a reason not to like Josephites; President Estevez's declaration of last month was enough to set the blood a-boil. When it came to turning over an entire state of the Union to an outside authority, the Prezz claimed he had consulted authorities throughout Utah, but nobody had asked Judge Thomas Longhome Colpepper anything. And the judge did not much cosy up to the idea of living along the Path of Joseph.

"Matthieu, Job," the judge said, "nobody asked me whether I wanted to be a citizen of Deseret and give up my cup of morning recaff, my slug or two of Colum's whiskey, my shot of Ferd's zooper-blast, or my Saturday evening hide-the-salami sessions with Miss Dolley. And, you know what, boys, I don't reckon I do want to give up those things. And nor, I would certainly wager, does anyone else in this lovely little city. I'm a peaceable man, but sometimes you have to fight for the little comforts you believe in. Do you get my drift?"

"Yes, judge."

Larroquette extended his arm, palm flat out, and flexed his bicep. There was a bang and a discharge of smoke, and the mangy cat twenty paces down the road flew to pieces. The deputy bent his elbow, then straightened out again, the spent cartridge popping out of the hairy slit in his forearm. It fell in the sand. Larroquette primed his pump-action arm again.

"I believe you do, Matthieu, I believe you do."

II
12 June 2021

JAZZBEAUX WOKE IN the dark, sun warmth playing over her. She was out of doors, mainly undressed, hair straggled over her face. On her back under a blanket, she felt soft pseudo-grass and sand beneath her. Through her optic sensor, the sun was a penny of heat in rust-red sky. Someone had switched her patch to cover her good eye. Probably Sweetcheeks. The dear girl always thought that hilarious.

She sat up, the aftershocks of last night's party still pleasurable as she unwound, and took a look at the heat picture. Recognisable ve-hickle shapes were warming in the sun, hot metal carapaces burning brighter than coolish engines. Otherwise, this was *terra incognita*.

Yesterday, after settling with the DAR, the 'Pomps had hit Spanish Fork and wound up in a motel a klick out of town, getting some serious party favours. Jazzbeaux's nostrils stung, reminding her she had been persuaded to backslide and snort a few jolts. Just Candy Z; she stayed off the zonk. Pretty colours ran across the surface of her occluded eye.

She slipped the patch back to the proper side of her nose and blinked. She had ended up outside one of a row of neat, off-white cabins. Up on a small hill was a gingerbread Gothic house: tall and wood and creaky.

The Katz Motel, she remembered. She toga-wrapped the blanket around her bod; otherwise, all the clothes she had on were go-go boots and a red star choker. The fabulous shades, as she had come to think of the pair scavved from the preachie, were stuck up in her hair.

Images and sensations from the party flickered back through her greymass: Cheeks stabbing a ruby pump into the non-abusable screen of the pornofeed, shouting how much she hated that satyrstud Billy Priapus as the set spark-destructed; Varoomschka strapping on a hardy boy, tying his hands to the bedboard with a leather bullwhip and riding him like a bronco for the full twenty minutes; Andrew Jean going weepy-sentimental about being all old and used up and having to be comforted with cuddles and kisses; Sleepy Jane, ripped on tequila, trying to shoot down spysats with a dart-gun; Cheeks singing "Long-Haired Lover From Leningrad" way out of key as a couple of the hardies tried to unpeel her without using their hands.

Just the regular Psychopomp Victory Good Tune.

Jazzbeaux found a black leather miniskirt inside-out on a window-sill. It fit her, so she ditched the blanket. Feeling sun warmth on untreated nipples, she wondered if this much exposure was good for her. Doctors recommended a six-monthly skinsmear against UV rays. She'd not been near a sawbone since her last amendment.

Thinking of amendments and worrying about her breasts reminded her that Daddy once told her that the Amazon warriors of old used to have one of their tits amputated. That way, the surplus gazonga didn't get in the way of drawing a bowstring and firing off an arrow. Jazzbeaux had used a crossbow a couple of times but never a longbow, so she couldn't tell if the Robin Hood act really twanged a nipple off every time you sank a yardshaft through one of the Sheriff of freakin' Nottingham's Norman dogs. Her rule for amendments was that they were all right so long as they didn't spoil the package. Her eye was an exception; she hadn't chosen to have the thing fished out so she had this hole in her face which needed filling. Doc Threadneedle, her favoured bio-surgeon, could jazz her up inside, but she wanted to stay as human as she was.

She pulled the shades down and took a quick scan at the landscape. Nothing was different. She had tamed the effect.

Humming "I Enjoy Being a Girl" from *Flower Drum Song,* she thought about her own victory celebration. Naturally, as the heroine of battle, she rated the best of everything: Colombian champagne, non-vat meatburgers, pick of the hardies and nancies, first go in the hot tub, and dibs on the cabins.

Jazzbeaux had selected a sweet-faced hardy boy, all cowboy hat and low-slung jeans and wispy face fuzz, and gentled him into the tub for a long, slow seduction. Having been on the road with the girls for so long, the boy was a nice change. She almost lost control when she flipped him over and, just as she was finishing off, kept forcing his head under the ripples. When it was over, she had to squeeze soapy water out of his lungs and give him tongue-to-tongue artificial respiration.

After that, she took her jolts and was carried in triumph around the complex by all and sundry, then turned over to So Long Suin and her acupuncture needles. With three precise jabs, So Long — without otherwise touching — brought her to a cataclysmax which thrilled her entire body. Now the warmth revived tactile memories of the pleasure paths her gangbuddy had mapped on her living body. And unlike the boy, three needles didn't half-drown when you showed them a good time.

She turned lazily around a corner and threw a startle into a birdlike, jittery young man whose face instantly reddened. She crossed her arms modestly and tried to smile.

The young man looked every way but at her, all at once, and stammered into an apology.

"We met yesterday?" she said.

"H-H-H-Herman K-K-Katz, ma'am. Like the K-K-Katz M-M-Motel."

"Ahh," she said, "that Katz."

"N-no ma'am, that K-Katz is my mother,' he darted a look up at the old house. "She runs the place, I just help out."

"Dutiful son, huh? A rare thing."

"A boy's best friend is his mother."

Jazzbeaux saw there was an uncurtained window in an upper storey, and a shadow figure looked down. Against the sunglare from the window, she instinctively slipped the shades on and regretted it. A black swirl of deathly evil seemed to pour out of the house, stretching tentacles towards them. Mrs Katz was probably scandalised her little boy was talking with a mostly naked woman. She lifted the sunglasses and let her hands fall to her sides, trying not to smile too broadly. For effect, she licked her lips.

"I, uh, found some, uh, ladies' clothes, strewn around," Herman said. "I guess you lost 'em during the, uh, party."

She shrugged, noting the way Herman's eyes kept being pulled back to her chest. This was pure wickedness, but hard to resist. She never got to flirt much; most people understood her straight off.

"It must be lonely out here, Herman."

"I have my mother, and my birds."

"Birds?" she raised the brow over her good eye.

"It's my hobby," Herman replied. "Stuffing birds. It's fascinating work, preserving life in death."

She was suddenly bored with tormenting this timid, inoffensive character. If anything, she wanted to charge up the hill and face the old lady. That black, swirling cloud must mean some oppressive force, some wrinkled and bony thumb pressing down on a butterfly life. Let the kid go, she should say, it does no good to keep him shackled like a slave. In the end, he'll turn. She was surprised Herman hadn't already followed the Jessamyn Bonney Rid-Yourself-of-a-Cloying-Parent Manoeuvre.

Perhaps Mrs Katz was cannier than Daddy Bruno. She was a woman, after all.

Jazzbeaux felt the grit she had slept on all over her. Like a cat, she needed to clean herself,

"I feel like a long, hot shower," she said.

That seemed to excite Herman even more. His mind was easy to read, even without the fabulous shades; every porn movie had a scene where some big-titted fillette takes a shower and gets intimate with the soap.

Amused, she used the glasses and looked at Herman, which was a shock. She expected slobbering prurience but what she got was death, a skin-covered skull with empty sockets. The gaze of the death's-head was stabbing, vicious, accusing...

Lifting the shades, she still scanned something dry and ancient looking out through Herman's eyes.

"There's a shower unit in your cabin," he said, with a slight croak. "We have to pay a huge kickback to Judge Colpepper for use of the well-water, but we offer the only decent facilities for klicks around."

She could almost hear water sluicing around her, feel the dirt sliding from the folds of her body, water gathering in her hair and turning it into a heavy tail that slipped down to her waist. In a precog buzz, she heard a strange shrieking and felt a shuddering chill. The skullface she'd seen loomed through shower curtains, blade-like nails shredding plastic and reaching for skin. Gooseflesh pricked her breasts.

"Well if that ain't pretty as a picture," a rich, deep voice said.

At the same time, there was a startled, startling animal sound. A rattling inrush of breath. Jazzbeaux instinctively assumed a fighting stance, hip tilted to launch a kick, hands apart and loose, fingers together like bone-blades. She must scan like an Amazon warrior of old now.

The rattle had been a horse almost whinnying. The man who spoke sat comfortably in the saddle, a roll-up in the corner of his mouth, leaning forward.

Herman shrank back against the bleached wall of a cabin as if he had seen a ghost.

The horseman wore a long duster, which was chalky with desert dirt. His face was deeply lined under his battered old hat, but she couldn't tell how old he was. He looked as if he'd been riding out here since the days of Billy the Kid and Jesse James.

Her Daddy claimed they were kin to Billy Bonney, Billy the Kid, but she'd looked the Kid up in a datanet file and found out his real name was probably Antrim or McCarty. Bruno also mentioned Anne Bonney, the female pirate, as an ancestor. It was a wonder he didn't rope Bonnie Parker and Bonnie Prince Charlie into the family tree.

"Don't see many critters like you out on the trail," the horseman said, grinning. "More's the pity."

Herman Katz had shuffled away. Jazzbeaux didn't feel like a shower any more. She also didn't quite know what had just passed between Herman and her. She thought they were both a little wiser and a little more scared.

"Do I know you?" she asked the horseman.

"Could be you *will* know me," he said. "Most everybody meets me one time or another. It's what comes with being a saddle tramp. I haven't been out this way in a while."

"You remind me of someone."

"I've got one of those faces, I guess," he said.

"John Wayne, maybe?"

"I don't know the feller. He's from these parts?"

She shrugged. "I don't think so."

He was hunched over on his horse, bent a strange way as if he had taken some bad wounds a long time ago and left them untreated. She was reminded of a lightning-struck tree that grows strong but crooked.

"You should cover up more, girl," he said, wryly. "In the desert day, you forget how cold it gets at night. You're begging for sunstroke or frostbite."

"This is not my *normal* get-up."

Wandering around in Barbie's Date Rape Outfit was beginning to get monotonous. Somehow, the desert got a lot less deserted if you wanted to sunbathe in the nude.

"I reckoned not, Jesse."

"Jesse?" Nobody had ever called her that before.

"It's one of your names, ain't it? You must have a lot of names, as if you were trying them all on for a proper fit. Like a hat or something."

"Jesse?" she said out loud, thinking about it. Just now, she wasn't really keen on being Jessamyn, and Jesse sounded like a shrivelled version of that.

"Who are you?" she asked. "Who are you *really*?"

The horseman grinned.

"I've got me a lot of names too. I've been around a while. I figure to move on now."

"No," she said, "who are you?"

The horseman's grin sparkled.

"You got the question right, Jesse. Maybe next time we meet you'll be ready for the answer."

Lazily, without seeming to take an order, the horse moved off. Jazzbeaux stood and watched the horseman ride off into the sand, away from town.

She used the glasses. The picture was exactly the same, only there were scarlet, bloody tracks where the horse's hooves had pressed.

III
12 June 2021

There was a sign up by the roadside. YOU ARE NOW ENTERING SPANISH FORK – A NICE, QUIET, LITTLE TOWN – PLEASE LEAVE IT AS YOU FIND

IT. Once the sign was passed, there was a sort of shift and the landscape changed. Brown-orange gave way to green. Large, picturesque houses stood on generous plots of grassy land. Signs on front lawns said KEEP OFF THE GRASS, BEWARE OF THE KILLER DOG, ARMED RESPONSE and TRESPASSERS WILL BE INDENTURED.

Yorke slowed and looked over at the Quince.

"Gas stop?"

"If there's a place."

It wasn't hard to find. Just inside the city limits was another sign. CHOLLIE'S GAS AND AUTO REPAIR, THIS WAY, with an arrow pointing to an old square building. Spanish Fork was obviously a big place for signs. Chollie's scanned like a cross between a livery stable, a junkyard and a dirigible hangar.

"This must be the place," Yorke said. Quincannon grunted and tapped keys on the dash.

Yorke turned the cruiser into Chollie's yard and the convoy followed. There wasn't room enough for all the motorwagons on the forecourt, so they spilled over up and down the street. It was early in the afternoon and quiet, so nobody minded much.

"Do we know anything about Spanish Fork, Quince?"

Quincannon was scrolling through Gazetteer. "Town used to be called New Canaan, a long time back. That rings a nasty historical bell. A bird named Colpepper more or less runs the place now. He calls himself a judge, just like Roy Bean. We don't have anything actually against him on the charge roll, though I doubt if any of these neighbourhood despots would pass muster if we mounted a full inspection. Of course, this is no longer the *United* States of America, so it's a moot point whether Colpepper is obliged to follow any of our laws on condoning drug traffic or immoral activities."

Elder Seth was outside, knuckles rapping like bird-beaks. It was a good thing the cruiser's screens were reinforced armaplas. Quincannon down-rolled the window and the elder's face dipped into view. His eyes were black pinpoints in the shadow of his hat.

"Why are we stopping?"

"We need a tank top-up, elder. Your motorwagons could do with a going-over, too."

The elder thought about it.

"We only have another fifty miles to go to Salt Lake City."

"Fifty is just the same as fifty thousand in this country if your auto don't run. Better safe than vulture meat."

The elder considered a moment.

"What is this place?"

"Spanish Fork, elder," the Quince said. "As a Josephite, you might better remember it as New Canaan."

Elder Seth's mouth curved into an approximate smile. He walked away without saying anything. Yorke had the odd impression his half-complaint had been for show. There was a quality about the elder just now that suggested he was home and knew exactly what he was doing.

"He remembers," Quincannon said.

"Remembers what?"

"You'll see. I'll just bet this town has a sign up about it. I never did see such a place for signs."

Nearby, a sign read: FOR YOUR OWN PROTECTION DO NOT ATTEMPT TO ROB CHOLLIE'S. Underneath the slogan was an airbrushed painting of two crossed pump-action shotguns and a neat row of symbols. Inside barred prohibition circles were startled cartoon thieves with stripy jerseys, domino masks and swag bags. Yorke got the impression the cheery little designs were grave markers.

Many of the resettlers were stretching their legs and kicking tires. More than one radiator was boiling over. Since the business with Sister Maureen, there was less smiling and hymn-singing. Their armour of faith was getting dented out here on the road, but a stubborn backbone of contrariwise determination was being shown.

Brother Wiggs caught sight of a stand of porno magazines and his face bloodied up, as if he were boiling to do some serious preaching and condemning. There was something weird about the Josephites when you looked at them close: Yorke would swear that two days ago, Wiggs had a regular face, with lumps and moles and marks. It seemed to be smoothing into a handsome mask. Maybe the Lord was clearing up the complexions of the chosen.

Tyree and Burnside rolled up and checked the place out. Tyree slipped her cashplastic into a vending machine and pulled out a can of Mountain Dew, which she opened with a thumb press, tested with her pen-end analyser and drank at a draught.

A scrawny kid with coke-bottle-bottom goggles ambled out of the armoured post by the gas-pumps. He wore oil-stained overalls with CHO LIE'S written on them. One of the Ls had peeled off.

"Fill 'er up," Quincannon told him, "and check the oil. What kind of mechanics you got in this town?"

"The best, sir. Chollie don't come cheap, but he don't come shoddy neither."

Another sign read: MOST OF OUR CUSTOMERS ARE STILL LIVING.

"You accept US Cav discount vouchers?"

"How's that again?"

Quincannon grinned.

"You don't mind my *amigo* Kirby Yorke here rubber-neckin' while you're workin' on the ve-hickles and shooting your dang head off if he figures you're sabotagin' or overchargin'?"

The Quince played with his holster flap for emphasis. The kid goggled with respect.

"Sounds mighty fair to me, sir."

"Excellent. Now where can a man get himself some brunch, in this burg?"

IV
12 June 2021

SOMETHING BUZZED UP and down Brother Wiggs's spine. These days of driving had bent his body into a new position, and it was hard to bend out of it.

The godless display of foul filth at the magazine rack still assaulted his mind. There were copies of Satanist propaganda like *Hustler*, *Derriere*, *National Geographic* and *Split Beaver* mixed in with good Christian publications like *Guns & Killing*, *White Dwarf*, *The Truth* and *Creation Science Monitor*. The glossy covers burned like vile flames of sin, searing his brain, reminding him of all he had abjured.

Sister Ciccone gave him succour, leading him back to the motorwagon and clapping his hands together in prayer, forcing him down onto his knees and making him bow his head against her belly. She shook with the fervour of her prayer.

Together on the filthy tarmac of Chollie's, they conjoined in worship of the Lord. Theirs was the Path of Joseph, and the things of the world were as far gone from him as the sinful flesh from which he had been freed. He felt a strange tingling in his amended groin, as if the rejected meat were knitting together in a new, purer form.

Elder Seth was not in the motorwagon. He must be about the Lord's work in this town. Throughout the nation of Deseret, towns like this must be awaiting news of the convoy's coming. There would be parades and processions and rejoicing.

Under his vestments, Brother Wiggs's skin squirmed and tightened. Months ago, he had been aswarm with bodily hair; now, only the barest wisps remained. Fasting and prayer had trimmed away the subcutaneous fat. His skeleton, even, was changed by the fire of faith.

Their prayer concluded, Brother Wiggs and Sister Ciccone stood and adjusted their garments.

He looked at the magazine rack and felt nothing.

"I thank thee, sister," Wiggs addressed Sister Ciccone. "Thou art ever my guide on the true Path of Joseph."

Sister Ciccone bobbed and curtseyed demurely, eyes downcast. Then she looked up at him. The woman had a spot – it might have been called a beauty mark – at the corner of her mouth. In his backsliding moments, Wiggs, had paid especial note to the black mark.

He reached out with his finger and touched the spot. It came away smoothly, leaving no scar. Sister Ciccone's face was now milky-perfect, lips as colourless as her cheeks, eyes as bright as a doll's.

He looked at the spot on his fingertip and flicked it away.

"We become purer," she said.

For a moment, Wiggs wondered what manner of life the sister had led before coming to the Path of Joseph. Knowing the worst sinners made the best saints, he suspected she had been mired deeply in filth and fornication.

"We must venture into the centre of this town and spread the Word of Joseph," she said. "Deseret will rejoice at our arrival. This place must be freed from the rule of sin!"

They walked past the motorwagons towards Main Street. There were people around. Ordinary, sinning people. Brother Wiggs and Sister Ciccone were courteous. Wiggs touched his hat-brim and the sister averted her eyes whenever they passed a citizen.

No one stopped to stare but Wiggs fancied a certain hostility from some of the townsfolk.

A sign identified a large building as the OLD CORN EXCHANGE VIDEO ARCADE. Outside stood a battered cross. Wiggs bowed his head to the cross.

"Arise and rejoice, thou brothers and sisters of Deseret," Sister Ciccone shouted, her voice strong and pure and almost musical. "The day of your deliverance is at hand. Let this be your holy holiday."

A fat man in dungarees spat a brown stream and looked put out. A small, thin crowd gathered.

"Follow the Path of Joseph," Sister Ciccone sang, "put away fleshly things..."

The fat man snickered. Several people, already bored, drifted away.

"I seen Spanish language cartoons that preach better'n that," the fat man said.

"This land is blessed. This shall be the Land of Joseph."

"I reckon you'd do yourself a big favour by reading that there plaque under that there cross before you mention the Path of Joseph again," the fat man said, snidely.

Wiggs scanned the plaque. It was a pack of blasphemous lies about the Brethren. Deadly drivel, poisoning the minds of all.

"Lies and filth!" he shouted.

The fat man just laughed.

The disappointed crowds went about their ways. As the people drifted off, they parted like a curtain. A woman stood still, hands on hips, looking straight at the Josephites. Wiggs recognised one of the she-fiends who had so abused the pilgrims.

She was tall, dressed in transparent sheaths that indecently displayed her body.

"Remember me?" she said. "Varoomschka?"

She was one of the killers. Elder Seth must be told the Psychopomps were in Spanish Fork. He would be interested in recovering his stolen spectacles and cashplastics.

"We have come to the place of our persecution," Wiggs said.

Varoomschka strode across to the monument. The fat man snickered as his eyes followed her long limbs and tight ass. Wiggs again had a twinge of the old sinful urges, but he conquered them with a blast of fiery purity.

The Psychopomp had a glossy fashion model face, and long, silky hair that looked like an implant. Though tall and powerful, she was dainty, like a dancer.

Varoomschka cupped Sister Ciccone's cheek with one hand and slipped her long fingers into the sister's bonnet, unloosing strands of mousy hair with her scarlet nails. Shockingly, the ganggirl kissed the sister on the lips.

Sister Ciccone suffered nobly, eyes raised to heaven. She knew that she would prevail.

"Mmmmm," Varoomschka said, licking her lips with a scarlet tongue. "You taste like a virgin."

"Thou art forgiven, harlot," Sister Ciccone said.

She launched a fist at the Psychopomp's chest. Varoomschka was knocked backwards with surprising force. Her immodest garments showed the plate-sized purple bruise on her upper ribs.

Sister Ciccone was changing. Like Wiggs, she got stronger as she got purer.

Varoomschka scrambled upright, a butterfly knife in one hand. She made a series of slicing passes before her as she moved towards the sister.

"I'll open you, hagwitch," she said. "I'll drink your *kravye* with cinnamon."

The Psychopomp struck like a scorpion. The knife slipped against Sister Ciccone's side and slid upwards across her torso. She would be wounded from hip to collar.

Varoomschka stepped back to admire her surgery.

The sister's vestments were rent and sagged apart. White flesh shone, but no red gash. Sister Ciccone's skin was inviolate and featureless.

"Lady, you ain't got no nipples," the fat man said. "That ain't natural."

Modestly, the sister closed the hole in her clothes.

"And you ain't got no navel either."

"What are you?" Varoomschka asked. "Some kind of clone thing?"

Sister Ciccone bowed her head.

"I am a Sister of Joseph," she said.

Wiggs realised his chest was itching and changing, and he felt his own nipples dwindling and receding into smooth skin. He was still flesh, but the flesh was better, stronger, purer. Untroubled by needs, he was fit for the struggles ahead.

V
12 June 2021

THE FEELGOOD SALOON was typical of a thousand other small-town joints where Tyree had wasted evenings. A couple of gaudy girls were bellying up to the bar, looking for trade. A few old-timers leaned chairs against the walls in the corners, mainlining the poison of their choice. Otherwise, the Feelgood wasn't doing much business this early, so the Cav managed to requisition a table. The Quince sat with his back to a wall and face to the main entrance, a shotgun stowed under his chair. From where Tyree was, she had a good view of the mirror behind the bar and thus of everyone in the room.

A green-faced waitress with vestigial gills took their orders. Some said the mutations were the legacy of those long-ago Bomb Tests, but there must be a reason they had grown more common these last few years.

Quincannon laid out kish for the hundred-dollar grill, while Tyree had the vat-grown eggs and Burnside plumped for gristle 'n' grits. Tyree's tasted OK. They had recaff all round. Fake coffee, but real water, a luxury this far into the sand. The Quince even remembered to have the girl send someone over to Chollie's with N-R-Gee candies for Yorke, who was minding the cruiser.

The green girl was friendly and efficient. It couldn't be easy adapting to an aquatic environment when there wasn't any large stretch of water left in the state.

The Quince lit up a Premier and offered the pack around. Tyree filled her lungs and had a good, healthy cough. She worried sometimes that she didn't smoke enough. Dr Nick said there were no noticeable physical benefits unless you were up to a pack a day.

It would be hours before the convoy could get moving again – one or two of the motorwagons were a refit away from the auto graveyard – so there was no sense in not taking advantage of the comforts on offer. They had been held up burying Sister Maureen yesterday, so they might well be looking to make camp here for the night. Tyree understood there was a motel outside town, so she might have a shot at a real bed.

This patrol had gone on way too long. Back at Valens, she would have earned some extra pay and a couple of vacation weeks on credit. After they'd hand-held the resettlers to Salt Lake, they'd still have to trek all the way back home.

Quincannon was talking ancient history again, not from experience but from books. In his down time, the Quince must be something of a library junkie. Tyree hadn't known that about him She hadn't read anything except forms, regulations and the odd comic strip since military school.

Burnside asked the sergeant his opinion of the Josephites' chances of making anything out of the Salt Lake valley.

"The Mormons did it once before," Quincannon replied, "round about 1848, just the same as the Josephites are trying to now. They'd been kicked out of everywhere else 'cause they believed in marryin' more than one gal at a time. I reckon they've given that up these days, along with 'carnal relations'. They found a place where nothing would grow and no one would live, and turned it into fertile land. The Lord knows how they did it. That church was founded by some fella named Smith who claimed an angel gave him some extra books of the Bible and a pair of magical spectacles to help him read it. The Josephites have some similar story. Different but the same angel. Something like that. Maybe that's why the elder's so steamed up about that gal who waltzed off with his shades. You notice how that riles them more than the fellers who got killed. More than the cashplastics she scavved. Hell, I don't know. The Mormons were straight-laced, but this lot are unnatural, if you know what I mean. They're like the Mormons, the Seventh Day Adventists, the Amish, the Moonies, the Scientologists, Jehovah's Witnesses and Stone-Crazed Baptists all rolled up into one. Me, I'm a good Catholic. Religion's been downhill since Martin Luther."

Tyree drank her recaff and ate her eggs. Burnside kept asking questions and passing comments. "You have to admire those old settlers, Quince, making something of nothing like that."

"Well, Wash, there was another side to the story. A side Elder Seth ain't gonna be too keen on hearin' told again. You can bet they'll remember it here in Spanish Fork, though. While the Mormons were settling Salt Lake, the Josephites were carving out claims for themselves in the Indian Territories. A feller by the name of

Hendrik Shatner, brother of the Joseph who founded the Brethren, was their head man, and he had some mighty strange allegiances. In the 1850s, federal troops were sent against the Church of Joseph, and the Josephites had a little war with the US of A. It seems the Josephites weren't so all-fired holy back then. No sir, when a group of regular Christian settlers moved in and staked a land claim right here, when this place was called New Canaan, the Josephites got together with the Paiute Indians, painted themselves up like redskins, and had themselves one of the bloodiest massacres in the history of the West."

She hadn't liked to say, but as Quincannon was speaking, the swinging doors opened silently and a tall man walked into the Feelgood. Elder Seth. The Quince must see him but he was into the flow of his story. She knew she should say something, try to shut the sergeant up, but somehow she found herself unable to open her mouth.

With Elder Seth were his two most devoted puppies, Wiggs and Ciccone. They looked different indoors, their faces harder.

Quincannon kept on talking. "Them Josephites carved up those regular Christians like you'd carve up a Sunday goatroast. The Prezz probably don't know much history or he wouldn't be handin' a state to these fellas. Who knows, maybe one day Seth will take it into his head to make war again against the United States of America. Then we'll be in a pretty pickle, 'cause I reckon any man who can haul a bunch of candy-ass resettlers a couple of thousand blood stained miles through the Des wouldn't be no pushover."

Tyree looked from Quincannon to Elder Seth, comparing the Quince's expressiveness, making handsigns as he spoke as if communicating with an Indian, and the elder's almost mechanical impassivity. If the Josephite was offended, he gave no indication of displeasure.

Indeed, Tyree thought that she could make out a real expression on his face, like the ghost of a smile around the very edges of his thin lips.

... and, in her mind, she had funny pictures. She thought she saw reflections in Elder Seth's eyes, but not the reflections of the saloon and its patrons. Under an open sky, in Elder Seth's pupils, red-smeared savages ran riot, hacking at fleeing men. Flaming arrows struck home, red knives did their work, kids fell under horses' hooves, women's hair came bloodily loose. Tyree thought she heard the echoes of screams and whoops and shouts. And, in the midst of the carnage he had wrought stood Elder Seth, dressed all in black with red on his face, a long rifle in his hands. The ground under his boots was bloodied...

"Leona?"

She snapped out of it. "Sergeant Quincannon?"

"Leona, you were dreaming."

Elder Seth walked further into the saloon, until he was standing directly across from Quincannon.

"No, I..."

The elder's shadow fell on the sergeant. Quincannon looked up at the man. He held a fork of mule kidney up at Elder Seth, then popped it into his mouth.

"I am given to understand the raiders who attacked us on the road are in this town," Elder Seth said, evenly, "staying at the motel. These people have stolen from the Brethren of Joseph. They have important relics. You will help me secure their return."

The Quince chewed slowly. "Hold on a moment. How many of these raiders are there?"

"That's of no matter. Sister Ciccone has already been assaulted by one of their number."

"It may not matter to you, elder, but I've got a troop strength of four."

"My people will help."

Quincannon swallowed and stood up. He wasn't quite as tall as the elder but he did his best to look the man in the eye.

"That's a comfort. If it comes to preachin' the crap out of the 'Pomps, I'm sure you'll be a big help."

That shadow smile was back. "In the Bible," Elder Seth began, "it says there is a time to every purpose under Heaven."

"So, now it's fightin' time."

"If needs be."

Quincannon shrugged, and hauled up his shotgun. "OK, elder, lead the way to the motel. I'll call Yorke in for backup with the cruiser."

Tyree and Burnside stood up, leaving unfinished meals, and unflapped their holsters. Tyree knew her piece was up to standard. She'd cleaned it twice since the patrol began.

"Sergeant, I said the raiders were staying at the motel. I did not say they were there at this moment."

Quincannon had been halfway to the door. He turned, looking highly fed up. Somehow, the elder had made a fool of him.

One of the gaudy girls turned on her barstool. She had an eyepatch.

"Hello preacherman," she said to Elder Seth. "Come for your shades?"

VI
12 June 2021

So, SHE WAS back here again, facing the preachie. She had his glasses on a thong around her neck. She was horribly tempted to look at him through the shades, but terror prevented her. She remembered Herman Katz's shrivelled skull and the bloody hoofprints. If inoffensive things were made horrible, what would be revealed of Elder Seth through his magic mirrorshades? The circuits of her optic implant buzzed, and she had the feeling it was too late, that having looked through the glasses, she would forever see more than she should.

"Hands away from those guns, yellowlegs," she said, pulling the rainbow scarf away from her semi-automatic pistol, "or I'll redecorate the saloon with your insides."

The sergeant and the two troopers held their hands out in front of them and looked at each other. The sergeant carefully set his shotgun down between plates of half-finished food and stood away. Jazzbeaux would rather not fight all three, since she knew a little about the Cav weapons training. Everyone else in the saloon was quiet. The jukebox was running down; some Bombs Not Burkas number slowing to a growl. The barman was backing away.

"And keep those pretty-pretty fingers off that scattergun you got down in the slops, darlin' dear."

The barkeep slapped his hands on the bar and left them there. Jazzbeaux nodded appreciation and blew him a kiss. He flinched. She turned back to the elder.

"If you want the shades, you'll have to take them, lover.

Elder Seth walked across the room. Jazzbeaux felt the Psychopomps with her – Andrew Jean, Sleepy Jane, Sweetcheeks – edge away, leaving her alone at the bar. It was between her and the preacherman. She flipped the safety and chambered a round.

The elder stood in front of her now. If she exerted just a hint of pressure on the hairtrigger, she'd fill his chest with explosive bullets. He'd be cut clean in two. She had the unhealthy feeling that his face still wouldn't move.

She flicked her tongue in and out. "Come on, preachie!"

He was as close to her as a dancing partner now, the barrel of her gun resting on his sternum. Jazzbeaux felt she was alone in the universe with the man.

His hands came up and he took the shades. She was sure he would rip them away, but he merely lifted them to her own face and eased the bars over her ears. She shut her eye but felt silly, then looked through the glass.

The elder's face changed in a second. The features became liquid, flowed into each other, and became features again. But different features. He had her daddy's face, she realised. Bruno Bonney's face when he was hopped up on zonk, and pulling his studded leather belt out of his jeans, *mishkin* drool on his chin, pain in his brain, death on his breath.

"Jessa-*myn*," Elder Seth said with her dead daddy's voice. "Gimme the scav. Gimme the scav now, or it'll go harsh with you."

Her forefinger had gone to sleep on the trigger. She tried to fire the gun but her godrotted finger was stone. It wouldn't move. The gun shook and she tried to gouge into the preacherman's chest with the barrel. His hands were on her now, fingers digging into her waist.

"Jessa-*myn*!"

Her cheek was wet, she knew. She was crying. No, her optic was leaking biofluid. She tried to singe through the patch, to blast the preacher's hat off. The amendment wouldn't burn and she had a feedback headache.

She had ripped out her daddy's throat when he had tried once too often to take things out on her. That had been her first, and she had done it with just claw-gauntlets. Now, when she needed to kill him again, she had a fine piece of high-precision deathware ready and couldn't bring herself to exert the pull you'd need to open a tube of Pivo.

Elder Seth had his own face back but her daddy's hung just behind his skin, ready to peer through at her.

Bruno Bonney wasn't done with, her yet.

Elder Seth took the gun away from her and put it on the bar, between shot glasses. His other hand crept up her side, sliding through her armpit, reaching around her back, pulling her to him.

He leaned his face close to hers. She thought he was going to kiss her and shuddered at the anticipation of his reptile touch, but he just let his eye loom as close to the lens of the spectacles as her own was behind it.

She didn't want to look into his huge eye. She knew she'd be dead if she did that.

But she looked…

… and she saw such horrors.

VII

OUTSIDE EVERYTHING, THE *Summoner held the girl by the shoulders and watched her face as the truth crowded into her mind…*

After the better part of two centuries, he was back. The name didn't matter: Spanish Fork, New Canaan. The place had other names. It was a site of predestined power. Once, he had put his mark here. Now, he would rekindle the flame.

Across the featureless, white plain rushed a crimson wave, driving before it hordes of ghosts.

The girl shivered and screamed, pestered by her own phantom. She was crying for her father, or crying against her father. It didn't matter. Nichevo, as she would say.

Horsemen passed by, their eyes shot away. Fanners trudged from the fields, hair askew on encrusted scalps. Pilgrims were borne down under the rush of blood, and embedded into the white sands. An eternal battle continued, as the living and the dead clashed, vast ignorant armies in a war only the Summoner truly understood.

Here, the Ruinous Ones walked, preparing themselves for the earthly plain. The desolation was magnificent.

This was, for the Summoner, a peaceful juncture, a moment of calm. He was poised on the lip of the next phase of the ritual, the mass, spilling of blood. At this second, he was alone with this tiny girl, almost intrigued by the rudimentary workings of her mind.

"Jessa-myn" he said to her, in her father's voice. "Now it's just us two, all alone and the evening ahead of us"

She was still horror-struck.

In the girl, the Summoner sensed the seed of something fine, something strong, something strange. When the moment was over, he should snuff her like a candle before her flame grew to a brush-fire. It was even conceivable she could hinder him. She had the makings of a spirit warrior inside, as a marble block conceals the statue that must be dug out by the sculptor.

But he would miss her. There were so few in his league. It would be a shame to finish her before she could truly test him.

That was sentimental nonsense. There were others, and they would come forth when it was time. They would give him enough trouble. There was a woman in Switzerland, a man in Rome. And there were men and women in the United States, already bloodied in the Dark Ones' killing grounds. The op in Memphis, the woman from Denver, the Navajo, the horseman…

He took Jessamyn's head and turned it away from his face, admiring her clean profile as she saw the plain extending away to infinity. Her white face was pinked by the reflection of the crimson wave that towered across the plain, rushing closer…

Jessamyn breathed something that might have been a profanity or a prayer.

In the torrent, creatures danced. They might be called demons and imps. Lost souls were turned inside out and left behind on the sands, exhausted forever. The wave ate everything.

The Summoner was unique. He could ride the wave.

VIII
12 June 2021

TYREE DIDN'T BELIEVE it but she saw it anyway.

The Psychopomps – one creature of indeterminate sex with an orange cockatoo haircut, and two shocked girls –

stood back and watched Elder Seth go to work on their leaderine. And he just glided across the floor and picked her up like the hero of a romance comic strip cruising for truelove in the disco hall.

The jukebox was stuttering into life again, some zonked version of "The Tennessee Waltz".

With a deep revulsion at herself, Tyree realised she was actually *jealous* of the one-eyed 'Pomp. There was something badly wrong, and Leona Tyree was part of it. Quincannon had his side arm out but wasn't doing anything with it.

Elder Seth, dancin' with his darlin', whispered something Tyree couldn't hear in the girl's ear and put her sunglasses on. Her mouth opened in a silent oval scream.

It was as if an invisible but blinding light filled the room. Tyree found herself blinking, rubbing her eyes as tears flowed. Everyone in the bar was doing the same. But there hadn't been any real light.

The Psychopomp was slumped over the bar, one arm hanging limp, throat exposed. Elder Seth supported the girl and heaved her up onto the stool. She was either dead or in a dead faint. He lifted her head and took her dark glasses off. They were the old-fashioned, metal-rimmed, non-wraparound kind.

He slipped the mirrorshades on and his face was complete.

The elder picked up the fillette's handbag and emptied it on the bar. The cockatoo laid a hand on him, but backed off instantly, face clown-white under make-up. Elder Seth sorted rapidly through the 'Pomp's belongings.

... *Tyree could see the burning village in her mind again. Sod huts, log cabins, cattle and goat pens, all ablaze. Horsemen riding through, whooping, swinging weapons. Men and women ridden down and killed. And the elder, on his knees, rubbing a small dead thing into the dirt, squeezing out the blood.*

Elder Seth found what he was looking for.

"My little demon, I believe," he said to the cockatoo, holding up a cashplastic. He made it disappear in his hand like a conjuring trick. He reached out and picked up the unconscious girl by the throat, hauling her upright as if she were a straw doll. Her arms dangled, her head lolled and her feet scraped the floor. Brother Wiggs and Sister Ciccone held the batwing doors open. Holding the 'Pomp like a plucked turkey, Elder Seth left the saloon.

Quincannon followed him and Tyree snapped to it, followed by everyone else in the saloon.

The sun wasn't yet down, but evening bugs were in the air. The street was crowded. Something had brought the people of Spanish Fork out of their houses. The resettlers were crowded around like a congregation, and a cadre of Psychopomps gathered like a gang spoiling for trouble.

The skies were darkening. There was a tang of blood in the air.

Elder Seth carried his prize through the ranks of parked ve-hickles and dropped her in the middle of the road. Her head cracked on the blacktop, and she moaned, stirring a little. Blood was smeared where she had fallen.

IX

Six hundred threescore and six! 666!

THE SUMMONER HEARD *the Number in his mind, ringing like a chorus, voiced by a thousand inhuman throats. It had been left for him in the writings, of all the religions, a sign to be read.*

There was blood on the road. The road to the Prime Site. And that was as it should be. The blood was the main ingredient of the ritual. It was there to guide the Dark Ones, to call them down, to help them gather at the City, the Shining City, the City of Dreadful Night, the City of the Last Days. He had the glasses now, and he had the Key.

666!

He knelt and took Jessamyn's head in his hand, gathering a fore-lock of her hair in his fist. The girl was unconscious, still terrified on the plain outside space. A pity. It would be better if she were awake. He slammed the back of her head against the hardtop. Her skull bounced a little, like a coconut.

666! The Number of the Beast!

The Summoner smashed Jessamyn's head against the road again. Blood flew, splattering in a neat arc, and sank in like butter on a griddle.

666! The Number of the Dark Sun!

He remembered New Canaan, remembered fighting alongside Old Hendrik Shatner and the Paiute. To him, 1854 was but a minute past. Then, he had been called the Ute. He had pulled a child out of a burning cabin. It had been grateful but started kick-ing and squealing when his mule-skinning knife came out. Burned flesh was no good to the Ruinous Ones, only spilled blood.

666! The Number of the Apocalypse!

He had seen so much blood, down through the centuries. He had been born in blood, continually rejuvenated in blood. There were many places, many names, many faces, but the blood was always the same. Whether on the Mutia Escarpment in Africa, or Judea under the Herods, or Pendragon's Britain, or Temujin's Eastern plains or Bonaparte's Empire or the fields of Kampuchea, the blood was always the same.

666! The Number of the Neverending Darkness!

In the Outer Darkness, the Old Ones heard the call. He spoke the words under his breath as his fingers spread the blood.

666! The Number of Blood!

He invoked the Names. He recited the Nine Names of the Beast. The creatures of the Outer Dark gathered around, pricking at the balloon of this reality.

666! 666 times 666! 666!

His hands were bloody to his shirtcuffs.

666!

★ ★ ★

X
12 June 2021

FLAT HAMMERS POUNDED the back of her head. Jazzbeaux awoke to mushrooming pain.

Her mind was blanked. A continent of blood funnelled into her eye and washed everything from her head.

Only fear remained.

A hand held her hair. Her head was being lifted up and slammed down. Again and again.

A black arm was responsible. It was as precise and impassive as a machine component.

More pain cracked inside her head. Something was breaking.

She scanned Elder Seth's impassive face floating above in the distance. The black arm that hurt her stretched up to the elder's shoulder.

She was getting motion sickness.

The rhythmic pounding echoed, beating time like a metronome. Her nostrils were full of blood.

She sent signals to her hands to come together around Elder Seth's throat, but the rest of her body wasn't at home when her greymass came to call.

The elder muttered something as he killed her. He chittered like an insect.

"… *Sicksicksicks sicksicksicks sicksicksicks sicksicksicks…*"

Her right arm convulsed and reached upwards, but Elder Seth brushed it away and bore down on her body with a bony knee. A stab of pain shot through her ribs.

She twisted her neck and her bloody hair slipped through the elder's greasy fingers. She grabbed the road and tried to pull herself away.

Hands took the back of her neck and the back of her head. Cruel fingers squeezed her wounds.

Jazzbeaux heard herself screaming again.

Elder Seth smashed her face against the road, twisting her head so the brunt of the blow was taken by her eye-patch. She felt crunching in the orbit around her optic burner.

If she could roll over, she could give the scumsucker a blast at the bridge of his cursed shades. She could bore a hole through his head and see the evening sky.

With the next thump, biofluid filled the inside of her patch and she felt the implant shifting, metal digging into her meat. Her nose was completely plugged with grit and blood and she was afraid for her teeth.

After this, she would not be the prettiest girl at the prom.

From her good eye, she saw the cracked ground, deco-rated with patterns in her own blood.

"… *Sicksicksicks sicksicksicks sicksicksicks sicksicksicks…*"

Elder Seth slammed her face against the road again. And again. And again.

XI
12 June 2021

ELDER SETH WAS methodically killing the one-eyed Psy-chopomp, without distaste or anger. As he smashed her face against the road, he looked as if he were baptising the girl in tarmac.

Everyone seemed only too pleased to watch. Tyree had her side arm out but didn't know who to shoot. Sergeant Quincannon had fetched his pumpaction from the Feelgood, but wasn't pointing it at anyone. The Josephites had beatific smiles on their faces, as if watch-ing their spiritual leader kissing a baby. The Psychopomps were appalled but made no move to help their gangbuddy.

"Hold on there a moment, your reverendship!" shouted someone.

Everybody turned to scan. Everybody except Elder Seth. He still beat the girl's head against the road. Each blow was like a drumbeat.

A short man, nattily dressed in a frock coat and a big black Stetson, stood in the street, flanked by two gorilla-shaped individuals with tin stars and datafeed Stetsons. The local heat.

The girl's blood made signs in the cracks of the road.

"I say I don't know if'n you have much familiarity with the law," the short man said, "but we take objection to this here sort of unruly behaviour in Spanish Fork, Utah."

The elder dropped the girl's head and stood up. His hands were red, but the rest of his outfit was as clean as it ever was. His face was empty.

"Deseret," he said, grinding the word between his teeth. "New Canaan, Deseret."

"We like proper names round these parts," said the short man.

The girl rolled away from the elder's legs, and the cockatoo creature went to help her. The fillette was still alive but had a bloody dent in her forehead. Her eyepatch was scraped away and a mechanical doodad hung out of her socket on multicoloured filaments. Tyree would guestimate severe concussion at the least, probably brain damage.

The short man took off his hat. "Permit me to introduce myself. I am Judge Thomas Longhorne Colpepper and we do things my way in Spanish Fork. Job, arrest this man."

One of the deputies lurched forwards, his clapperclawed right hand held out. Circuitry hummed inside the bulky bio-amendment.

There was quite a crowd. Most of the Josephites were there, looking bewildered but not surprised at their elder's activities. Kirby Yorke was with them, goggle-eyed and slack-jawed, derelict in his duties for leaving the cruiser unguarded. That worried Tyree almost more than anything; it was like seeing a baby crawling in the road. There were more Psychopomps, pouting with indignation and fingering home-made shooting and stabbing irons. The townsfolk of Spanish Fork all turned out to see the show.

Shutters went up over breakable windows and guns were handed out like burgers at a BBQ. This situation had all the fixings of a medium-sized bloodbath, Tyree thought.

The clawed deputy reached out to take Elder Seth's wrist. With an easy movement, the elder pushed the big man in the centre of the chest. It looked like a playground shove to Tyree, but there must have been deadly force behind it. She heard bones snapping and the deputy dropped like a felled tree.

Brother Wiggs and Sister Ciccone darted forwards and fell on the deputy. Wiggs's knee smashed into the man's throat and Ciccone's hands dug into his guts. The cyberfeed overloaded and blew its circuits. The deputy's head caught fire, burned bright for a few seconds, then turned into a reeking, charred blob. The rest of him was still twitching.

There was more blood on the road.

Elder Seth said something that sounded like *"Sicksicksicks"*. The resettlers gathered behind him. Wiggs and Ciccone, dirtied and bloodied, were back in line. One or two of the faithful looked scared out of their tiny minds, but they still backed him up. Tyree had to fight the impulse to go stand beside the elder. She got the impression Brother Baille, for one, was fighting an impulse to get out of the line-up and stand against Elder Seth. The man had some sort of unnatural influence.

"Get your kicksssss," hissed Elder Seth, *"on Route Sicksicksicksss…"*

The remaining deputy shot his arm out, flat-handing the air. He had a shotgun implant, an impressive piece of work. There was an almighty bang as he discharged himself. He cocked his elbow, filling the chamber again, and fired a second time.

"… *Sicksicksicks sicksicksicks…*"

He had taken one of the blasts full in the belly. The other had glanced off his right shoulder. Brother Baille, who had been standing behind him, was on the ground with his face in his hands, trying to press it back onto his skull. Elder Seth was still standing, clothes a ruin, body still whole. Tyree saw patches of his skin blackened from the discharge, but unbroken.

"… *Sicksicksicks sicksicksicks sicksicksicks sicksicksicks…*"

Elder Seth wasn't human. That explained a lot.

XII

THIS WAS THE *site of the Great Invocation. The Summoner ignored the stinging in his flesh and advanced on the man with the gun in his arm. Deputy Larroquette reminded him of a Roman legionary he had pulled apart when he rode with Attila. If you lived long enough, everybody reminded you of somebody else. The Roman's insides had felt slippery and yet tough in his fists. He had been less strong then.*

He took the next blast full in the face. His hat flew off and he shook the flattened fragments of the charge out of his hair. His spectacles were not destroyed. He fixed the deputy with mirrored eyes.

The deputy saw the worst thing in the world and lowered his arm. For Larroquette, the worst thing in the world was a man with two buzzing chainsaws, surprised in the boiler room of an Albuquerque elementary school. The Summoner let the man with the chainsaws carve the deputy's mind into sections.

He took Larroquette's wrist and tore his gun-arm off, as easily as he would rip a silk neckerchief in two. He dropped the useless thing on the ground.

The deputy bled from the shoulder, bright jewels splashing to the tarmac. More blood for the Dark Ones.

They were in the air now, squeezing onto the earthly plane through rips in the fabric of this reality. He saw them swarming around in multitudes. The clawed, crawling, winged, stinging, horned, spiny, toothed hordes. The Vanguard of the Beast.

This would have to end now. It was the place of sacrifice, and the time. Those who would not follow him must die.

The deputy, dead but moving, lunged out with his remaining arm and clawed the spectacles from the Summoner's face. His nerveless fingers couldn't grip the sacred objects, which flew away and skittered across the ground towards the crowd.

The loss didn't matter. As always, it was temporary.

XIII
12 June 2021

PEOPLE WERE SUDDENLY dying all around Yorke. Attacked as if by invisible creatures and torn apart. It was as if the Dancing Death had descended among them and laid about himself with a vibrating scythe.

Yorke discharged his side arm into the air until his wrist was wrung out, spinning around trying to draw a bead on something insubstantial. Hot cartridge cases pattered around his feet, bouncing on asphalt like Mexican jumping beans.

Brother Baille, sorely wounded, staggered out of the ranks of the Josephites, sobbing with pain and terror, face leaking through his fingers. He froze and was pulled up into the air. His clothes ripped and red rain fell around him. He twisted in the air as if mangled, and thumped to the ground in several large pieces.

One of Yorke's ankles was kicked out from under him and he went down, eyes hurting as if he had stared full into the sun for a full minute. His head throbbed and someone jabbed him in the side. One of the ganggirls, a weepy-looking fillette with lazy eyelids. As he fell, he lost his grip on his probably empty side arm.

The ganggirl, taking to her spike heels, got about a dozen yards before scratches appeared in the back of her shiny Russian smocktop. Material parted around deep rents in her skin. Her hair was pulled out of its tight knot and ripped up. A diamond-shaped wound appeared in the bare nape of her neck, a tunnel into her greymass. She dropped like a puppet.

Yorke gasped. Someone stepped on his hand and he heard, but could not feel, a crunch. The boot-heel had come down on his plastik fingers

Scrabbling for his gun, Yorke found something else. The spectacles the shotgun deputy had struck from Elder Seth's face. Not really knowing why, Yorke opened them and slipped them on.

… And the world looked different.

He screamed.

He could see the things that had killed Brother Baille and the ganggirl.

A fat citizen was covered with the creatures, like a man smeared with honey and left for warrior ants. They buzzed and burrowed, sharp little teeth digging into cloth and skin, a million tiny tears shredding down to bone, verminous little wings crawling. Their buzzing was horribly like cruel laughter.

Because he could see them, they left him alone, left him to watch. In his skull, torrents raged. Synapses burned out. Memories wiped. A scream began in the pulsating centre of his being and radiated outwards, disrupting everything, shaking his greymass into jelly.

He knew the killing things for what they were. The Bible Belt had taught him to recognise the demons of pain and sorrow. They danced and circled in the air, insubstantially hideous, working violence and destruction. They swirled around Elder Seth, alighting gently on his shoulders and outstretched arms like doves flocking to St Francis. They gave him offerings of the dead.

Trooper Kirby Yorke screamed and screamed until his mind was gone, and nothing mattered any more.

XIV
12 June 2021

JUDGE THOMAS LONGHORNE Colpepper looked into the eyes of the man who was killing his town, and saw the hood of the hangman. Again, the Josephites had come in blood to Spanish Fork. There would be a fresh plaque on the monument, for this was not a new thing, this was merely a continuation of the massacre of 1854. Then, the Brethren of Joseph had come with savage Indians; today, they came with lawless gangcultists. The blood was the same.

The judge knew what he had to do to end the bloodshed, end the lawlessness, end everything.

His own voice sounded. "You be taken from here to a place of lawful execution…"

He picked up Larroquette's free arm and pressed its hand to his chin. In a reflex, the fingers curled up around his jaw, locking into his mouth. His false teeth shifted. He felt the hot aperture of the barrel against the soft fold of his dewlap.

"… and there you be hanged by the neck till you are goddang dead…"

There was a snap, and another, and another. The sound continued, like the popping of flashbulbs around a celebrity on opening night. Men fell through hatches in his mind. Behind Elder Seth they all stood, heads loose, tongues out, eyes showing only white.

"… and that's m'ruling!"

Judge Colpepper had tried and hanged three hundred and seventeen men, twenty-five women, two indeterminate and one intelligence-raised dog. They all waited for him. They had a necktie party ready.

Elder Seth looked at him, terrible eyes burning. The neck-tie party crowded in his mirrored pupils.

The judge held Larroquette's elbow in one hand and the ragged stump of his bicep in the other. He pumped the arm, chambering a round in the forearm, and straightened the limb out.

The last snap was louder than all the others.

XV
12 June 2021

THE JUDGE'S HAT came off the top of his head with most of his skull wadded into it. He stood for a moment, eyes opaque, and crumpled at the knees. He hit the road before his hat, which plopped with a sickening splat against the side of a wall ten yards distant and slithered redly towards the ground.

Tyree didn't believe what she saw, but took stock of the situation. Kirby Yorke, those strange shades clamped to his head, wouldn't stop screaming. The Quince had his back to the Feelgood and was levelling his shotgun at any who might rush him. Burnside was lost somewhere in the melee. People screeched and died indiscriminately. Buildings were on fire.

The cockatoo creature ran past Tyree, flaps of fair skin falling away as if a flock of invisible, sharp-beaked birds were attacking.

In the midst of it all, the elder stood calm, surveying his flock. With him stood a small knot, the rump of his faithful and new converts. There were Psychopomps with him, and a few of the townsfolk.

She made a snap judgement, and decided whose fault this all was.

Holding up her side arm with both hands, she circled around the outskirts of the killing zone, shouldering through floundering fools. Quincannon covered her, shotgunning a 'Pomp who tried to get in the way. This was a proper Cav action.

Stepping over the ganggirl, Tyree took careful aim and shot Elder Seth three times in the small of the back. The thing that looked like a man turned and she had the sense not to look into his eyes. That seemed like a good way to go mad or get killed.

But the Mark of Death had been put on her. She knew she could run but she couldn't hide.

One day, soon…

Ciccone flew at Tyree, hands contorted into claws. Tyree shot the sister in the chest, and what looked like pink plastic exploded through her robes. She slowed, but didn't stop. Tyree put a bullet in her head, just above the left eye. She saw the nailhead of the round embedded in the Josephite woman's head. A trickle of clear fluid welled around the wound, but Ciccone just seemed disoriented when she should be dead.

These people were getting less and less human. The elder put a hand on Sister Ciccone's shoulder and she calmed, bowing her head. He scanned Tyree and smiled.

Unseen claws didn't come to rip her apart. The elder stretched out an arm and beckoned. Ice-water dribbled down Tyree's spine. Ciccone and Wiggs and the others were smiling, beckoning her. She could be forgiven her sins.

She did not have to die. If she joined the faithful.

Elder Seth was walking away, trailing his flock of resettlers, They were singing "Shall We Gather at the River", with explosions instead of drumbeats to keep time.

Her voice came to her and she found herself singing too. Miraculously, she knew the words…

"… *the beautiful, the beautiful river.*
Yes, we'll gather at the river

That flows from the Throne of God"

Quincannon, who had broken away from the Feelgood, struggled with a Psychopomp and a little man in a blue suit. They were both trying to get knives into his throat.

Tyree shot the panzergirl and the Quince took care of blue suit with a shotgun-stock heartpunch. The sergeant shot her a salute and floored another assailant with a slash from the gun.

She didn't return the salute. She was still singing.

Her gun fell from her grasp and she lurched towards the Josephites as if pulled by puppet strings. Her hair was disarrayed by things rushing through the air. She knew she had to go to the elder, go *with* the elder. Her whole life had been designed to bring her to this point, to set her on the Road to Salt Lake City.

If she went with the elder, the Mark of Death would be wiped from her forehead. She could live...

Chollie Jenevein's gas tanks went up and fire was falling all over Spanish Fork. A nice, quiet, little town.

She saw Burnside slumped against the drug store, dead without a mark on him, side arm still holstered. Yorke was still screaming. The elder stood over the trooper and retrieved his spectacles, raising them up to his face like a sacrament. Yorke scratched Oedipus-fashion at his eyes, and kicked at the ground. Elder Seth walked away.

Tyree stood over Yorke, fending off the streams of people with the threat of her gun. Quincannon got to the kid and slapped him, but it had no effect. He dug out a squeezer of morph-plus from his belt-slung medikit and put the trooper to sleep. Yorke shut up but still writhed. Quincannon tried to get a grip on him.

Tyree still fought the impulse to go with the music. A tall Psychopomp, an elegant girl in see-through plastic, shoved past her and fell in step with the Josephites. She marched off like a catwalk creature. Tyree knew she should follow.

Elder Seth walked towards the city limits, ignoring his flock. Everywhere he went, he could guarantee new converts. Whatever his religion really was, she guessed it had nothing to do with Jesus H Christ.

She was hearing him right now. "Six six six."

With a lurch, her legs were moving, and she was among the multitude. A ticking calm settled around her. Quincannon and Yorke would be left behind with the dead. If she went with the Josephites, she would be saved, she would atone for her sins. She followed.

The Quince called for her, but she ignored him,

She knew it was madness but she marched with the crowd. They were united by love. She knew she was like them, another sacrificial lamb, more meat for the juggernaut that rolled down Route 666 to the Apocalypse, but she was happy with her lot. There were arms around her. To her left was an old man, a Josephite, to her right the 'Pomp she had seen join the resettlers. Together, they walked towards the desert. The old man fell, and his brothers and sisters walked over him. He was still singing, *they* were still singing, as their feet broke his ribs.

Tyree and the tall, thin girl embraced. Her name, Tyree gathered from the gush of welcome, was Varoomschka. Love was all around, and old enmities were strewn in the blooded dirt. When she stumbled, she was held up by Varoomschka and Brother Wiggs. Both had burned away their sins and imperfections and had become beacons of purity.

The Feelgood blazed away like a Fourth of July bonfire, and the courthouse began to smoulder. There was a five-man gallows that would burn up beautifully. It was a shame nobody was in a mood to appreciate the fireworks and bake potatoes in the ashes later.

She saw Elder Seth leading his Indians and his saints away from the blazes of massacre, his footprints filled with blood, spirits in the air.

And she saw him now, exactly the same.

Someone had hold of her, pulling her away from the ranks of the pilgrims. Varoomschka tried to rescue her from the new tugging, arms slipping around her neck in a bear-hug. Tyree struggled, possessed by the need to be with the elder, and took a slap in the face.

She closed her eyes and concentrated hard. She didn't want to be a sacrifice for anyone's God.

The Quince was with her now, red face pale. He was the only other citizen in sight not dead or crazy. He had hauled her out of the procession, and was holding her back.

Brother Wiggs, smiling, reached out for Tyree. Putting all his meat into it, Quincannon stuck a huge fist into the Josephite's face. Wiggs's smile caved in like an abusable TV screen and cracks appeared, but no blood burst through. He drew in breath and his face filled out, beatific expression popping forth.

The Quince was ready to fight, but Tyree didn't want to be fought for. She struggled to be with Wiggs and Varoomschka and Ciccone and Elder Seth. Most of all, Elder Seth.

Then, it snapped inside. She realised how insane this all was. It would be better to die than go to Salt Lake like a zombie. She clung to Quincannon and scanned the pilgrims with loathing.

As Wiggs began to march her off, Varoomschka mewled for her lost new friend and cried out "*Suestra, suestra*", sister, sister…

Tyree took the fillette's hand and pulled her away from Brother Wiggs. Perhaps she could save someone. Varoomschka squirmed and got loose. She stumbled a few steps, then fell in line with the others. She would find more new friends in the throng.

Damn.

"What…?" Tyree began.

"Hell, Leona, don't ask."

Elder Seth's party was nearly out of sight now, beyond the walls of fire. Shame flooded through her, self-disgust at what she had nearly been. She shuddered and Quincannon embraced her.

The courthouse exploded, and flaming timbers fell out of the sky like pick-up-sticks.

Quincannon hauled her through the fires and into the wake of the pilgrim procession. They found Yorke, still out cold, curled up on the sidewalk. Taking an arm each, they hauled the kid off towards Chollie's Gas and Inferno. The cruiser was parked opposite, unharmed by the explosions, Tyree's motorcyke was melted metal by now, though.

"Burnside?" Quincannon asked.

Tyree shook her head.

Yorke moaned in his troubled sleep. His eyes leaked blood where he had clawed.

Quincannon punched the access code into the doorlock, and the cruiser opened for them. They hauled Yorke into the back and slipped restraints on him for when he woke up.

The Quince sucked in his belly and got behind the wheel. Tyree took the weapons console and fired everything up. Then they drove steadily out of town, careful to avoid the fires in the road. A mass of twisted, smouldering wreckage blocked their way, and Quincannon had Tyree use the directional cannon to blast a clear path through it.

When they were out of range of flying debris, they stopped, and the Quince pressed his head to the wheel. It was cool in the cruiser after the heat of the day and the fires, and the soundproofing cut out most of the noise.

"Jesus, Mary and Joseph," Quincannon said. Before them, on the road, the crowd walked. They were thousands strong, a column winding away into the distance. Whoever they had been before, they were Josephites now, marching off to whatever Elder Seth had in store at Salt Lake City.

Tyree's fingers flexed on the keyboard. She could unloose the chainguns, the maxiscreamers and launch a couple of missiles. She had the impression she would be doing these people a good turn by killing as many of them as possible now.

But she did nothing. Elder Seth followed the Path of Joseph.

XVI
12 June 2021

DYING IS EASY, as her old man used to say. *It's the coming back that's hard.*

Inside her head, there was darkness. A red darkness. She was sinking slowly into it. Her optic implant was dangling useless on her cheek, her durium skull platelocks were bent uncomfortably inside her head. That wasn't supposed to happen. They were under guarantee. Doc Threadneedle had used only the best scav medtech from the Thalamus Corp.

There were deadfolks in the road with her. The Feelgood Saloon was burning, and there were overturned ve-hickles all around. The whole town was going up in flames.

All you need to be a freedom fighter, Petya Tcherkassoff sang on his "The World We Have Lost", *is a fiddle and a bow and cigarette lighter.*

Somewhere in the darkness outside her head, something – an animal or a person – was howling in pain.

There was a dull *whumpf!* as a gastank exploded. Jazzbeaux felt specks of heat on her face. The blacktop shuddered with the impact of flying debris. She knew she was lucky not to have been cut in half by a razor-edged car door playing frisbee.

Her father, of course, was dead. He had never come back.

The longer she lay here, the shorter the odds became.

She tried to open her eye and found it glued shut. She had blood on her face, dried-up and mixed with grit from the road.

The road. All her pain came from the road.

Get your kicksssssssssssssssss, the preacher had hissed, on *Route SixSixSixxxxxxxxxxxxxxxxxxxxxxxx!*

She had a skullcracker of a headache, and guessed she'd been opened in several places by knifecuts, branded in others by dollops of fire—

SHE KEPT LOSING herself, losing her train of thought. She wished she had listened when Doc Threadneedle tried to tell her about her brain. *It's where you live,* the Doc had said. *You should take care of it.* Well, she had tried. A durium skullsheath doesn't come cheap. A year's worth of fenced scav had brought her the treatment. It was supposed to be like armour inside your head.

But the preacherman had opened up a crack and got into her greymass. Somehow, he had wormed his way into her private self, the place where she lived. And he had done a lot of mischief in there. She knew her body could be fixed, but she wasn't sure about the important stuff. Doc Threadneedle couldn't replace neurons and synapses. Even the GenTech wizards, Dr Zarathustra and WD Donovan, could only reconstruct a ruined face; they couldn't do anything about a shredded psyche, a ruptured personality, a raped memory—

★ ★ ★

SOMEWHERE IN THE distance, there was gunfire. Shots were exchanged. Then, nothing. She could hear fires crackling. The thing in pain was out of it now. Spanish Fork was another ghost town. She was probably the only thing alive in it. Soon, the predators would lope out of the desert for her. On the road with the 'Pomps, she had seen some pretty weird critters: wolfrat coyotes, subhume vermin, sharkmouth rabbits. They had to eat red meat one day out of seven.

Jessamyn.

Amanda.

Bonney.

She held onto herself, trying to come to the surface of her cranial quicksand.

Jessamyn Amanda Bonney.

Nobody called her that any more. Nobody but cops and ops and soce workers. Not since her old man.

Jessa-MYN, her dead daddy whispered in her inner ear, *cain't you be more sociable?*

No, not Jessamyn. She didn't live here any more. Jazzbeaux. She was Jazzbeaux. That was her name in the Psychopomps, that was who she was. Jazz–*beaux!*

She brought her right hand up to her face. A numbed pain told her two of the fingers were broken. She rubbed her eye, and tried to open it again. The blood crust cracked, and she saw the night sky.

Star light, star bright, first star I see tonight…

Pushing hard with her elbows, she half-sat in the road. Her back ached, but her spine was undamaged. That was something. The Feelgood was a stone shell full of glowing ashes. A half-burned corpse sprawled on the steps, the top of its head gone. A wind had come through with the Josephites, and blown away the man's whole world.

I wish I may, I wish I might…

The starlight and the firelight went to her head like a blow, and she blinked uncontrollably. Her damaged implant was leaking biofluid. Delicately, with an unbroken thumb and ringfinger, she eased the ball-shaped doodad back into its socket. The connections were loose, and the optic burner didn't respond to her impulse command. No prob. Doc Threadneedle could fix that. At least, he could if the fault was in the machine rather than in the meat.

She found her eyepatch on the ground, and slipped it on over her optic. She pulled her hair out from over the patch-cord, and passed her fingers through it. Blood, dirt and filth came loose. Her broken fingerbones ground painfully.

Have the wish I wish tonight.

SHE WAS MORE in control now. Soon, she would be able to stand up, able to walk out of here on her own two legs.

The Psychopomps were finished, she guessed. Andrew Jean, her lieutenant for the past two years, was a few yards away, skin in shreds, orange beehive hairdo picked to pieces. The corpse looked as if it had been attacked by dagger-billed birds. She found So Long Suin and Sleepy Jane Porteous too, both killed. The 'Pomps who weren't dead had gone off with the preacherman.

Citizens, Psychopomps, Cav. There were lots of casualties. Jazzbeaux had been out of it for most of the fighting, but she could tell from the leavings that things had got serious. Some of the people looked as if they had been torn apart by animals with more in the way of teeth and claws than the Good Lord intended for them to have. Sweetcheeks was literally crushed flat into the road, dead eyes staring from a foot-wide face. A farmer was burned to the bone inside his unmarked Oshkosh B'Gosh biballs. A black cavalryman was slumped against the front window of the drugstore, dead without a mark on him.

She unbuttoned his holster, and took out his side arm. She had lost her own gun back in the Feelgood.

The official killing iron was heavier than she was used to, but it would do the job. She unbuckled the yellowlegs' gunbelt, and cinched it around her hips.

Then, she picked up a half-brick and threw it through the drugstore window. Picking the glass away from the display, she reached for a squirter of morph-plus. She exposed her wrist, and jabbed the painkiller into her bloodstream.

Her head clearing slightly, she filled her jacket pockets with pills and jujubes. She popped a glojo capsule into her mouth, and rolled it around on her tongue, not biting into it. The buzz seeped through her body. Some of the pain went away. Some—

THERE WAS A well nearby. Her waterdetector – now lost – had twanged when they crossed the Spanish Fork city limits. She would need a drink soon, and food.

She couldn't find a ve-hickle that worked. Her prized Tucker Tomorrow was somewhere in a block-sized scrap metal bonfire. She supposed Elder Seth must have taken everything with him when he left in his motorwagon train. He would be half-way to Salt Lake by now.

Now, she was coming for him. He had done his best to destroy her, and she was still here. She was still Jazzbeaux.

She squatted by the mess that had been Andrew Jean, and said her goodbyes. Andrew Jean had been a good 'Pomp, a good gangbuddy. Nobody deserved to die like that.

Except the preacherman. Elder Seth needed to die slowly. He had been invincible earlier, when he had changed – the real self pushing out from behind his human mask – but now he was her meat.

The preacher had taken a girl out to kill her, but made of her a weapon which could be used against him.

Jazzbeaux walked away from Andrew Jean. Just off the main street, she found the first of the carrion creatures. It was a bad one, a mew-tater. There was some kind of housecat in there, but it was the size of a moose, had white skunkmarks down its back, and the buds of vestigial extra heads hanging in its neckfur. It had gathered three or four corpses, and was playing with them, slicing them out of their clothes. Its saliva was corrosive, and etched patterns in the pale, dead skin of its supper.

Jazzbeaux stretched her fingers and lightly rested them on the butt of her scavved gun. The creature turned its head to look at her with slit-pupilled eyes the size of saucers. It showed its needle-sharp teeth, and flared a furry ruff. It could have leaped. With her broken fingers, she probably couldn't have outdrawn the thing.

But she met its eyes. It recognised a fellow predator, and backed down, returning its attention to its food. She walked away.

For the first time since she'd iced her dad, Jazzbeaux felt she really had a *purpose* on this dull earth.

She hoped the old man would be proud of her.

epilogue

12 June 2021

"Report it in full, Leona, and we'll be Section-Eighted out of This Man's Cavalry faster than the Prezz can tell a lie. The way I see it, we were attacked by Psychopomps and had a bad time of it. They jolted us full of zonk, and that made poor Kirby Yorke lose what sense he had. But we got away, and so did Elder Seth and his resettlers. They'll be in Salt Lake by now, those that made it through the Des, and they'll be building. Whatever the elder is, he's got himself a plan, and you and I ain't no part of it. Let's get back to Fort Valens and on with our lives. We'll need to live fast and live full, 'cause I reckon we're about near the end of our times. There's something going down out there that's gonna affect all of us in the end. When the time comes, maybe we'll take up arms again and find out just what Elder Seth is made of. Maybe not. Maybe we'll just be swept away by the fires. This here is the road to Armageddon, and maybe we can just turn round and go back to Valens and hope nothing comes of it, because there sure ain't much else we can do against someone who can do what he's just done to Spanish Fork. Six six six. That's in the Bible, I reckon. Something to do with the Beast of Revelations. The end of the world. Maybe that's what's coming. World's been going to Hell for long enough, maybe we're just about there now. Maybe... fuck, there's too many maybes."

Quincannon gunned the motor, and drove south. To the west, the sun was rapidly sinking, turning the sands the colour of blood. Tyree slumped in her seat, trying to forget Elder Seth's eyes, trying to ignore the urge to join him in his mad march.

They'd had to sedate Yorke again. His watery, empty eyes suggested permanent trauma. Tyree thought the kid was as dead as Bumside. Fifty per cent casualties on this patrol. Not good.

The Quince took something down from his rooflocker. A bottle of Shochaiku Double-Blend. He twisted off the top and drank from the neck, then passed it to her.

"I was nearly one of them, Quince!"

"I know. The way I figure it, Elder Seth was painting the road with blood, as a marker for something."

She took a swig of the booze, and felt warmth in her stomach. In the back, Yorke shifted, crying out in his sleep. She held the bottle.

"There were invisible things—"

"Don't think, Leona."

Quincannon picked something up off the floor. A piece of paper. It must have fallen from the locker. Tyree craned her neck, trying to get a look, but couldn't. Quincannon rolled his window down a crack, and threw the paper out. It was whipped away in the air, and lost in the desert.

She swallowed whiskey, focusing on the burn in her gullet. She could not *not* think.

Outside, full night had fallen and the Des was dark. Quincannon gunned the cruiser into the visibility funnel of its headlights

"Goodbye, Marilyn," he said, almost under his breath.

ABOUT THE AUTHOR

Besides his contributions to BL Publishing's
Warhammer and Dark Future series, the seldom-
seen Jack Yeovil is the author of a single novel, *Orgy
of the Blood Parasites*, and used to fill in occasionally
as a film reviewer for *Empire* and the *NME*. Kim
Newman seems to have Jack under control at the
moment, but the stubborn beast flesh occasionally
comes creeping back.

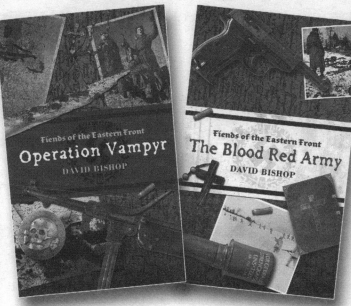